I0671063

The Blood Red Line

Alfie Robins

Kings Town Publishing

First Published by Kings Town Publishing. 2017.

British Library Cataloguing in Publication Data

A CIP catalogue record for this book is available from the British Library

ISBN:978-09927594-7-6

About the Author

Alfie Robins was born and raised in the English east coast city of Kingston Upon Hull, known locally as, 'Ull. Alfie left school at 15 and started work as a ships carpenter working on the trawlers on Hull fish dock. Over the years he has had a varied career, carpenter, production manager in the caravan industry, sales manager with a radio communication and a postman with Royal Mail. He is married and has three grown up children, four grandsons and lives with his wife and son in rural East Yorkshire, England.

Also by Alfie Robins

Reprisal

Snakes and Losers

A Winning Hand Loses

Just Whistle

Funeral Rites

Why Won't You Stay Dead

Coming soon

Heads She Loses, Tails She Loses.

Acknowledgements

As always, I would like to give special thanks to my family for their encouragement and constructive, but not always welcome criticism, during the process of writing this book.

Thank you all.

Once more the novel is based in the present day in and around Hull and East Yorkshire. Also references are made to Hull as it used to be during its heyday as the country's premier fishing port. The majority of locations mentioned do exist in Hull and the surrounding area, whilst other exist purely in my imagination.

This one is for all the boys.

The Blood Red Line

Chapter 1

The evening was closing in. Darkening clouds scudded inland above the River Humber threatening a storm as the sun sank towards the west. Eight Officers of The Humberside Police Firearms Unit, travelling in a nondescript Ford Transit, followed a top specification, black 4 X 4 Range Rover at a discrete distance. They had picked the suspect vehicle up as it left the North Yorkshire Police jurisdiction west of Goole and had been sitting on the tail of the Range Rover for approximately thirty miles.

Chatter was kept to a minimum as the team leader gave a live commentary over the communication system to the Gold Command Centre.

'Zulu-Alfa-2-Zero to control, we are maintaining visual contact with target vehicle, continuing west along the A63 Clive Sullivan Way, passing under the Humber Bridge – continuing along A63 towards the city,' the team leader relayed as the vehicles passed the industrial and retail parks along the banks of the River Humber. 'Vehicle signalling to leave the A63 at the Brighton Street junction - repeat, leaving A63 at the Brighton Street junction. Control - approaching Freightliner

1

Road roundabout, target vehicle turning left, left, left onto Freightliner Road.' Tension built as the vehicles slowed.

The team leader, a sergeant, turned to face the officers in the rear of the van. 'Get ready.' Face visors were pulled down into position, helmet cameras activated and carbines made ready. The Range Rover slowed as it approached the roundabout, signalled and turned left into the industrial area. The sergeant spoke to the driver. 'Okay, Dave, on my mark.' No further words were needed. 'Control, about to engage with suspect vehicle.' He banged a fist on the dashboard. 'Here we go,' he said quietly as the van accelerated and overtook the Range Rover, the police driver pulled the Ford Transit across the bows of the vehicle and slammed on the brakes. The driver of the 4x4 braked hard, tyres squealing on the tarmac as he stopped. Immediately the back doors of the van flew open. Officers dressed in black combat gear and kitted out with Heckler & Koch automatic carbines, swarmed around the vehicle. The sergeant shouted instructions to the occupant of the 4X4. 'Turn off the engine - remain in the vehicle - place your hands on the steering wheel.'

To all intents, it appeared the driver was being compliant. The vehicle engine was turned off and the occupant placed both hands on the steering wheel in full view. The sergeant placed a hand on the shoulder of the officer standing next to him. The signal was confirmed with a nod of the head. Cautiously, the officer walked slowly over to the 4X4, Heckler and Koch carbine primed and pointing towards the vehicle.

Slowly and steadily he approached the vehicle. He reached out with a leather gloved hand to open the vehicle door – that's when the shit hit the fan. The single occupant of the Range Rover dropped his right hand into his lap and picked up a weapon. At point, blank range he discharged his weapon as the door opened. The officer, stunned, staggered backwards, but remained standing. Then the screaming began - but it wasn't the officer.

When the occupant of the vehicle discharged his Eastern European pistol, the weapon exploded – his right hand hung in shreds. The gunman fell from the vehicle, landing heavily in a bloody heap on the tarmac - screaming. His name was Dave Scabies. The situation was contained.

Number 56, Hendon Street was just like the house next door and the house next door to that. A row of semi-detached houses with postage stamp front gardens and satellite dishes high on the walls, UPVC double glazing and long gardens at the rear that backed on to the Dairycoates railway sidings. To all intents and purposes the prefabricated shed at the bottom of the garden of number 56, looked nothing more than a home for the householder's gardening equipment. There was one significant difference, it was no longer a store for plant pots and lawnmowers. The place was a one man hive of activity, often buzzing to the sound of machinery. Visitors weren't welcome and nor were they allowed to enter without telephoning in advance. Aptly enough, the man who owned the shed was named Gardener, Bill Gardener.

The work was easy for a man with Gardener's skills and the money had been good - was good. But the truth was he no longer enjoyed the work, nor did he need the money the work brought in any longer. The trouble was it was a tricky situation to get out of - alive.

This day Gardener was expecting a visitor, yes, the visitor had telephoned in advance. He walked down the garden path bordered with spring flowers and shrubs, towards the shed, as he neared he could hear metal machining against metal. He knocked on the solid hardwood door and waited. A moment or two later a key turned in the lock and bolts slid open. The visitor gave a quick glance over his shoulder, then stepped inside the shed and locked the door behind him. Gardener returned to the lathe and continued with his work.

His guest placed his briefcase on the workbench, then settled himself on a tall stool and watched Gardener work.

'You heard what happened to Scabby Dave?' he asked. The man was a regular visitor to the shed, an old acquaintance of Gardener's from their army days and more recently an unwelcome business associate. The visitor's name was Neil Powers. Once upon a time, both men served in Her Majesty's Armed Forces as sergeants in the Royal Logistic Regiment. Now, Powers was a gangster, not the "wanna be gansta" type, but the real deal, a proper gangster. He was the man you didn't want to know; the man nightmares were made of.

'It happens,' Gardener replied, his back to Powers as he focused on the job in hand. 'You get what you pay for, if you buy crap for peanuts, you can't expect anything else but a job done by a monkey.' He wound back the cutting tool and pressed the stop button on the lathe. The whining motor slowed and cut-out. Gardener pulled a rag from his overall pocket and wiped his hands, then dropped the rag on the workbench and picked up his tobacco tin. Just like in his work, he rolled himself a cigarette with precision. Stuck it to his bottom lip and flicked his Zippo and lit up. 'What have you brought?' The small workshop began to fill with a blue haze that clung to the low ceiling.

'The usual, five Baikal 79s, no rush - as and when.' Powers opened the briefcase, took out the firearms and placed them on the workbench. He shifted his position on the tall stool, took out his cigarettes and sparked up.

Gardener wrapped the pistols in an old curtain and locked them safely away.

For operators like Powers, the Baikal could be a money spinner, it could be bought legally in Russia for around £40, or if the cash was available you could buy them in bulk for around £10 each. The cost to convert them into 9mm killing machines was a mere £50 or so, depending on quantity. The big risk was bringing them into the country. Powers was careful; he left the hands-on importation to others in his organisation. After half an hour in Gardener's workshop the Baikal would become a reliable 9mm automatic weapon, demanding a price of anything up to £1000.

The Baikal was a Russian weapon that originated in Izhievsk, an Urals backwater some 2500 miles from Hull. Izhievsk is - was the centre of the Russian arms industry, the birth place of the AK-47. The Baikal had started its life as the Markov pistol, used by both the

5

Soviet police and military although production ceased in the 1990s, there were still plenty to be had. From the Markov, the CS gas cartridge firing Baikal was born, primarily a weapon for self-defence after the collapse of the Berlin Wall.

The weapons were then transported to a small town called Alytus, in Lithuania. In a small hub of workshops belonging to the notorious criminal gang known as the Bauble, the weapons were converted to fire live ammunition. Powers, however, preferred the conversion to be taken care of by his own men, he needed to guarantee the products he sold. Gardener was one of these men. For a man, as skilled as Gardener, an ex-munitions expert in the armed forces, the operation to re-bore the barrel and make other minor adjustments was a piece of piss. Of course, Powers wasn't one to miss an opportunity, a "dirty" weapon was always available for hire at a substantially reduced price.

'How they got onto him, that's what I'd like to know.'

'Always did have a big gob that one. You want a brew?' Gardener flicked the switch turning on the kettle.

'No thanks, I'm not stopping, people to see and all that.' Gardener was relieved, doing business with Powers was one thing, socializing didn't even come into it. Back in the day when they served together at equal rank things were different. Now he could only tolerate Powers in small doses. Gardener was hardly squeaky clean himself, but since their return to civvy street, he made every effort to keep things strictly business. 'I'll have them picked up next week and the next batch dropped off.' Powers stood up to leave and dusted down his suit trousers. Picked up his briefcase and unlocked the shed door. 'Be seeing you,' he said as he opened the door.

'See you next week then,' Gardener said with his head down and back towards Powers.

Powers shut the door behind him as he left. Gardener walked over to the door locked it once more. He took a tin down from a shelf, opened it, took out a teabag, dropped it into his mug and filled it with boiling water, stubbed out his cigarette and went back to his lathe and pressed the start button leaving his tea to brew. Just another day in the life of Bill Gardener.

Chapter 2

The weather had taken a turn for the better. The cold wintery conditions of the previous days had been replaced by a warm spring with unseasonably warm humid nights. The high humidity made for an uneasy night for Detective Sergeant Greg Warren, it was a night of tossing and turning well into the small hours. He lay on his back atop of the duvet, arms behind his head, watching through the gap in the curtains, waiting for daylight. It was a case of mind over matter, mind won, he made a move. Reluctantly he kicked his legs over the bedside and sat on the edge for a couple of minutes as he gathered his thoughts. He had lots of thoughts.

He eased himself off the bed and took the two steps to the window, pulled the curtains aside slightly and peered into the street. Darkness was beginning to give way to dawn. Naked, he walked to the bathroom, ran the basin tap and dowsed his face in cool water, then returned to the bedroom and dressed in shorts and a running vest. Downstairs in the kitchen, he opened the fridge, took out a carton of fresh orange and drank straight from the container to slake the overnight thirst. Sitting on a kitchen chair he put on his trainers. While most normal people were still in bed, he left the house for his regular four miles pounding of the streets, with his iPod strapped to his upper arm. Only today he had no intention of breaking any records, there was no hurry, a steady jog was the order of the day, he had issues to mull over.

Warren, born and bred in Camden, North London, had followed a troubled path through his school years and beyond, finally coming to his senses at the age of twenty-one and joining the Metropolitan Police Force. After completing his initial training at the police college in Hendon, Warren was assigned to Clapton Road nick. His stay at Clapton Road was an enjoyable one, providing the recruit with experience in most aspects of police work. He'd worked and studied hard, and realising his ambition, promotion into the Criminal Investigation Department followed. Warren continued with his studies and passed the sergeants promotion board. Alas, due to fierce competition in the London area, promotion was slow in arriving. Hence, his move up north to Hull, hoping his fortunes would change. They did, but not always for the better.

For the past three months, Detective Sergeant Greg Warren had endured enforced "gardening leave", his superiors had called him reckless with no regard for authority, which, in his opinion was a total load of bollocks. Okay, so he'd had to make one or two questionable decisions, but he stood by them. His leave had been spent doing nothing out of the ordinary. He drank too much, ate too much, and certainly pondered too long over the "what ifs" of life. Today was to be the day that defined the rest of his life, the day of reckoning, his future was in the balance. Warren was to appear before the Police Internal Disciplinary Panel, they would decide his future in the Police Force, that's if he still had one.

Some months earlier, Warren had realised his dream of promotion and excitement, both came faster than he could have ever anticipated, when he was introduced to the two 'suits' who were to change his life. Now, it looked as if the promotion was going to be short lived, and maybe his job along with it. All the things he strove towards since joining the police force, now on the verge of being flushed down the toilet.

Warren had been drafted into a clandestine government department operating under the cover name of Gemmell Strategies. Unfortunately for the newly promoted Detective Sergeant, things hadn't worked out the way he had hoped they would. He'd stepped over the 'thin blue line', perhaps with the blood that had been spilled it should have been renamed the 'blood red line'. Of course, all in the call of duty, or so he truly believed. Others didn't necessarily agree.

Warren's run was steady, along the pavements of Anlaby Road, with a circuit of the K.C. Stadium and home again, he had hardly broken into a sweat. He let himself inside and headed straight for the kitchen, where he retrieved the carton of orange juice from the fridge. He drank deep before going upstairs to the bathroom, and setting the shower running while he stripped off. Standing under the pulsing power shower, he considered his options should things not go the way he wanted. He couldn't think of any. The shower did little to ease the tension. With a towel around his waist, he stood in front of the mirror and shaved, he studied his reflection, his bright blue eyes seemed pale - watery, he was sure there were more grey hairs than he had previously.

He padded through to the bedroom. Opening the wardrobe, he took out his best suit - his only suit, a dark grey fine pin stripe with three buttons and a single vent. After deliberating, he picked a pale blue shirt and navy tie to match, he wanted to - had to make a good impression. Warren dressed and went downstairs to the kitchen, put two slices of bread in the toaster and put the kettle on to boil while he gave his shoes a quick polish. Sat at the kitchen table, he watched the morning news on the television while he ate his breakfast. He glanced up at the wall clock and sighed, still an hour to go before he had to leave. The way his nerves were feeling, he thought maybe this was an appropriate time to start smoking. The clock ticked its way around, time to go. He took his jacket off the hanger, put it on and checked his appearance in the glass door of the built-in oven then straightened his tie.

'Okay, matey,' he said to the reflection, 'let's go and find out what they have to say.'

The meeting was to take place at the new Humberside Police headquarters, a state of the art purpose built building on Clough Road. The building looked more like a place of learning, a modern education Academy than a place of law enforcement. Warren drove into the car park and showed his ID to the Private Security Officer manning the barrier and was told where to park. Warren shook his head. 'Private security, what was the job coming to?' he said out loud. 'Maybe I'll find out when they sack me.' He thought he might be better off out of it anyway. That said, he really didn't fancy working security in a supermarket looking out for tow-rags shoplifting. He parked up and walked around to the front of the station, again, he was annoyed at having to 'buzz' to be admitted into the building. The reception was manned by a Civilian Support Officer, not a copper in sight. Eventually Warren was booked in, given a visitor's badge, which he attached to the top pocket of his jacket and was escorted up two floors and through a maze of corridors.

'Please wait here,' the CSO said, inclining his head to a row of chairs along one wall. 'Shouldn't be too long,' he said, then he was gone, leaving Warren with a thudding in his chest and butterflies in his stomach.

Two minutes later the door opposite opened. 'DS Warren?' a uniformed inspector asked, holding the door ajar. 'Please come in,' he stood aside to allow Warren to pass.

'Here we go,' Warren said under his breath as he entered the conference room.

'Take a seat, Detective Sergeant,' said the inspector, as he headed towards his own seat behind a highly polished solid wood table. A single chair had been placed in the centre of the room facing the officers behind the long conference table. Warren stepped forward and reluctantly sat down, he'd never felt so conspicuous in all his life. 'The officers to my left are Superintendent Bales, Superintendent Hargreaves and Assistant Chief Constable Nail, of the Internal

Disciplinary Department and my name is Inspector Wellington.'

Warren looked from one face to the other, he'd had bollockings in the past, but this was in a totally different league, to say it was intimidating would have been an understatement. The silence in the air was so dense it could have been cut with a knife. Assistant Chief Constable Nail broke the silence. He slammed the folder he'd supposedly been reading shut with a slap of his hand for dramatic effect, and sat upright with his hands palm down on the table before him.

'DS Warren, I won't beat about the bush, to say I am disgusted with your conduct would be putting it lightly. Burglary, robbery, grievous bodily harm, an assault on a senior officer and even discharging a firearm into a senior colleague's foot - I could go on but what would be the point?'

You haven't mentioned the spook I shot through the back of the head, Warren wanted to add but decided maybe keeping his gob shut was the better option.

'Is there anything you'd like to add in your defence?'

Warren sat straight backed, with his hands resting on his knees military fashion and made a brief statement. 'Sir - gentlemen,' he said, as he looked at his senior officers in the eye one by one, 'I have nothing more to add to my original statement. As far as I am concerned my actions were warranted and lawful.'

'Shooting a fellow officer in the foot and leaving another with two broken legs - lawful?' challenged the Assistant Chief Constable.'

'Sir, am I correct in believing this Board has in its possession, a statement from the senior officers concerned that exonerates me from the action I had to take?' Warren said confidently.

'Don't be clever, DS Warren, you know we have. I tell you now, if it hadn't been for that statement you *would* be facing criminal charges. Charges that would have led to you serving a custodial sentence.'

Warren kept position as the Assistant Chief Constable continued.

'We have studied the evidence before us very carefully and reached a decision, a decision we have not made lightly.' Nail cleared his throat noisily. 'It is the decision of this Board that you resume your duties immediately. This, however, was not a unanimous decision.'

Warren gave out a loud sigh, surprised. There was no way he had been expecting the outcome to be in his favour.

'This Board is now concluded.'

Warren stood, he felt relieved as the tension left his body. 'Thank you, sir...' he never had a chance to finish the sentence.

'There's no need to thank me, DS Warren, as I said, it was a Board decision. If I'd had my way the case would have been brought to the attention of the Crown Prosecution Service.' The ACC kept his composure and added. 'It is my opinion that you are not fit to wear the uniform. But then, who am I?'

The Assistant Chief Constable pushed back his chair, stood up and nodded to his fellow Board members. He left the room without another word.

Superintendent Bales shook his head as Nail left the room, closing the door heavily behind him. 'DS Warren, Greg - don't take it personally, we're not all of the same opinion, the evidence speaks for its self, maybe you were shall we say a little over zealous in your actions, but there was no other option other than to exonerate you. Strictly speaking, you were put in an impossible situation, and not one of your own making.'

'I appreciate your honesty, sir, thank you.'

Inspector Wellington now spoke for the first time. 'Consequently, with no loss of rank, you are to resume your duties immediately. We didn't think it appropriate in the circumstances for you to return to Central Police Station at Queens Gardens. You are to report to the Priory Road Station at 9am tomorrow. You should find it interesting to say the least, it's a new department in the final stages of development. It should be right up your street.'

'Sir?' Warren was puzzled.

'It's a department that will allow you to, for want of better words, use your more unorthodox skills.

'Who's the SIO, sir?

'Someone you know, just report to room 2A on the 2nd floor at 0900 hours. That's it. I bid you good day, DS Warren.'

Arse, thought Warren as he stood. He nodded his thanks and made to leave the room. 'You will need this.'

Wellington handed over Warren's warrant card. He had been doubtful that he would ever see it again.

Warren smiled as he accepted the card and nodded his thanks

Out in the corridor, he gave the biggest sigh of his life, he could hardly believe what had just happened. The best he had hoped for was a demotion back to being a uniformed PC, and working in some backwater for the rest of his career, he wouldn't have been happy, but he could have lived with it. But joining a new department and keeping his rank, he was over the moon with the outcome.

Exonerated. If only by default, Warren was in no mood to go out on the town in celebration and besides who was there to celebrate with? Since his escapade into the darker side of policing, he'd lost contact with the few friends he did have. Rather than go out for a lonely celebratory drink, he decided on a quiet night in with his new-found friend *Jim Beam*.

Chapter 3

Warren rose early as usual, but unlike usual, he didn't give the paths of Hull's West Park and the streets of Anlaby Road a pounding. He showered, shaved and picked out some smart casual clothes. On his first day in a new department, he didn't want to appear too starched in a three-piece suit. Sitting at the kitchen table, he contemplated his immediate future over one too many mugs of instant coffee. He pottered about the house for a while, doing jobs that didn't really need doing, anything, to pass the time. If the truth was known he was feeling a little on the nervous side, not like him at all, after all it had been a while since he'd felt someone's collar. Eventually he gave up clock watching, put his empty mug on the draining board and grabbed his jacket. It was time to earn a crust.

The feeling as he drove into the Priory Road nick car park was one of déjà vu and trepidation. At the car park entrance, he flashed his ID at the Civilian Support Officer in his sentry box, then drove around the back of the building and parked up. Standing by the side of the car he looked up at the four-storey building. 'Here we go, kid, don't cock it up,' he said out aloud and clicked the key fob locking the car, then confidently walked towards the main building. At the main door, he took a couple of deep breaths before pushing it open and assertively walking into the reception area. Another CSO manned the desk, once again he showed his warrant card and waited to be admitted into the secure area. It had been a while since he'd last been in the Priory Road Station but nothing appeared to have changed. Once inside the secure area he stood for a second or two to get his bearings then took the stairwell to the upper floors. On the second floor, he checked the door numbers.

Walking toward him was an attractive young woman with brown shoulder length hair, styled in the unkempt look, which had obviously taken an age to create. She was wearing a "Debbie Harry" logo T-shirt, bomber jacket, skinny jeans and heeled boots. 'You look lost. Can I help?'

Warren gave her his best smile, glanced at the ID badge hanging around her neck on a lanyard, but couldn't make out her name. He lifted his eyes and stared into her brown eyes. 'I'm DS Warren – Greg,' he said, extending his hand. 'I'm looking for 2A?'

'DC James,' she replied, flicking the ID so that Warren could see it before taking the offered hand. Subconsciously he held the hand for a second or two longer than he should have. 'My hand?' she said, looking straight back in his eyes.

'Sorry - 2A?' he repeated.

'Straight ahead on the right.'

'Maybe I'll see you around?' He smiled.

'Sooner than you think,' she said in a whisper as she carried on walking.

Warren stood in front of room 2A. Once more he took a controlling breath, knocked once on the glass panel and confidently walked in. It was just like any other squad room, only smaller, much smaller. The lay-out was open-plan, with five desks loaded with computer monitors and the obligatory white board dominating the far end of the room. The only thing missing were the occupants, it was like the *Mary Celeste*. As he closed the door behind him a familiar face appeared from beneath the desk furthest away.

'Greg, it's good to see you.' It was his old Detective Inspector, Bill Grimes, previously stationed at the Queen's Gardens nick. Grimes stood up and wiped his hands down the side of his trousers. 'Just sorting out some wires,' he said, as he walked over to Warren with an outstretched arm.

'Bloody hell, Bill, they told me someone I knew would be running the team, but you're the last person I was expecting to see this morning.' Warren held out his hand and shook. He was pleased to see a familiar face. The last time Warren had seen Grimes was just before he used his given code word *Suits and Bullets* and 'came in from the cold'. If truth were known, Grimes had put his own neck on the block to keep Warren out of trouble, more than Warren would ever know.

'Thought you'd be surprised. When they asked me to head this team up I had one or two reservations, but it seemed too good an opportunity to turn down. I told them, if I'm doing this I pick my own team, which,

19

much to my surprise was sanctioned, that is until I said, "I'll need Greg Warren", now that didn't go down too well, I can tell you. They said no chance, and I quote, "not a cat in hells chance, he's going to be out on his arse". I stuck to my guns, told them point blank, "if you want this to work I need someone with first hand undercover experience", and that person was you.'

'Undercover?'

'Yep, street level stuff, nothing too heavy like the Gemmell fiasco.'

'Seems I owe you, thanks for sticking your neck out.'

'No need for thanks, I really *do* need you on the team. Anyway, come in and make yourself at home, such as it is. That's your desk,' he pointed towards the one piled high with files.

Warren looked and raised his eyebrows. It didn't go un-noticed by Grimes. 'They're not all yours, we're still getting organised' he said, smiling.

'Where's the rest of the team?' Warren had been expecting a busy squad room full of serious detectives.

'You probably passed her in the corridor.'

'Her?'

'Yeah, she's just gone for coffee.'

Warren hoped it was a slip of the tongue. 'So that's it, just the three of us? Seriously, where *are* the rest of team?'

'That's it, the full team, the four of us.'

'Four of us, I thought you were taking the piss when you said three?'

Grimes let the remark pass.

'Saying that, the budget will stretch to another DC when we find a suitable candidate. In the meantime, we'll draw on the uniform pool as and when we need an extra pair of hands. If anyone stands out we'll keep them.'

'Sounds like a plan.' He was thinking this must be the smallest team in the force.

'Grab the end of this,' Bill passed over the terminal end of a computer cable. Warren held onto the cable as the DI disappeared under a desk. 'Oh, and did I mention the fourth member of the team is a Civilian Advisor?'

Warren gave him the look, when he surfaced from underneath the desk. 'Civilian?' *Bloody hell, not even a copper.*

'I use the term Advisor loosely, he doesn't know a lot about police procedures, but he has a wealth of information on the local criminal community, he'll be here in a minute.' He didn't bother to explain further, the door opened and DC Trish James entered carrying a tray with four coffees. 'DS Warren, this is our colleague, Detective Constable Trish James,' he said as Trish walked in.

'We've already met,' she said, putting the tray of canteen coffees on the desk and shook hands once again.

There was someone behind her, a slight figure who Warren couldn't quite see. Then a skinny young man wearing smart chinos and a denim shirt stepped out from behind DC James.

'Ta-daaaa,' a voice sang out.

21

Warren was almost struck dumb, he couldn't believe his eyes. It was James Boland, AKA, Jimbo. The young man with whom he'd formed a friendship, a friendship that had been very beneficial for both. Boland may have been a bit of a scally, working on the wrong side of the law, but he had also assisted Warren in some of his more dubious pursuits. As Grimes had said, Jimbo was a handy lad to know, especially when unlocking unlockable doors were involved. The young man had also proved himself by saving Warren's skin on more than one occasion.

'Well, I bloody never - two surprises in one day! Civilian advisor, what's that all about?'

'That's me, official advisor to the police, who would have thought it, me working with the law instead of trying to break it.' Warren went over and gave Boland a man-hug. 'Give over you tart,' he said, as Warren's arms wrapped around his skinny body. 'Man, it's good to see you again, Greg.'

'You too, pal.' Warren disentangled himself and stood back. 'You're looking well. When did you get to look so healthy?' Jimbo had always had a half-starved appearance that seemed in keeping with his unkempt scruffy look.

'Healthy eating and early nights, that's me now.' He made a play of smoothing the creases in his chinos. 'Cool, huh?'

Warren still couldn't believe Jimbo was on the team. 'So, how is that fat twat of a mate of yours, Conway?' Pat Conway was an 'associate' from Warren's last undercover job, a villain and all-round bastard. All in all, a prominent figure in the northern criminal fraternity.

'Last time I saw him he was okay, but I haven't seen him for a while, suppose that's a good thing. Oh yeah, I do remember the last time I did speak to him and he didn't say anything good about you.'

'I can live with that.'

The four of them pulled up chairs and sat around the nearest desk.

'So, Jimbo, you managed to keep your nose clean?'

'It wasn't easy considering the mess you left me with.'

'What made you come over to the Dark Side?' Warren asked, pushing back his chair and stretching out his legs.

Boland looked to Bill Grimes, who took the story forward.

'When you eventually turned yourself in, there were still a multitude of questions about some of your antics that needed to be answered - unofficially of course and I was tasked with debriefing Jimbo. I told the power's to be what I wanted them to know. Bloody hell, if I told them half the stuff Jimbo told me, they would have locked you up and thrown away the bloody key.' The DI looked from Warren to Jimbo and back again. 'Jimbo here was ready to sing your praises and fill the gaps. Anyway, I needed a little unorthodox help with other things and who better to assist?'

Warren smiled, it seemed that Jimbo had come good after all and not returned to work for his former mentor and employer Pat Conway. 'All the same I'm surprised,' he turned to face his pal, 'pleasantly surprised of course,' he added. 'How the hell did you manage to get it authorised, I mean, Jimbo's not what you'd call squeaky clean?'

Jimbo sat with a serious look on his face. 'You know how to offend a bloke, Greg.'

'No offence meant...'

'I'm not serious, mate, just pulling your pisser,' Jimbo smiled and chuckled.

'If you two have finished?' Grimes said, looking to both of them in turn. 'The answer to your original question is – they don't actually know who our advisor is, well they do, but they're not fully aware of his background.'

'Dangerous ground, Bill,' Warren's expression was serious.

'Yeah, well, Jimbo hasn't actually got a criminal record.'

'Seriously?'

'You obviously never checked him out carefully enough when you worked together.'

'I just put two and two together - assuming that anyone who worked for Conway must have had a record as long as your arm.'

'Well, that goes to show, doesn't it? Trish spoke for the first time.

'Goes to show what?' asked Warren.

'That you're no good with maths.'

The comment lightened the atmosphere that was in danger of becoming sombre.

'Okay, I'll give you two ten minutes to do some catching up, then we've got work to do,' DI Bill Grimes stood up. 'Trish,' he nodded towards the door.

Warren stood up and walked over to the window. 'It *is* good to see you, pal,' he said, as he turned and faced Boland. 'To say I was surprised was an understatement. So, how long have you been working for Bill?'

'It must be around a couple of months now.'

'But bloody hell, Jimbo, why?'

'Cos of you.'

'Because of me, I don't get it?'

'Let's just say I found out that not all coppers are bastards.'

'Nice of you to say so.'

'Yeah, well, I kinda got the taste for all the ducking and diving we did.'

'Jimbo, you've always been one for ducking and diving, that's how you survived.'

'Yeah, I know, but what we did was sort of legal, and we made a great team, right? When me and DI Grimes had finished sorting all the shit out you left, he asked if I'd fancy doing a bit of work, unofficial like, off the books. I told him straight, I'm no grass, not even for a mate of yours. He explained he didn't want a "grass", he had plenty of those, he just wanted sound info, so I said I'd give it a go. At first it was things like who's new on the streets - had I heard anything about so and so, stuff like that.'

'When was all this made official?'

'Soon after, he said there was a new department starting up and he'd be running it, asked if I'd fancy making it permanent. He reckoned he could get me a job as a civilian advisor, like, I mean, *me*, working for the Police. No way, I said - not for me. But he told me he could help look after my interests, keep my name out of the shit we got into. I owed him. He reckons if it hadn't been for him sticking his neck out, I could have been charged with all sorts of crap that could have put me away for a long time, and I have my mum to think about.

Well, it got me to re-think things; I did need to get my life sorted and when he said he was in a position to get you assigned to the team, well that clinched the deal.' Jimbo sat back in his chair and smiled as he carried on. 'It went something like, "no other idiot would be prepared to take you on", and if he didn't you would be heading to the Job Centre to sign on. So, I said okay.'

'Cheers for that.' Warren was genuinely touched by the comment. At least he still had two mates who were willing to stick their necks out for him. 'You'll have me getting all sentimental in a minute.'

'You sentimental? The bloke who took out a hit-man, shot a spook in the foot, and broke another officer's legs, in several places I might add - like fuck you're sentimental.'

'Correction - who drove a van into the bloke breaking his legs?'

'Yeah, well, I was saving your life, man, you'd be brown bread if I hadn't.'

Warren smiled, he couldn't do anything but agree with Jimbo's comments, his association with the clandestine operation run by Gemmell Strategies, had been nothing less than a total fiasco from start to finish.

'Touché. So, how's your mum doing?' Warren said, changing the subject.

'Tops, really good thanks to the help you gave me.' During their previous escapade, a quantity of illegal Blood Diamonds had come into their possession, which, with the help of Pat Conway, were turned into a very substantial amount of cash. Warren, not too sure of how his own future would pan out, gave the lion's share of the proceeds to Jimbo. 'Thanks to you, and the cash you gave me I managed to get her into a first-class nursing home, they really look after her. Plus, I got myself a SmartCar.'

'Good on you, what sort?'

'Just said, a SmartCar.'

'Yeah, but what make?'

'Told you, a SmartCar.'

'You are taking the piss?' Warren started laughing out loud.

'No, seriously it's cool - and economical.' He was surprised Jimbo knew what the word economical meant.

Warren did his best to curb the laughter. 'I'm pleased things have turned out okay for you. And I see you lost a few of the piercings along the way?'

'Yeah, well, I didn't want to look *too* obvious working in a nick, thought they might take one look at me and throw me in the cells.' Jimbo subconsciously touched his left ear that used to be decorated with rings and studs.

'DC James, what's she like?' asked Warren.

'Trish, she's cool, hot, out of your league, man. Now it's my turn to ask a question, how come you didn't get in touch?'

'It was nothing personal, mate. Once the shit hit the fan they kept me incommunicado for a while in a safe house. Then I thought it best if I kept my head down for a while, didn't contact anyone - especially didn't want to get you involved more than you had been. To be honest with you, I thought about my future, what was going to happen to me, and, what would I do if I got kicked off the force.' A short silence followed. 'I would have got in touch - eventually. Anyway, it's all academic now, water under the bridge; I'm here now, aren't I?' Warren picked up his coffee cup and held it high. 'Here's to us, and our future. We'll have a proper catch up later over a pint in *The Eagle*.'

'Sounds like a plan,' Jimbo replied, holding his cup high in a toast.

The office door opened. 'You two caught up?' asked Grimes as he and Trish came back into the squad room. He smiled. 'I'll take the grins to mean yes.' The DI went over to his desk and picked up a buff coloured folder. 'Right, work to do. Trish, will you do the honours?' Grimes passed the folder over.

Trish pulled out a chair and sat opposite Warren and Jimbo. She flicked dark curls from her face, as she laid the folder on the desk. She opened the file and spread out a batch of crime scene photographs. 'These are the stills taken from the helmet-cams of an armed response unit who stopped a 4X4 they'd had under surveillance.' She shuffled the photographs across the desk. 'The vehicle was driven by David Scabies, he's better known on the streets as Scabby Dave.' Jimbo raised his eyebrow, that was a blast from the past that he wasn't expecting.

'Nice name,' Warren said.

'Yeah, well, following an anonymous tip off, an armed response was dispatched to intercept his vehicle.'

'Some tip off,' said Warren.

'Intelligence verified the information.'

'How?'

'Come on, Greg,' said Grimes, 'as if they'd tell me - way beyond my pay grade.'

Trish carried on. 'As you can see the operation was text book. Everything went like clockwork. Then the shit hit the fan. Scabies attempted to discharge his weapon at one of the team as he approached the vehicle. Luckily for our bloke the gun blew to bits in Scabies' hand as it was discharged, not so lucky for him, it blew his hand off.' Trish placed her hand palm down on one of the photographs then slid it across the desk.

'Jesus, Trish, it's not long since I had my breakfast,' Warren grumbled when he saw the close-up photograph of Scabies's bloody stump, mangled bits of flesh and ligament hanging where his hand used to be.   He pushed the photograph back across the table and turned to Jimbo. 'You know him, Scabby Dave?'

'I sort of know of him. A little shit who pretends to be a big shit. Never worked with him though, too much of an arse even for my liking.'

Warren picked up his coffee and sipped, spat it back in the cup, it was cold. 'This Scabby, has he any history with firearms?'

'No, not that we're aware of but he isn't opposed to violence, this is the first we've heard of him branching out.' Trish gathered up the photographs.

Grimes stood up and put his hands in his pockets. 'The thing is, there's been a couple of these exploding firearms. If the intelligence is right, it looks like we might be expecting more incidents like this in our neck of the woods. What's more worrying are the non-exploding weapons.'

'Never knew there was a gun culture in our neck of the woods,' Warren said, as he made eye contact with the DI.

'As I said before, you've been out of it a while, Greg, things move on quickly. Intelligence suggests there are more weapons out there than we know about. But saying that, not all the firearms out there are actually fired, just used to define status, kudos, earn respect from other gang members.'

'Respect - respect my arse, if you carry a weapon, at some point in time you'll use it.'

'And you'd know all about that,' Grimes said sarcastically, referring to an incident where Warren had shot and killed in cold blood the man sent to gun him down.

Warren ignored the jibe. 'What type of firearms are we looking at here?'

'You name it and it seems to be on the streets. The trend seems to be supplier driven, whatever the dealer can get hold of. The flavour of the past few months are Eastern European blank firing pistols, the Baikal. A Russian weapon originally used for crowd control firing gas cartridges, that was until someone cottoned on to how easy they are to convert. They're bought for next to nowt on the continent, sometimes converted over there, others when they get them back in the country. To put it simply, we've been asked to do our bit in nipping it the bud.'

'Why us?' asked Warren.

'Why not us, we've got to earn our keep.'

'Fair enough.'

Warren was the first to admit that it was good to catch up with Jimbo, but at the same time he was sceptical about him being a police employee. He could understand the logic behind the idea, but for Christ's sake he was a villain, thief, burglar and everything else in between. Before things went any further, he needed to clear the air with Grimes. Turning to Jimbo, he asked. 'Are we having another coffee, mate?'

'Here we go, things never change, Jimbo do this - Jimbo do that...'

'Oh, stop the whining, you know you're glad to see me,' Warren joked.

'Yeah... yeah.' Jimbo stood up and razzed to himself. 'Glorified office boy, that's me,' they heard him say as he closed the door behind him.

'More coffee?' asked Grimes.

'No, not really, I just wanted him out of the way while we had a chat.'

'O-k-a-y, what's bothering you?'

'Jimbo, just how far are you willing to go with him? I mean he's a good lad and I wouldn't like to see anyone taking advantage of him.'

'Like you did?' Grimes answered back.

'Come on, that's not fair, you know that was different; he was on the other side of the fence then.'

The DI stood up. 'I'll use him as far as he's willing to go.'

'What's your take on this, Trish?' Warren asked.

'Not for me to say, is it?'

'That's right, just sit on the fence...'

'Now hang on a minute, Greg, you know very well Trish has no say in this whatsoever. Let's get this much clear, I'm the SIO and Jimbo is employed as a Civilian Advisor...'

'I can sense a "but" coming.'

'Greg, let me finish. I know the term advisor can be used to cover a multitude of things, but I can assure you, I have no intention of putting Jimbo in any situation that he's uncomfortable with, or, any position that would knowingly put him in danger. After all, as you've just pointed out he *is* a civilian and *not* a copper.'

'We got there in the end, that's all I wanted to know. As you've probably found out already, he's keen and just wants to please. If you keep it that way I'll have no problems.'

'I'm pleased to hear that - now can we concentrate on the job in hand?' The tension now eased, Grimes took his seat again.

'Yep, as soon as the coffee arrives.'

Jimbo came back with a tray of coffees no one wanted and placed them on the desk where they remained to congeal.

Trish stood up and went across to the whiteboard and attached the photographs of the armed "stop and search".

'So, back to what we were talking about. The latest trend is to have the weapons dismantled and sent into the country by post, bit by bit, concealed with car parts and agricultural machines seem to a good favourite. God knows how many have come in that way.'

Warren sat forward in his chair, resting his elbows on the desk and faced the DI. 'I take it you have a plan? Other than open all the parcels sent via Royal Mail.'

Grimes sat back and folded his arms across his chest. 'I'd hardly call it a plan, but I do have an idea to help get the ball rolling,' he turned to face Jimbo. 'I was thinking along the lines that Jimbo hit the streets and start asking around.' Jimbo nodded. Grimes hesitated slightly before carrying on. 'Also, I was thinking maybe, and it's only a maybe, that's if you agree...'

'Stop waffling, Bill.'

'How do you fancy contacting your old pal Conway - see if he knows anything?'

Warren sat upright in his chair, this was not what he was expecting. 'For fuck's sake, Bill, you don't make life easy, do you? He's the last person I want *any* contact with.' Warren had been taken by surprise, first day back on the job and the DI wanted him to face his nemesis. Pat Conway was a significant player in the world of organised crime in the north of England. A man with fingers in many pies, a dangerous man to cross. 'I take it by contact, you mean you want me to bring Raymond Cole out of retirement?' Warren unfortunately had an uncanny resemblance to Raymond Cole, a villain in the know, one with many Stratergies in the underworld, this resemblance led to Warren being recruited into Gemmell Stratergies. Thus Warren's alter ego, Raymond Cole was created, and created very successfully.

Raymond Cole, the real Raymond Cole was dead - murdered. He died in prison whilst being held on unofficial remand, all it took was a bent screw with a gambling problem, and a 'lifer' who wanted his wife to be rewarded financially for his deed. She was - handsomely and anonymously, she never knew where the nest egg came from.

In his foray into the underworld, Warren had formed an unusual relationship with Conway. Assuming the identity of the fugitive on the run from the law, he had wormed his way into Conway's trust. Surprisingly, Warren had taken to the role like a fish to water and became 'close' to Conway, for a while anyway. Then, as quick as he'd appeared on the scene, Warren, still in his assumed role of Cole, disappeared from circulation. Now Bill wanted him to reappear. Warren was not a happy man.

'You have objections?' Grimes wasn't surprised at the response.

'Only the obvious ones.'

'Such as?' asked Grimes.

'How long have we got - you know bloody well the history between us,' Warren protested.

'I appreciate where you're coming from, Greg, but you've got to admit, if anyone knows anything, there's a damn good chance it will be Conway.'

'I'm not disagreeing with you, Bill. I just don't fancy getting reacquainted. What do you reckon, Jimbo?' Boland shrugged his shoulders noncommittally. He was glad he hadn't been tasked with contacting his old employer. 'If, and I say if, I was to make contact, I'll need a decent back-story.'

'Thought about that, we book you a few sessions on a sun bed and to all intents and purposes you've been sunning yourself on the Costas.' Warren shook his head at the comment. He came from a mixed-race family; his father was Jamaican and his mother was the stereotypical blonde English rose. Warren had inherited his father's dark genes, but he had his mother's blue eyes. What was stranger, so did the 'real' Raymond Cole. 'Just thought you'd enjoy a couple of sessions on a sun bed, brighten you up a bit,' Grimes said, through a smile.

Warren tried to put on a serious face but failed. 'You disrespecting my heritage?' He responded giving the DI a serious look. Then laughed out loud.

'Prat,' said the DI, turning to the younger man. 'That leaves you, Jimbo.'

'Wondered when you'd get around to me. So, what have you got in mind for a civilian advisor?' Boland asked sarcastically.

'Come on, mate, don't be like that, you've just got to do what you do best - hit the streets and see who knows what, you know the game, you did it for long enough.'

Jimbo nodded his agreement, at least it was better than being cooped up in the office.

As if on cue, there was a knock on the door and a uniformed constable entered. 'Sir,' he said as he crossed the room and handed a file to the DI. 'Just been asked to give you this,' he nodded, turned and left the room.

'Cheers,' Grimes said as he accepted the file and opened it. 'Shit,' he said, when he looked at a full colour crime scene photograph.

A young man lay in a pool of blood, he couldn't have been older than seventeen, a dark red stain in the front of his chest. He took out the photograph and placed it on the desk.

Warren leaned across the desk. 'Where is this?'

'The McDonalds' car park, Hessle Road. It was a drive-by, seems he was shot in the early hours of this morning, 2am.'

'Apparently, some of these guns do work,' Trish chipped in.

'So it would seem,' Warren picked up the report and read out loud. 'Witness said he heard two shots, turned and saw a vehicle drive away at high speed. He thinks it was a dark blue or black 4X4, possibly an Audi, with two male occupants. The witness went to see if he could help, but no joy. Paramedics confirmed him dead at the scene.'

'What was the witness doing at McDonalds at that time in the morning?' asked Trish, sceptically.

'He was a member of staff. The restaurant is open 24 hours. The bloke was just coming off shift.'

'That's a crime in itself.'

'What is?' Warren asked, puzzled.

'Calling McDonalds a restaurant. The dead lad, who is he?'

Grimes read from the folder. 'Alan Browning, 22 years old, he has a record for possession. He'd been pulled in a couple of times on suspicion to supply, clever lad, he was never caught with a significant amount on him. Browning - had a flat on Hawthorn Avenue.'

'Is he one of your old pals?' Trish asked Jimbo.

'No, never heard of him.'

Grimes closed the folder and handed it to Trish. 'Have a look on the PNC and see what you can come up with. Check for any known Strategies, family background, the usual stuff, specifically is there a link with Scabies. Looks like we're going to be busy.' He closed the folder.

Chapter 4

Warren took a breath, put on his best smile and pushed open the door to their old haunt, *The Eagle* on the corner of Coltman Street, mid-way along Anlaby Road.

'Haven't seen you for a while,' said Kirsty, the young barmaid. Her face lighting up as Warren and Jimbo walked towards the bar.

'Hi, it's good to see you, too,' Warren said, a broad smile on his face. Resting an elbow on the mahogany bar top he looked around the room, just the same old.

'Been working out of town?' asked Kirsty.

'You know what it's like, have to earn a crust, I go where the work is,' he replied turning back to face the girl. 'Give us two pints of lager will you please, Kirsty, take one for yourself.'

Kirsty held a glass under the pump. 'Thanks, I'll just have a half. How long are you going to be around?'

'A while I should think.' Warren gave her his warmest smile. Again, he looked around the bar where he used to be a regular.

'Alright?' asked a face he recognised.

'Not bad, pal. You keeping okay?' Warren couldn't remember the old bloke's name for love nor money.

'Aye.' End of conversation.

There were other faces he recognised, he nodded and received acknowledging nods back. He thought back to the first time he walked into the *Eagle*, every head in the place turned and eyed him with suspicion.

'So, are we going to see a bit more of you then?' asked Kirsty, returning the smile and passing the drinks across the bar top.

Warren placed a ten-pound note on the bar top. 'I'll have to see what I can do,' he collected his change, put it in his pocket and picked up the drinks. 'See you in a bit.'

Jimbo had found them a table with seats facing the door. Old habits die hard. Warren had taught him well.

Drinks in hand, Warren walked across the room and set them down on the table. 'So, mate, what do reckon?' He said, as he sat down and picked up his pint of lager.

'To what?' asked Jimbo as he sat back in his chair.

'The job you div, the team, everything?' Warren's eyes constantly scanned around the pub, as well as nodding acquaintances. He'd made one or two enemies during his last stay in the area, one being Jimbo's cousin, William Boland - AKA, Billybob. Billybob, with a trimming knife in his hand, had lain in wait for Warren, a decision he was to regret and resulted in him occupying a bed in the Orthopaedic ward in Hull Royal Infirmaries having his leg rebuilt.

'Like I said, I've been getting on with Bill, he seems a decent enough bloke for a copper, and Trish, well, she's cool as well as hot. A good laugh when you get to know her, and from what I've seen she seems good at her job.'

'And you're happy with the way things are?'

'What's with the all the questions, Greg?'

Warren was serious. 'Look at what happened last time you got mixed up with me? We got into one or two awkward scrapes if my memory serves me correctly - and it does.'

'But we had a bloody good time doing it, didn't we?' Both men laughed. 'So, how do you think we should play this? I reckon we should pair up.'

'There is one difference, Jimbo, this time I won't be running the show.'

'Yeah, but once we're out of the office, it'll be just you and me like old times, the "A" team - right?'

'If you say so, Jimbo, if you say so,' replied Warren, eyeing the girl behind the bar as he spoke.

'So, what do you think to Bill's plan?'

'As good as any I suppose, like he said, bringing Ray Cole back from the dead is the best option. I'll try and worm my way back in with that fat twat, Conway. I take it he's still working out of the flats on Ice House Road?'

'Not heard any different, but not for much longer there's talk of knocking them down.' Jimbo inclined his head towards Warren's glass. 'Want another?' He finished what was left in his glass, stood up and went to the bar without waiting for an answer.

Warren was pleased the way things had worked out, it could have been a lot worse, he could have been working security in some supermarket or another, and it was good to be working with the lad again. Although he did have reservations about being thrown back into the fray as his alter ego, Ray Cole, thug and killer. He'd hoped Cole had been dead and buried once and for all. Getting reacquainted with Conway wasn't something he was looking forward to.

'That bird behind the bar was asking about you.' Jimbo said, when he returned. Warren turned his head and smiled. 'C'mon man ... you didn't ... you never ... you did, didn't you?'

'Jimbo, if all that mumbo jumbo coming out of your mouth means did I sleep with her? That's for me to know and you to keep guessing.' He hadn't of course, but Warren reckoned if he'd played his cards right the opportunity had been there and maybe it still was. But he was going to keep the lad guessing. 'Now be serious will you, how do you feel about going on the streets, meeting up with your old cronies?'

'I'm cool, it's not as if I don't know my way around. Been there, done that. Get rid of the glad rags for a while,' he said, as he brushed away imaginary crumbs from his Ben Sherman shirt. 'I'll dig out my old street clobber and put a few piercings back in, more like the old me, look the part.'

'Sure you're definitely okay with it?'

'I am, Greg, I am.' Warren needed to hear this said away from the nick.

'It's a good job I kept this,' he said, holding up a second mobile. Warren had a second phone, the undercover mobile he'd used while assuming the persona of Ray Cole. 'Down to me then,' he said reluctantly, holding up the phone. 'Suppose I'd better give Conway a bell, pave the way. I don't just want to turn up unannounced on the paranoid twat's doorstep and get my head caved in with a cricket bat.' He turned his head and smiled at the girl behind the bar - again, much to Jimbo's amusement.

'Give over, old man.'

'In for a penny ...' Warren scrolled through the contacts, stopped at Conway's number and hesitated for a second or two before pressing the dial button. The call was answered almost immediately.

'Who the fuck is this?' Warren's number wasn't recognised.

'Is that any way to speak to an old friend?' Warren said in a West Yorkshire accent, when taking on the role of Cole he had perfected the dialect and found it easy to adopt on a whim.

Silence for a second or two. 'Cole - that you?'

Warren sat back in his seat. 'None other, pal. Listen, I'm in the area, can we meet?'

'You've got some bleedin nerve, I thought I'd seen the back of you,' Conway almost spat down the phone. 'The cops still looking for you?'

'I heard they gave up, bigger fish to catch and all that. Can we meet or what?'

'Na, I had enough of you last time, bye.' He hung up. Warren laughed and put the mobile down on the table.

'Well, what's he have to say?' Jimbo asked, leaning over the sodden table top.

'Can't say that he was pleased to hear from me, the cheeky sod hung up.'

'Got you sussed alright.'

Warren gave a grin, picked up his phone and dialled again.

Conway picked up the call right away and didn't bother with small talk. 'Be at the flat tomorrow - one time offer, 10 o'clock, don't be late.' End of conversation.

'Nice speaking to you too,' Warren said into the dead mobile, then put it down on the table between the beer spills.

'Well?' Jimbo asked, as he picked up his pint of lager and sipped through the frothy head.

'Meeting him at the flat tomorrow.'

'Rather you than me. You are going tooled up?'

'I'll have a word, see how we're fixed legally regarding firearms, but I can't see it's something Bill would want authorised.'

'Greg, there's no way you can go in there without insurance, you know what a mad fucker he can be when he wants.' He leaned in closer across the table and spoke in low voice. 'I've still got the Glock.' The concern was genuine. 'Just let me know - okay?' The Glock had been acquired during their run-in with a senior member of Gemmell Stratergies.

'Bloody hell, Jimbo, you *have* been listening to all the shit that's been going around today? Now you're offering me an illegal firearm!'

'Just trying to look after your welfare, that's all.'

'Thanks for the concern, pal. But I reckon he'll think I'm carrying, that should be enough insurance.' He hoped. 'Are you still living in the same flat?'

'You must be joking, with the money you gave me, I've got myself a proper place now, a one bed roomed flat in Hessle, bought it cash on the nose.'

'Good for you, the other place was a bloody dump!'

'You never thought that when you were dossing down on my settee.'

'Thought it - but never said it. And the car well, enough....,' Warren said smiling.

Chapter 5

Warren called in at the office briefly to keep the DI informed on his plans to meet Conway, after a quick catch up he was away to his meeting. Conway never conducted business from his home, always from a flat on Ice House Road, close to the city centre. Some 100 metres short of his destination, a high-rise block of flats, Warren pulled his Ford Escort into the kerb and killed the engine. He had that feeling of déjà vu as he sat staring through the windscreen. Nothing had changed, there was nothing in the area to change. The pub was still closed and boarded up, and the local shops still sported steel security shutters over the windows. Through the smeared glass of the windscreen he stared at the high rise. He thought back to his first visit to the flat, his first meeting with Conway posing as Raymond Cole - that was something he wouldn't forget in a hurry. It was also the first time he met a young scally called James Boland, AKA Jimbo who was now a trusted friend and of all things, a Civilian Advisor to the police.

He checked his watch, it was coming up to 9.50am, his meeting with Conway was scheduled for 10am. His hands were damp, sweaty, he held his arms out in front of him, he was sure he could detect a tremble, some hard man he was - if only Conway could see him now. He wiped the palms down his jeans. He shook his hand to try and rid them of the feeling, turned the ignition key, selected first gear and moved off. Two minutes later he turned into the parking area of the tower block. He climbed out of the vehicle and locked it. He kicked away a beer can as he picked his way through the debris scattered about the parking area. Looking up he could see the CCTV camera high on a single pole, on his last visits some old codger unaware of what it was, had grumbled on about the council and the flood light that didn't work.

True to expectations the entrance foyer of the flats was clear of the usual rubbish, empty fag packets and beer cans, undoubtedly down to Conway's influence. Warren crossed the lobby. It looked as if the lift was working. He pressed the call button and watched the floor lights change as it journeyed down. Unlike the foyer, the lift left a lot to be desired. The stench of piss invaded his nostrils as the lift doors opened, he watched them close again and headed for the stairwell.

After taking the stairs two at a time he stood in front of the door of number thirteen. A few angry people who Conway had crossed swords with had left their mark on the door over the years. He took a deep breath, clenched his right hand into a fist and banged on the steel plated door. Warren could sense someone checking him out through the door spy-hole. He heard the locks click and the bolts being drawn on the inside.

The door opened. 'You've got some fucking nerve coming back here.' Warren flashed him a confident grin. 'Pissed off without a bye or leave, and now you turn up out of bloody nowhere.' Conway said, as he stood aside to allow Warren to pass.

'But I left you a wealthy man.'

'And that, Ray, is the only reason I agreed to see you.'

He noticed Conway hadn't got any thinner, porky as ever, but still sturdy with it. Warren was committed - he had no option other than to face it out. He smiled. 'You know me, Pat, don't give a fuck about anything or anyone. How have you been keeping?'

Fat maybe, but Conway looked as if he could still look after himself if the occasion arose. According to rumour Conway had been a half decent bare knuckle fighter in his time, Warren couldn't see it himself - but you can't always judge a book by its cover and he had no intention of finding out.

Security conscious as ever, Conway re-locked the door, slid the bolts tight shut before following Warren into the living-room and sat down in his large leather easy chair. Warren, who stood in the centre of the room, took this as his cue to sit and flopped onto the sofa, not before moving a pile of boxing magazines onto the floor.

'Put anyone in hospital lately?' Conway asked sarcastically.

'Not since I rearranged your man's hands and face. Have you?' Warren replied through a half smile. During his time working for Conway, the need to assert himself arose and he had needed to lay down some rules as to who was in charge. His authority was questioned by an employee of Conway's, a local hard-case, Warren never did find out the name he had given to hospital staff -

when they attempted to put his face and hands back together.

'How *is* that employee of yours these days, still taking his food through a straw?'

'Oh, he was eventually discharged from the infirmary. He's lodging on Chanterlands Avenue now - in the Garden of Remembrance. You're not the only one who had to lay down some ground rules. I had to send a message to anyone else who thought about grassing me up to the cops.'

Jesus, thought Warren, and Bill wondered why he didn't want to get involved.

'No loss there, then,' he said, feeling a twinge of guilt - but not too much, the bloke had been an arsehole, no mistake.

Conway stood up and went through into the kitchen, returning with a couple of cans. 'Beer?' he asked as he passed over a can of strong export lager.

Warren accepted the can from a knuckle damaged hand. Maybe he had been a scrapper? Warren thought as he accepted the tinny. 'Cheers,' he pulled back the tab and sipped from the can. He wasn't having problems keeping up the pretence, he'd slipped back into the persona of Ray Cole with no problem - it was easier than he thought.

'So, what brings your black arse back to my neck of the woods?' Conway asked, as he put his can on the floor beside his chair and sat forward, elbows resting on his knees.

'Can't I just pay an old pal a visit?' Although calling Conway a pal was a bit extreme.

48

'Fuck off, Ray, I didn't come down in the last shower! You don't pay social calls. What are you after?'

'You're such a cynical old bastard - you know that?'

'Look, if we're just going to see who can piss the furthest you might as well sod off now, I'm a busy man.' Conway had little patience.

'Don't get snappy. Information. I'm looking for some info that's all, I'm not here to cause any bother.'

'Well, I'm pleased to hear that.'

'A pal of mine up Newcastle way is in the arms market, the problem is we heard someone from around here is supplying unreliable goods, you know how the word spreads. It's sort of tarnishing my friend's good name and he wants it stopped.'

'Suppose that's where you come in?'

'Yep, that's where I come in, you could say I'm a sort of trouble shooter - it's good that, 'trouble shooter',' he laughed a little, not too much.

Conway didn't find the pun funny.

'So, tell me what is it you want from me?' He fished in his pocket and took out his cigars.

'You're top dog, around here. You must know someone or something that can help me.'

'Come off it, Ray, why the fucking hell would I want to help you?' Conway lit his cigar with his old-fashioned Zippo. The room filled with a blue fog. The smell always reminded Warren of Christmas time at his grandparent's house.

'Old time's sake?' He splayed his hands palm up.

'Yeah, right. Old time's sake? You'll be swinging the lantern and playing a fucking violin in a minute. If I did have a mind to help - what would be in it for me?'

'My gratitude, Pat, my eternal gratitude.'

'Gratitude's no fucking good to me, can't spend fucking words. Now if there was to be a finder's fee that would be a different kettle of fish altogether.'

'You're a hard man to bargain with, I'll give you that. I'm sure we can come to some amicable understanding.'

'Has this got anything to do with that young fucking idiot who got his hand blown off, Scabies?'

'Sort of, as it happens, he's not the only one its happened to, what concerns us is that some of these crap pistols have made their way further north, what's more it doesn't look good for trade.'

Warren never noticed the twitch in Conway's face. 'One of them things. Shit happens, you know that.' The fat man blew smoke up to the ceiling.

Warren was relieved; it looked as if Conway had swallowed his spiel. He sat back on the settee and relaxed a little.

'Just like the old days, Pat, you and me having a beer and chewing the fat.'

'Just get on with it, Ray.'

'My colleague, in Newcastle, reckons things could escalate pretty quickly. The trouble as he sees it, is the number of independent operators getting into the game is getting a little bit out of hand. Not that he's afraid of competition, he thrives on it. What he wants is these dodgy weapons stopped, once and for all - not doing the trade any good at all, not for anyone.'

'Okay, so somewhere in the city we have amateurs converting guns, and you think I might know who.'

'Come on, Pat, you run the city - if someone's converting and selling imported firearms you're bound to hear about it at some point, all I want is for you to put some feelers out. I need to know sooner, rather than later.' Warren played on Conway's vanity - it usually worked.

'That's as may be, but you know I do my best to keep out of other people's business. As long as they keep out of mine and don't get in the way, I leave them alone.' Conway stood up and walked through to the kitchen and retrieved another two beers from the fridge. 'Like I said, if I was to help, what's in it for me?' Conway asked, as he came back into the living room and sat down.

'I'll make sure you get well paid. Have I ever let you down?'

Conway raised his eyebrows. 'Don't even go there, Ray ...'

'Look, all we want is for you to put the word out, anybody new on the scene, anybody dealing who shouldn't be dealing, offer a cash incentive for information, I'll make sure you're reimbursed - you know the game. Got anything stronger?' Warren asked, holding the can up.

'Yep, but you're leaving soon.'

'You will ask around?'

'I'll see what I can do.'

'Thanks, Pat, I appreciate the help.' Warren stood up ready to leave.

'Whoa, not so quick, fella, there is a little something you can help me with in the meantime.'

'You never change, do you?' Warren sat down again. 'What *is* this little something you want me to help with?'

Hoping he wasn't going to get drawn into deep trouble - again.

'First off, you sure you're not still wanted by the law, right?'

'In a manner of speaking I suppose I am, but I honestly don't think they're putting much effort into it. According to my passport, birth certificate and driving licence I'm someone else. I've been coming in and out of the UK every few weeks or so from the Costa del Crime, never had any problems since we parted ways.'

'So, you reckon that there's no chance of you getting picked up then?'

Warren wondered where the conversation was going. 'Nope, not a cat in Hell's chance, unless *someone* grasses me up.' The emphasis just brought a scowl to Conway's face. He was many things, but not a grass where people like Raymond Cole were concerned.

'I need someone I can trust.'

'Here we go, tell you what forget it, I don't want to get mixed up in any of your business.' He was about to stand up, calling Conway's bluff.

'Calm down, Ray, it's kosher, I just need a favour.'

'I thought you were all out of favours?'

'I just need someone to collect my daughter off the London train in the morning. It gets in around 10am.'

'Bloody hell, I never knew you had a kid?' Warren was genuinely surprised.

'Long story,' he took out his wallet and removed a photograph and passed it over. 'She's seventeen and lives with her mother, over in Toronto, Canada. Me and Maggie - well, you don't really want to know, but me and her mother, we've been getting on quite well recently, been Skyping and stuff.'

Warren gave a laugh. 'Skyping?'

'What's so funny? I'm not a complete moron you know, I can use a computer.'

'Sorry, mate, never took you for the techie type.'

Conway ignored the jibe. 'As I was saying, the problem is Rachell seems to be going through a rebellious stage, a bit more than that she's driving her mother barmy. You know what teenagers can be like?'

Indeed, Warren did know, he'd put his parents through hell before finding his vocation in the Police Force.

'We thought it would be good for her to come over here and visit for a while. She's been staying with some relation or other of her mother's down in London.'

'She's a good looking young woman,' Warren said, looking at the photograph of the slim girl with an oval face, long blond hair and piercing green eyes.

'That's why I need someone I can trust. You know the type of people I employ, deadheads, druggies and wankers. There isn't one of 'em I'd trust to keep their hands off me granny, never mind my seventeen-year-old daughter.'

'How come you aren't picking her up yourself?'

'I've got a meeting with the Inland Revenue, I've managed to swerve it twice. My accountant says if I try to put the meeting off again I'll be right up shit creek. Bastards.'

'You turned legit?'

'Hardly, but some things have to look to be done by the book, keep things sweet.'

'And that's it? You just want me to meet her off the train and bring her - to where?' he said looking around. 'Not here surely?'

'My home, you div, you don't think I'd want her to know this place exists, never mind see it.'

Conway's official residence was a smart, four bed-roomed, detached house down north Boulevard, an area once the home for the wealthy trawler owners and skippers. 'Okay, I think I can manage that, just let the girl know it will be me collecting her. I don't want arresting by some British Rail cop for abduction.'

'Will do, thanks.'

'You seen anything of Jimbo since I've been away?' He had to ask, Conway would have thought it strange if he hadn't.

'Just the once, didn't have much to say for himself. Didn't expect to see him again, not after he went off with you on the great adventure.'

'Yeah, well, it didn't last long. We parted company after a couple of weeks.' Some quick thinking was called for. 'We went up north to Newcastle, as I said, I've still got contacts up there. He didn't much like the company I was keeping, and after a couple weeks he'd had enough packed his bags and was away on his toes. Probably back to his old ways by now.'

'If he is I haven't heard about it. So, Ray, as I said, things to do people to see, so, piss off and I'll see you tomorrow.'

'Fair enough.' Warren stood up, shook a fat hand and left.

He felt relieved as he walked out of the flat, the first and hardest hurdle over. He took a deep breath when he heard the heavy steel plated door close behind him. He had been dubious about what kind of reception he'd receive. The meeting had gone better than he ever expected, in fact it couldn't have gone any better. A favour for a favour, he wouldn't have expected anything less from Conway. The Escort was still in the parking area, a big plus was it was undamaged and still had all its wheels. The local 'boys' probably recognised it as belonging to a pal of Conway's.

Chapter 6

James Boland had undergone a transformation, he was back to the way he used to dress, Jimbo the scally. He was wearing denim jeans and a jacket that had seen better days, beneath the jacket he wore a faded 'Iron Maiden' T-shirt and generally looked as if he'd had a makeover in a charity shop - except for his favourite Doc Martin boots. Not mentioning the piercings had been reinstated in his ears and nose and finished off with a safety pin through his left eyebrow.

He walked along Springbank towards the city centre glancing in doorways, looking for dossers he knew in his past life. Every now and then he would stop and look in a shop window, checking the reflection to see if he was being followed - a habit he'd picked up from Warren. He kept walking and watching. Not far from the city centre, he ducked down an alleyway between a betting shop and Chinese take-away, stepping over take-away cartons as he went. Around the back of the bookies, he looked over his shoulder once more, then strode over a low fence to the building next door and hammered with his fist on a rotting wooden door. The door shook in its frame, green paint flaked away from the rotting timber and floated to the ground. No answer, he banged again. He could hear movement inside the squat. The semi-derelict building had been home to several dead beats and junkies over the years. Those people who over time had escaped or evaded the system for one reason or another.

'Yeah, who's that?' a rasping voice called out.

Jimbo recognised it immediately, it was Lee Etherington, a mate from way back, the man he wanted to see.

Jimbo and Lee's friendship pre-dated the multitude of piercings and tats they both had in common, back to when they were fresh faced school boys.

'It's me, open up,' he yelled back.

'Who's me?' the croaky voice questioned suspiciously.

'For fuck's sake, Lee, it's me, Jimbo.'

The key in the lock turned, a head poked out of the open door and scanned both directions before speaking.

'Bloody hell, mate, haven't seen you for a while, where you been hiding yourself?' He growled out, his voice sounded as if his throat had been scraped with sandpaper. The foul smell of poverty, damp and decay invaded Jimbo's nostrils. Lee yanked the sticking door wide to let Jimbo in.

'Been in Wakefield,' Jimbo lied, as he entered the filthy hallway, following Lee further amongst the grott. He tried not to breathe too deeply, the place stank of the dispossessed. He was surprised at the state Lee was in, his mate was in desperate need of a hot meal and bath – not in any particular order. His hair was lank, lifeless and he was in need of a razor. He stank of stale cider and over-rank body odour. It was obviously way too late to take better care of his personal hygiene – way too late to make a difference. On top of that the smell of Cannabis resin seemed to be oozing out of his skin.

'What the fuck was you doing in Wakefield?' he asked, as he shuffled his way like an old man along the torn lino into the front room, where he dropped down onto a moth eaten, manky old settee. Jimbo pulled a wobbly legged kitchen chair and sat facing his one-time best friend. As he looked around the squalid room he thought how lucky he was to have been taken under Conway's wing. This could have easily been his life, no question about it. When his old man, suffering from the Big C had taken his own life, Conway gave him a job - even if that job involved working on the wrong side of the law, it saved him. Living in a shit hole of a squat could have easily been his misfortune.

'Three months for possession with intent to supply,' the comment brought a hoarse smoker's laugh from his old mate, who splat phlegm into a dirty handkerchief.

'What did you have on you?' Lee asked as he wiped the dribble from his mouth

'Only 8oz of Moroccan Black, intent to supply, a measly 8oz.' Boland could lie well when he had to. 'The only reason I had so much on me was cos I'd come into a bit of cash. I mean, for fucks sake I was just stocking up on my stash while I could.'

'Bastards,' Lee could hardly get the word out without spluttering and coughing, he didn't sound too good. Lee picked up his tobacco tin off the floor and opened it, took out the king-size cigarette paper and spread tobacco on the sheet. Then produced a small scrunched up ball of tin foil, opened it and rubbed the contents between well practised fingers, spreading the Cannabis resin onto the tobacco. The result was a well rolled spliff. 'So, you looking to score, matey?' he asked as he hung the roach to his bottom lip.

'Maybe, but I thought I'd call on my old mate to see what's been going on while I was away?'

'Fuck all to speak about. Just the same shit,' he flicked a cheap plastic lighter and lit his smoke and took a deep draw - held it, swallowed, then coughed again as he let the smoke drift from his mouth.

Lee offered the roach to Jimbo. There was no way in the world he was putting that in his mouth.

'I'm cool, cheers all the same. How's Mouse doing? He still around?' Mouse was another contact from the old days.

'Yep, the little shit's still causing mayhem, ducking, diving and dealing. Reckons he's in with a 'face', heading for the big-time. Oh yeah, and he's taken up with some of these skinhead types, going around saying all this racist shit.'

'Who's the 'face'?'

'Won't say, least ways not told me.'

'If he's dealing I might pay him a visit, I take it he is?'

'Does a scabby dog have fleas? He reckons he's made a fair bit of cash, or so he says.' He put his hand down his tracky bottoms and scratched his scrotum. 'Just told me he's moving up in the world, goin' places.' Jimbo remembered Mouse as being a small-time dealer and paranoid with it. 'Can't see it me self.'

'No, neither can I.' Mouse usually pissed away any money he made up against the wall, as quick as he got his hands on it. But he was curious about the 'face', someone had been reading a Martina Cole novel. 'Changed my mind,' he reached across and held his hand out for the smoke. 'Cheers, so how come he's in the money?' He feigned taking a deep drag and passed back the soggy ended roach. He wanted the conversation to keep going, but it looked like Lee was near to losing the plot, his brain was too fuddled with the weed and White Lightening cider.

'Never said.' Lee coughed phlegm again - it dribbled down his chin, he wiped it with the sleeve of his shirt.

Jimbo thought he'd try a different tack. 'Shame about what happened to Scabby Dave.'

'Fucking hell, man, he got his hand blown right off.'

'You know where he got the gun?'

'Na, too heavy for me, man, don't know. But it wouldn't surprise me if Mouse doesn't know something or other.'

'What makes you say that?'

'Dunno really, I mean it's just a feeling, could be this geezer he keeps going on about?' Then Lee lay back on the settee cushions and closed his eyes. It looked like this was the end of the meeting.

'The 'face?''

'Hmm, maybe.'

Jimbo stood up. 'Ok, mate, I'm off now and you get that cough sorted,' Jimbo stood up and was about to leave. 'Take care of yourself.'

'Can't let me have few quid 'til my social comes through can ya?' Lee asked, his eyes still closed.

Jimbo took a twenty-pound note from his wallet and pressed it into Lee's hand. He knew it would be spent on his next fix.

Eyes still closed and sprawled on the settee. 'Cheers, mate. Drop the latch on your way out,' he drawled.

What a fucking state to be in thought Jimbo, he genuinely felt sorry for Lee, he was sure it wouldn't be long before someone found him dead.

Jimbo had been in the office an hour or so reading through Blackstone's *General Police Duties*, Trish was busy with her head stuck into research on illegal weapons and Warren wasn't expected anytime soon, the perfect opportunity to nip into the car-park for a smoke thought Jimbo. Standing in the car-park, back against the wall with his face up to the sun, and the roll-up clinging on to his bottom lip for all it was worth, he enjoyed a few minutes alone time. Then he heard it, the familiar growling engine of Warren's Ford Escort, he heard it long before it turned the corner into the car-park.

This was the day Warren was to see Jimbo transformed to his old self - clothes wise. The transformation couldn't be missed, unless you were as short-sighted as a mole. He had received more than a few strange looks that morning, as he punched in the security code into the keypad and walked through the station. He was half expecting to be challenged but it never happened. He stood and watched as Warren parked.

'Jimbo, you do realise what you're wearing is totally inappropriate clobber when you work in a police station,' Warren said jokingly. He couldn't help but notice the numerous facial piercings had also returned.

Jimbo totally ignored him. 'Still got the speed machine then?' he said, as he walked over and gave one of the front tyres a kick.

'Yep, wouldn't part with it.' It may not have been much to look at but the Ford Escort with its formula 1 type engine had served them both well in the past. 'For some reason or another nobody's asked for it back. Someone's obviously keeping it taxed and insured.' The Ford was the service vehicle issued to him whilst he was in the "employ" of Gemmell Stratergies, nothing much to look at but as fast as a rat coming down a drainpipe.

Jimbo took a drag of his smoke. 'How did you get on with Conway?' He dropped the fag end to the floor and crushed it underfoot.

'Surprisingly well, better than I expected - look.' He held up his hands, palms facing Jimbo and wiggled his fingers. 'Still got all my digits!'

On the way back to their mini squad room, if it could really be called that, they called in at the station canteen for coffee and cakes. Jimbo garnering more than a few funny looks along the way, he looked as if he should be in the cells not walking around the place with a security pass hung around his neck.

'Excuse me, love,' the assistant behind the counter had said, when she saw Jimbo standing in the queue, 'are you allowed in here?' Jimbo tutted and held his ID for her to see. 'Sorry, love,' she replied, 'got to be careful.'

Warren was very close to bursting out laughing. 'Never mind, mate,' he said, patting Jimbo on the shoulder only to have his hand shrugged off. He was still smiling to himself as they reached the office.

'Cakes and refreshments,' Warren said as he kicked open the office door and placed the tray down on the desk. 'No Bill?'

'Nope, just me,' Trish answered as she eyed up the cakes.

'Help yourself.'

'Thanks, I'm starving.' She dived in and helped herself to the largest fresh cream bun on the plate. 'So, how did things go with, Conway?' She picked up a paper tissue and wiped the cream from around her mouth as she made a crumby mess on the DIs desk.

'Better than I expected, it went very well in fact, as I've told Jimbo I've still got the use of my hands and legs, so I reckon things went okay. I spun him a story about a colleague in Newcastle, not being too pleased with the dodgy firearms that are floating about. He reckons he'd see what he can find out.'

'Just like that?' Jimbo asked. 'Too easy.'

'However' Warren paused, 'he does want a favour in return.'

'I guessed as much, whose legs does he want you to break?'

'No, nothing like that - did you know he has a daughter?' Warren took out the photograph from his wallet and passed it across.

'Nice looking girl,' Trish acknowledged.

'Heard something but never actually met her,' said Jimbo. He looked over Trish's shoulder at the photograph. 'Nothing like her fat twat of a father. He sure he's her dad?'

'Apparently, she lives in Canada with her mother and is visiting for a while. The fat man has a meeting in the morning with the tax-man. All I have to do is meet her off the London train, keep her occupied for an hour or so, and then take her to his place, simple.'

'And that's it?' asked Trish, who was by now in an even bigger mess with the cream bun. She licked her fingers, and wiped them on another paper tissue, before picking up a pen and updating the daily action log.

'That's all there is to it, London train 10am tomorrow, coffee, show her the city's sights then back to his place - all done and back here for lunch time.'

'Why you and not one of his own blokes?' Jimbo asked.

'Jimbo, you've worked for him, would you trust any of them?

'Point taken.'

'Right, Jimbo me lad, your turn what did you find out?' Trish asked, pen poised over the logbook.

'I paid a visit to an old dope head friend of mine, Lee Etherington, you should have seen the fucking state of him. Half stoned and coughing up phlegm, I didn't get a great deal out of him. The best was that a psycho who goes by the name of Mouse...'

'For the log, what's his real name?'

'Sebastian London.'

'Ooh, Sebastian, sounds a posh boy,' said Trish.

'Hardly, that's why he goes by a nickname.'

'Why Mouse?'

'To be honest, I don't really know, cos he's got a face more like a bleedin rat, pointy and big ears,' he shuddered at the thought. 'Anyway, Lee, reckons Mouse keeps going on about some bloke he's working for, 'a face'.

'Sounds as if he's been reading too many Martina Cole novels,' Trish managed to mutter through the cream.

'That's what I thought, great minds and all that. So, it seems Mouse is flashing the cash. Believe me, from what I remember about him it's not like him having any cash to brag about. He's the sort of piss head psycho who can't hang on to it.'

'Worth checking him out?' asked Trish.

'Somewhere to start at least.'

'Sounds like a plan,' Warren turned face her, 'what are you doing tonight?'

'Washing my cat - take Jimbo.'

'Thought you might say that - what do you reckon Jimbo, me and you, a night on the town?'

'Like a date, you mean?' He tried his best not to crack his face into a smile.

Jimbo winked across at Trish. 'Sorry to disappoint you, fella, I've told you before, you're not my type. Seriously, Mouse is one nasty fucker. We'll probably find him in the *Rose* on Beverley Road, he usually ends up in there at some point.'

'Okay, matey, I'll see you in the *Eagle* about eight? Sure, you won't come, Trish, so I don't have to look at his ugly mug all night?'

'I'd like to, Greg, but like I said, I'm bathing the cat tonight.'

'Nice one, Trish,' then Jimbo turned to Warren. 'Ugly mug, me, wait until you see Mouse.'

'Why wait?' said Trish as she brought his details from the PNC up on her laptop. 'You have something there Jimbo, it's a face only a mother could love - I think.'

'What's his form?' Warren asked as he helped himself to the remaining cream cake, Trish threw him a look, she obviously intended working her way through everything on the plate.

'GBH, ABH, TWOCKING, burglary, possession with intent, you name it this lad has done it and got the tee-shirt, but no mention of firearms.' She turned to Jimbo. 'How the hell did you get involved with a scrote like him?'

Jimbo just shrugged his shoulders. There had been times when Jimbo had been desperate for cash, and, needs must as the saying goes, but he wasn't going to expand on the subject.

'What about this Scabby and the lad shot in McDonalds, Alan?'

Trish opened her A4 pad. 'I've done a bit of trawling about but there's not much to link them together apart from the obvious, namely they both did a bit of dealing. Scabies and the lad did run in the same gang when they were younger, but parted ways a while back.'

As arranged Warren and Jimbo met up for a pint in the *Eagle*, the place was quiet. They sat at a table with a good view of the exits. 'How do you want to play this? And

66

will you please stop eyeing up that barmaid?' Jimbo taunted, as he picked up his glass.

'Window shopping, just window shopping,' he turned and smiled across at the girl and back again. 'As to how we play this, the ball is in your court - he's your mate.'

'I tell you he's no bleedin mate of mine, well not for yonks, he's a nasty twat.' Warren kept looking across toward the bar. 'Oh c'mon, you look as if you're getting settled in here, let's get going before you try and get into her knickers,' Jimbo said, being the responsible one.

'Crude, Jimbo, that's what you are.' Warren picked up his glass, finished it one swallow and stood up and gave the girl another wink. 'Well what are we waiting for?'

Jimbo sighed, shook his head, gave the girl a wave of the hand and followed him out of the door.

'Been a while since we last drove through the city,' Warren said as he negotiated the Escort through the town centre traffic.

'Hmm, at least we haven't got anybody shooting at us and no one tucked up in the boot.'

Warren drove along Beverley Road, the main road north out of the city centre. Polish supermarkets, Romanian bakeries, and various eastern European shops now dominated the area. Turkish barbers seemed to be the flavour of the moment. Warren turned the Escort into Park Lane, pulling up around the corner of the *Rose*.

'You ready for this?' he asked as he killed the engine. Jimbo nodded, he wasn't looking forward to it one little bit. 'Right, let's see if this Mouse is in his hole.'

'If that was your attempt at a joke, it was sad, even for you,' Jimbo said, as they climbed out of the low-slung car. 'And Greg - if he's there, let me do the talking.'

'Why's that?'

'You can come across as sort of - aggressive at times.'

'Cheeky, sod. You really know how to hurt me, hurt me right here,' Warren punched himself in the chest, all the time suppressing a laugh. 'But can I smack him one if he gets too clever?'

'Fucking southerner, always want to let your fists do the talking.' Jimbo said just loud enough for Warren to hear. The *Rose* was an old-fashioned pub, the exterior, cracked green glazed bricks with frosted glass windows.

At the green painted door Jimbo stopped and paused, took a breath, then pushed the door open. The voices stopped and heads turned as they walked in.

Warren didn't take much notice, just stared straight ahead, ignoring the British National Party poster on the wall. He'd seen it all before. Where he came from, it was a usual occurrence when a stranger walked in for voices to pause, especially when it was a tall, handy looking black guy. The *Rose* was no different - a "locals" pub although it did look a little on the racist side. Ignoring the stares they went across to the bar and stood side by side, resting their elbows on the mahogany bar top. Jimbo constantly looked about.

'Two pints of lager please, mate,' Warren said to the scruffy fat youth of a barman.

'Yes, pal, what can I get you?'

'I just told you ...' said Warren, looking the barman in the eye.

The youth completely blanked him - looked over Warren's shoulder as if he didn't exist and proceeded to serve the skinhead who'd followed them in, this to Warren, was like showing a red rag to a bull. 'Hey, fat boy, you deaf or what?'

The barman carried on pulling the skinheads pint. Enough was enough. Warren reached across the bar with both arms and grabbed him by the front of his shirt, glasses clattered to the floor as he was hoisted half way across the bar top, and spilling beer as he did. Heads turned. In the mirror behind the bar, Jimbo could see movement.

'I knew it - I fucking knew it,' he said under his breath. Warren obviously didn't have the anger management thing under control.

Two of the regulars stood and pushed back their chairs as if they were going to intervene. They were stopped in their tracks as a smaller figure pushed between them.

'Oh shit, shit, shit,' Jimbo said in a low voice. Warren immediately looked at the reflection coming toward them. It was Mouse.

'What's goin' on here, Jimbo? And YOU, let go of fucking Charlie,' said the smaller man as he prodded Warren in the back. Mouse was small in stature, but hard with it. His motto was the bigger they are the harder they fall.

'With pleasure.'

With an exaggerated flourish, Warren flexed his arms and pulled Charlie forward and then threw him backwards to his own side of the bar, taking half a dozen bottles of beer with him as he crashed into the bottle shelf behind him before collapsing to the floor in a heap.

'Look, Mouse, we just came in for a quiet …'

'And this is a quiet drink?' Mouse questioned threateningly, holding his arms wide looking up at Warren.

Warren was struggling to keep his temper in check, arms down by his side clenching and unclenching his fists, breathing slow and deep, just like his therapist had shown him. In his previous life his fists and his feet had landed him in more trouble than he cared to admit.

'If this is your idea of a quiet friggin drink - I'd like to see it when you have a proper night out!'

Warren stared into the smaller man's eyes willing him to try and throw a punch, it may have been something subliminal that Mouse recognised in the gaze.

'Well, get up off your arse Charlie and get these blokes a drink,' he told the barman. 'When you do have a proper night out you let me know, cos I like a fucking good fight.' Mouse laughed and gave Jimbo a man-hug. Jimbo reluctantly responded at the same time turning his face away from the coffin breath and blackened teeth.

'Aren't you going to introduce us?' Warren asked, standing to his full height of five eleven, to emphasise Mouse's short stature.

'Yeah, right, Ray, this Mouse - Mouse, Ray.' Warren reluctantly held out his hand, he was pleased when Mouse ignored the gesture.

'Sebastian,' corrected Mouse.

Warren was now in full character. 'Some fucking pub this is when the barman ignores the customers,' he said looking down on Mouse. He could see a swastika tat on the side of Mouse's neck, boldly placed for all to admire or loath.

'We don't get many of your sort in here,' Mouse told him.

'What do you mean - my sort?'

'Take a look around, mate, what do you think I'm on about?'

Warren turned, looked at the walls covered in BNP and Keep England White posters. He gave Jimbo a look that said, *what the fuck are we doing in here?* Before he counted to ten.

'Sorry,' he silently mouthed an apology.

Mouse stood between Jimbo and Warren and put his arms around their shoulders, sort of in a group hug. 'But then again, any mate of Jimbo's and all that, even if he is black.' Warren was really itching to give the bloke a smack in the face.

'C'mon, Charlie, chop, chop, get them pints, these blokes are dying of thirst here.' Warren watched closely, never taking his eyes off the barman, he wouldn't have put it past him to spit in his glass. Once Charlie passed over their pints, Mouse then led them down the pub between the staring faces. Faces that questioned why Warren was even being allowed in the place never mind drinking their beer. With full lager glasses before them, they sat at a table as far from the front door as possible - not where Warren would have chosen to sit in any pub, never mind in a den like the *Rose*. He preferred quick access and an even quicker get away.

'So, Jimbo, what's the idea, bringing your mate in here?'

'Business, what else?' Jimbo had regained his composure, and his confidence. 'Ray's looking for a certain type of merchandise, I told him, there's only one bloke in the city with those sort of contacts - you.'

Mouse loved the praise, his strangely sculptured face glowed with pride, this was what he liked to hear. 'So, Mr Ray, what sort of business you looking to do, drugs, a white girl, or maybe a little white boy?'

The fist clenching continued, it was taking all of Warren's willpower to stop himself from reaching across the table and pounding the shit out of Mouse's face. Jimbo's brain was working overtime, it could turn volatile at any moment, he was just waiting for things to explode - he'd seen it happen once too often. Sensing what was about to happen next he briefly placed a hand on Warren's arm. Warren relaxed at the touch. He rested his elbows on the table amongst the beer spills and took a few deep breaths before he dared speak.

'I'm looking for a new supplier. Jimbo here reckons you might be able to put me on to someone.'

'Depends what you want supplying with, I don't usually do business with ... people like you, know what I mean?'

'People like me?'

'Yeah, people like you. Look around the place, you stand out like a vicar in a brothel, know what I mean?'

'I know exactly what you mean.' All the time Warren could feel the tension still building inside. With his right hand, he picked up his pint and sipped to stop himself from reaching across the table and throttling the little bastard. His left hand, under the table, was still clenching and unclenching

'So, tell me, what you after?' Mouse asked cockily.

'A colleague of mine is in the market for firearms, his current – former supplier can't deliver.'

'And why's that?'

'If you really want to know - I ripped his fucking head off and shit down his neck for selling shite.'

A long silence followed while Mouse digested what he'd just heard. Then he made a loud forced laugh.

'If, and I say if, I was to put you on to someone it'll cost ya, I don't do owt for nowt, know what I mean?

Warren smiled. *Oh, I know what you mean, wanker, and I'll let you know what I mean once this deals sorted.* He could see the rough prison tats on Mouse's fingers as he grasped his glass. He was tempted to reach over and squeeze Mouse's hand until the glass shattered. He liked the idea, he was in half a mind to do it but held back.

'So, are we doing business or are we gonna fuck off and I find someone else who wants to make some easy money?'

'Don't get arsey, man, I reckon we can do a deal, but it'll cost you a ton.' Warren put his hand in his jacket inside pocket to get his wallet. 'Fucking hell, man, not in here, I'll meet you outside in five.'

Without saying another word, Warren and Jimbo finished their drinks and stood up.

'In five, know what I mean?' Warren said.

They left the pub to racist chants of hoots and jeers.

'Fucking hell, that was scary, I know he's a twat but I didn't reckon on any of that,' Jimbo said, and sighed with relief as the pub door closed behind them.

'Yeah, well, we ain't there yet, keep your eyes open in case any of those Neanderthals fancy taking a pop at us.'

They walked a short way down the side of the *Rose* and stood by the side of the Escort. Jimbo took out his tobacco tin and skinned up while they waited. 'Here he comes,' said Jimbo and lit his fag.

Mouse nodded for them to walk further down the street. Warren half expected to be jumped on by the racist morons any minute.

'Got my money?' Mouse held out his hand.

Warren shook his head. 'When you give me the number, you get your cash.'

Mouse glanced over his shoulder, satisfied no one was watching the transaction, he didn't want to be seen doing a deal with a black man. 'Fair enough.' He shrugged his shoulders, then passed over a scrap of paper with a mobile telephone number scrawled on it. Mouse held out his hand, rubbing his fingers together. 'Money?'

'Who is this bloke?' Warren kept a firm grip on the notes.

'Someone you really don't want to know, know what I mean?'

'Just give him the fucking name, Mouse, then we can all be on our way,' Jimbo said, as he continued scanning around.

'Told you before, it's Sebastian now. The bloke you want is called Powers, Neil Powers, now where's my fucking money?'

'Just one more thing.'

Mouse sighed and rocked back on one leg showing disinterest, he just wanted his money and to get back to his beer. Then, caught off guard, he was floored by a quick one two - one in the gut and number two to the face. The fist smacked him in the mouth splitting his lip and loosened a couple of teeth at the same time.

Now on his knees, Mouse brought his hands to his face. 'Bastard,' he mumbled through his fingers, his lips swelling immediately.

All the time Jimbo was hopping from one foot to the other, looking over his shoulder expecting the pub's heavy mob to come around the corner any second.

Warren crouched down in front of him and stuffed two fifty-pound notes into his bloody mouth. 'Here you go, pal, KNOW WHAT I MEAN?' Then he gave Mouse an extra kick that sent him sprawling across the paving stones.

'Well, I think that went well, don't you?' Warren said, as they drove away. In the rear-view mirror, he could see Mouse getting to his feet.

'Went well? I was near on shitting myself. I thought you was gonna pummel him while we were in the pub.'

'Nearly did, mate, had to take a few deep breaths I can tell you, the only thing that stopped me was the other dozen blokes itching to have a go at us. You heard of this Powers?'

'Can't say as I know the fella.'

'When you get into the office in the morning, ask Trish to do a PNC check on him, see what it throws up. And I'll give Conway a call and see if I can get the *real* story.'

'And you'll be doing what?'

'Doing that favour for your mate - meeting his daughter off the London train. Fancy a pint in the Eagle?'

'Fancy that bird behind the bar more like!'

His second day back in the job was one to remember - despite everything that had happened, he'd enjoyed it.

Chapter 7

Warren woke early, he was looking forward to work. If the previous day was anything to go by, anything could happen. This was the day he was determined to return to some sort of routine, he was resolute to get back into the habit of looking after himself, with early morning pounding of the pavements and maybe find himself a gym. As his trainers slapped the flagstones he knew he'd made the right decision by coming back to the "job", on the other hand, maybe he *should* have given it more thought? Too late now, a couple of days in and he was already up to his neck in the mire and he'd let his quick temper get the better of him - not a good thing. Too many questions were cluttering his head, he even wondered how Mouse was feeling? Not too good, hopefully.

He was in no rush; Conway's daughter's train wasn't due to arrive until 10am. After a leisurely shower, he dressed in the style of Ray Cole, off the peg casual gear, cheap chain store clobber, but not quite Primarni. The snazzy suit stayed in the wardrobe. He took his time over breakfast, a mug or two of tea and toast with a poached egg on top.

Despite taking his time Warren was early. Conway's daughter's train was not due for another fifteen minutes. He wandered over to one of the hot food vendors to top up his breakfast with a bacon roll and a hot drink. With a cardboard cup of something impersonating coffee in his left hand and hot roll in the other, he stood next to the bronze statue of the poet laureate Philip Larkin and waited for the London train.

'Don't know how you do it mate, standing here day in day out, winter and summer,' he said to the non-responsive statue as he people-watched. He was surprised to see a couple of "working girls" out so early, short skirts and flimsy tops with their arms huddled around themselves trying to stop the cold draught that always blew through the concourse. The train was due anytime, he checked his watch hoping it would be on time, he had more important things to do than babysit Conway's daughter.

'Looks like you're on your own again, mate,' he said, to Larkin's statue when he saw the London train arriving at platform eight. Roll finished and coffee in hand, he stood by the metal security gate as the passengers disembarked, many dragging wheeled suitcases behind them as they began to make for the platform exit.

Warren scanned the faces of the female passengers as they made their way to the gate. The girl was nowhere to be seen. Then he saw a young girl at the far end of the platform struggling with her luggage. About bloody time he thought. She came closer, it wasn't Rachell. Warren elbowed his way onto the platform, getting annoying looks as he pushed through the throng of travellers jostling against him. He walked the length of the platform, looking through the carriage windows. When there was no sight of Rachell panic set in. At the far end of the platform he boarded the train, checking each carriage as he made his way back down the length of the train. Still no Rachell. Once again standing next to Larking, he took out his unregistered second mobile and dialled.

Less than half a mile away, Pat Conway along with his accountant, sat in an institutional magnolia painted office before two Inspectors from HM Inland Revenue. Both parties had reams of paper spread on the desk before them. If truth was known, it wasn't going as well as Conway hoped, it looked as if they were going to hammer him for unpaid taxes. The fat man was feeling the heat of the situation despite the room being air-conditioned. He loosened his tie and ran his finger around his shirt collar. His mobile switched to silent, lay amongst the papers on the desk. He glanced down as it started to vibrate and skid around the desk.

'Sorry about this,' he said. He picked it up to turn it off, then he saw the caller ID, it was Warren. 'Excuse me, I have to take this it's important.' This did *not* please the Inspectors, when he stood and walked out of the meeting into the corridor, leaving his accountant flabbergasted.

He pressed the accept key. 'This better be fucking good, Ray, or you're dead meat,' he said, holding the handset to his ear.

'Rachell, she wasn't on the train.'

'What do you mean she wasn't on the train, of course she was on the fucking train - she'd have let me know if there was any change in her plans,' Conway told him.

'And I'm telling you she wasn't...'

He cut him short. 'Stay fucking put, I'll ring you back.'

'One question before you hang up, Neil Powers?'

'For fuck's sake, not now.' he hung up.

Warren shut down the phone, there was only one thing for it - another bacon roll and dubious coffee while he waited.

Ten minutes later, his mobile rang once more.

'Just been on with her mother in Vancouver, she wasn't fucking pleased I can tell you, still middle of the night over there. She reckons Rachell never let her know about changing her plans. She's going to ring the folks in London see if they know anything.'

'Ok, I'm heading off,' Warren said, through a mouth of full of bacon roll. 'Let me know what's happening. Before I go - Neil Powers?'

'Don't go there, stay well clear, hear me - stay well clear?'

Warren was pissed, he was sure Conway would have come up with something a bit more constructive. What a waste of the best part of the morning, it wasn't as if he didn't have anything else to do. He'd no sooner settled himself into the driving seat of the Escort with a sigh of frustration, when his phone rang again. He answered without checking the display, expecting it to be the nick. 'Yep.'

'It's me, I'm telling you she *was* on that bloody train, check again,' Conway sounded as if he was ready to hyperventilate.

'And I'm telling *you*, Pat, there was no sign of her,' he sipped the liquid, it was fairer to call it liquid than coffee. 'She's probably stopped off for a bit of sightseeing. If you hear anything give me a bell, okay?'

Conway tried to protest. 'The rellies down in London watched her get on the train, she *did* get on the train - so where the fuck is she?' He was beside himself, there was no way he was going back into the meeting with the tax people - fuck the consequences.

Warren ended the call, opened the car window and tipped away the cold coffee. Dropped the cup in the passenger foot-well and drove off, none too pleased with the start to the day.

'Every time I drive into the car-park you're out here having a fag,' Warren remarked to Jimbo as he walked over towards the Escort.

'So, you paying my wages now are you?'

Warren raised his eyebrows. 'Sarky, let's get a coffee, that stuff at Paragon Station is like manky piss.'

'Never had manky piss, mind you if it's anything like the coffee you make ....' Warren was impressed with Jimbo's new confidence in the way he answered back - up to a point. 'Don't remember you drinking so much caffeine, you do know it's not good for you?'

'Bloody hell, Jimbo, next you'll be telling me you've started drinking those fancy herbal teas?'

'So what if I have?' he answered, slightly embarrassed.

Warren wanted to laugh, but he could see the lad was deadly serious. 'Well, I need some caffeine - you coming?' Jimbo shrugged his shoulders and followed him to the canteen.

Jimbo was still garnering a few strange looks in his "new", old attire.

'Sorry, love, staff only in here,' the assistant behind the serving counter told him. It took all the restraint he had to stop Warren from laughing.

'And what's this?' Jimbo showed her the security ID that hung around his neck. This was the second time it had happened.

Warren leaned across the counter top and read the name on the assistant's badge. 'It's alright, Carole, we haven't house trained him yet,' he said with a smile.

Jimbo tut tutted, picked up his fruit tea and walked out.

'Oh c'mon, Jimbo, you have to see the funny side,' he said when they were in the corridor.

Jimbo did think it funny, a little, but he wasn't going to let on to his mentor.

Warren pushed open the squad room door. 'Morning, Trish.'

'Is it? According to my watch it's nearer afternoon,' she replied sarcastically.

'Who rattled your cage?'

'You have - okay?'

'Sorry I spoke. Have you got the PNC report I wanted on Neil Powers?' The DI's desk had been cleared. 'Where *is* Bill?'

'Greg, give it a rest with all the questions will you, you have noticed I'm working solo here?

He had noticed. 'Bill?' Greg asked again.

'Can't tell you.'

'Can't or won't?' questioned Warren.

'Seriously I've no idea,' Trish replied, as the phone rang. 'DC James,' she said into the receiver, 'yes ma-am, I'll put him on,' the Super she mouthed silently and passed over the handset.

For me, he mouthed back poking himself in the chest. 'Morning Superintendent, how can I help?' Trying to make a funny face into the receiver. He listened quietly, his face turning serious as the one-sided conversation played out. 'Have you any idea how long?' he asked. 'No, no problem ma-am, just let me know if we can do anything.' End of conversation. Both Trish and Jimbo looked on with serious expressions.

'Well?' asked Trish.

Warren sat on the edge of the desk. 'It's Bill, he's had a stroke, don't know any of the details yet, but it's not looking good.'

'Bloody hell, poor bloke, what's brought that on?'

'What usually brings on a stroke - stress, it's the nature of this bloody job,' said Warren. 'So, in the meantime she's put me in charge of the team - such as it is.'

'Well there goes the rule book,' Jimbo chipped in.

Trish brushed away the hair from her face. 'We're definitely going to need another pair of hands.'

'Is there anyone in uniform you fancy?' Warren asked.

Trish raised her eyebrows. 'One or two I wouldn't mind ...' and then laughed.

'Give over, woman, you know what I mean.'

'As a matter of fact, there is, and they both work at this nick.'

'Okay tell me.'

'First of all there's Bernard Philips, a PC, currently working in Missing Persons ...'

'Bernard! What's the other bloke's name?'

'Elvis,' she said light heartedly.

'Elvis, tell me you're joking?'

'Straight up, Detective Constable Edward Dixon, aka Elvis.'

'Go on, I know you're dying to tell me,' Warren said playing along.

'It's because of his love for the King, and his Elvis quiff.'

'I can hardly wait to meet him.'

'Do you want to have a word with them?'

'Not at this stage, you know them better than I do, what do you think about giving them both a go, see who's more suited to the team?'

'Sounds like a plan, I'll sound them out. What if they both look like they'd make it?'

'Well, we are a man down, and we haven't got clue as to when and if the DI will be back, under the circumstances I think I'd be able to swing it with the Super, but let's see how they get on before we make any plans.'

Warren eased himself off the corner of the desk. 'Bloody cramp,' he said as he danced around the room like a loon, Trish and Jimbo laughed showing no sign of sympathy what so ever. 'Well that lightened the mood - for all of a couple of minutes.' Then with his serious head on. 'Back to business, what's the report say about Powers?'

'Surprisingly, not a lot.' Trish said as she opened the file and slid it across the desk top

'I didn't get anything out of Conway, either.'

Trish carried on. 'Born in Driffield, that's a market town about twenty miles north of Hull if you didn't know,' she said looking directly at Warren.

'You are winding me up aren't you, Trish?'

She smiled, he was so easy.

'Just checking, you being a southerner.' Mr Cool didn't bite this time. 'Anyway, Powers, thirty-three years old, he did a six year stint in the forces, the Royal Logistics Regiment, trained as an Ammunition Technician and rose to the rank of Sergeant.

'So, he knows his way around firearms.'

'Certainly does and he's a bit of a tough nut, two tours of Afghanistan, Iraq. Seems he's also a bit of an adrenaline junkie, failed twice to get into the Special Forces, by all accounts it left him with a chip on his shoulder. It was after the second attempt that things started to go shit-up. Drinking, insubordination, even went as far as striking a senior officer.'

Jimbo sniggered. 'Sounds a bit like you, Greg.

'Piss off. I take it he served time before he was discharged?'

'Six months in the Military Corrective Training Centre, that's the army nick, Jimbo.'

'I know that, why does everyone around here think I'm thick?' They ignored the comment.

'What about a civilian rap sheet?' Warren asked as he sat cracking his knuckles.

'He does seem to like to use his fists - and his feet.' This made Jimbo look towards Warren. Something else he and Powers had in common. The DS shook his head. 'No arrests, because no one actually followed through with their statements.'

'So, he sounds like a thoroughly nice bloke. That's it?'

'The rest is just the usual crap, pulled in on numerous occasions, but never enough evidence to charge him.'

Trish slid the file across the desk, Jimbo reached out, but Warren beat him to it. 'Got to be faster than that, mate.' Warren opened the file and studied Powers personal details. Six feet two tall, well-trimmed brown hair and a trendy stubble beard.

'Hardly looks like your typical ex-squaddie, looks more like he should be working in the financial sector.' He slid the page over to Jimbo.

'You could take a leaf out of this bloke's book,' said Jimbo, with a big grin on his face.

'Jimbo, are you asking for a thick lip?' He said keeping a straight face. 'Mind you, I can see where you're coming from.' Acting out his alter ego, Raymond Cole, Warren had let his appearance slide in keeping with the character, enforcer, thug and fugitive and slowly the persona was creeping back. 'See if there's any more info on him, I'm sure there must be some other department looking into him.' He said turning to Trish. Then his mobile vibrated in his pocket, he took it out and checked the display screen. 'Conway,' he put his finger to his lips. 'Yes, Pat, what can I do for you?'

'Rachell - she *was* on that bloody train. Greg, I'm at my fucking wit's end here - I don't know what the fuck to do?'

'Calm down, give me a half hour and I'll meet you at the house - okay?'

'Just fucking get here sharpish.' Warren could sense the urgency and anger behind the finger that hung up the call.

'Trouble?' Jimbo asked.

'You could say that,' Warren replied, still staring at the phone's display.

'Like what?' asked Trish.

'Like it seems Conway's daughter has gone walkabout.'

'Oh fuck - just fucking perfect.' Jimbo stood up almost pushing over his chair.

'Calm down, Jimbo.'

'It's alright for you saying calm down, you've never seen him when he goes ballistic, and believe me this will turn him into the psycho from hell.'

'Well, maybe, when I go see him I should take along my new friendly colleague, see if she has a calming effect on him?' he said as he turned to Trish. 'What do you say? Fancy a drive out, get some fresh air?'

She rolled her eyes, she knew she didn't really have a choice. In Bill's absence, Warren was in charge, and as Jimbo had said, the rule book went out of the window with the phone call.

Chapter 8

'Not exactly built for comfort, is it?' Trish said, as she was bounced about in the bucket seat of the Ford Escort.

'Maybe not, but it comes in handy if you've got to make a quick exit.'

'And who am I supposed to be again?' Trish asked, as if she didn't know the answer he would give.

'Let's keep it as near the truth as possible - girlfriend?'

'In your dreams, DS Warren - in your dreams,' she turned to stare out of the car window, smiling.

'How do you know you're not already?'

She quickly turned back to face him.

He gave her a wink.

'Yuk, let's not go there,' she replied, trying to sound affronted.

'Seriously, he'll probably kick off when he sees you, I'll tell him you're my girlfriend and we were just on the way out when he rang. More importantly, remember I'm Ray Cole, for Christ's sake, don't call me Greg.'

'I'm not stupid you know!'

'I know you're not, but please remember.'

Warren pulled the Escort into the kerb outside Conway's, large detached Boulevard home. The front door opened before they'd even had a chance to get out of the car. Conway stood on the doorstep waiting. Trish was glad she was wearing jeans, the undignified way she had to clamber out of the low slung car.

'About time,' Conway said, as they walked down the path towards the house. He moved aside to let them pass. 'Who the fuck is she and why have you brought her?'

'Language, Pat, okay? This is, Trish, my girlfriend. Trish this Mr Conway,' he said by the way of an introduction.

She held out her hand, Conway ignored the offered hand, as if she wasn't even there. Warren put an arm around Trish's shoulder. 'We were just about to go out when you rang. Let's sit down and you can fill me in.'

'Do *not* patronise me, Ray.'

Conway led the way through to the lounge.

'Okay, mate, didn't realise I was. Go put the kettle on will you, love?' he said to Trish.

The *little woman* threw Warren a look and forced a smile as she went through to the kitchen - it was more of a grimace than a smile.

'So, what's going on?'

'Like I said, Rachell, she *was* on the train, end of.'

'And I can tell you she wasn't by the time it pulled in. I walked the full length of the platform and the train, checking every carriage - I'm telling you, Pat, if she got on the train, then she got off again.'

Trish came back from the kitchen and unceremoniously placed the tray of drinks on the expensive looking coffee table.

'Careful luv, do you know how much that cost?' She just shrugged, she didn't know and what's more she didn't give a toss. 'If she got off the train where the fucking hell is she?'

Trish passed him a mug. 'Listen Pat, I've got one or two contacts, if, and I say *if*, she was on the train I'll find her.' Trish gave him a raised eyebrow. 'Just stay calm, give me twenty-four hours and I'll get back to you - keep cool.'

'Cool, keep fucking cool! Easier said than done. Her mother will fucking kill me if anything happens to her.'

'Pity she's in Canada,' Trish mumbled under her breath.

'You say something, luv?'

'Poor woman, she must be out of her mind with worry,' she lied. 'How's the coffee?'

'Prefer tea.' Arse, thought Trish. The mug was back on the tray and he was heading for the whisky bottle. 'Ray, what the fuck am I going to do?' Holding his glass he gestured to Warren, who shook his head, it was way too early in the day to start hitting the hard stuff.

'Look, Pat, try not to worry, she's a big girl...'

'Big girl - she's fucking seventeen, barely out of nappies.'

Strange how things change, thought Warren, it wasn't so long ago since Conway had been involved with people who didn't think twice about pimping girls Rachell's age.

'Just try and keep calm, I have an idea or two - we'll find her I promise,' Warren said as he stood up.

Conway jumped from his seat and stood almost nose to nose with Warren. 'Where the fuck are you going?'

'To set things in motion and try to find your daughter. Where do you think? Pat, you've got to keep a grip on things. Just let me make a few enquiries.'

'Enquiries? You sound just like a fucking copper.'

This prompted Trish to raise an eyebrow.

If only you knew. 'If anything develops give me a bell. You ready, love?'

'Right behind you, babe,' she said all girly, making Warren smile.

They left Conway nursing his glass of whisky. 'I almost feel sorry for the man, even if he is an arrogant, self-centred, sexist pig.' Trish said as they walked down the garden path.

'That's what I like about you, Trish, never mince your words do you, *babe?*'

She laughed. 'I thought it was a nice touch. I nearly smiled when he said you sounded like a copper. Anyway, what are these enquiries you're going to make?' she asked, as the Escort pulled away from the kerbside.

'When I was down south I did a liaison stint with the Transport Police at Liverpool Street Station. I'll give one of the lads a bell and see if they can come up with anything. The trains have cameras on them these days, never know we might come up lucky.'

'If not?'

'Not a clue, Trish, not a clue,' he replied as he concentrated on his driving.

Chapter 9

'Can I have some hush PLEASE,' Warren asked Jimbo and Trish who were having some animated conversation about Jimbo's nose ring of all things

'Well, I think they're bloody ridiculous,' she told him. 'What happens when you have a cold and your nose runs?'

'I wipe it. Some people just don't have any class...'

'Give over will you, I'm trying to think here,' Warren told them.

'That'll be a first,' Jimbo muttered under his breath.

'Heard that, I'm not deaf.'

'No, just daft.'

Warren shook his head, took his wallet out of his jacket and examined the piece of paper Mouse had given him. 'Give me some hush,' he said as he dialled the number scrawled down. 'Shush.' The call was accepted.

'Who is this?'

'Cole, my names Raymond Cole, I'm in the market for...'

'Sorry, you've got the wrong number.' Powers hung up.

Powers didn't seem unduly bothered by the call, but Warren knew that when he found out who'd been giving out his number there would be serious repercussions. He obviously wasn't used to accepting unsolicited business calls.

'Well?' Jimbo asked.

'Hung up on me,' Warren looked at his watch. 'I'll give him two minutes and call again.'

He did. The mobile at the other end rang. Powers picked up. 'Mr Powers please don't hang up, this a onetime only offer, an offer that could be financially lucrative.'

'Speak, I'll give you thirty seconds, say your piece.'

'Five hundred pounds just to talk to me, no strings, how does that sound? Then we'll see where we can go from there.'

'I don't do business on the phone with strangers, if you want to discuss business I suggest we do it face to face. I'll call you back in twenty-four hours.' He hung up.

This gave Powers a full day to find out all he could about Raymond Cole.

'Where the hell are you going to get five hundred notes?' Jimbo asked.

'Let me worry about that.' He did after all, have his own illicit stash.

'You think he went for it?'

'Time will tell.' Warren knew full well, that Powers would have a contact somewhere in the police force, someone, who for a cash payment would run the name Raymond Cole through the system. Warren wasn't unduly worried, he still had the contacts of his own from when he was working undercover, all it took was a quick telephone call.

Warren made the call.

Less than a minute later he received an email, his alter ego was resurrected - Ray Cole was back in the system. 'Now we wait for him to call back.'

'If he calls back,' Jimbo said depressingly.

'Don't be so negative, Jimbo, he'll call back. In the meantime, I'll bell my mate at Liverpool Street Station; see if he can trace Rachell Conway's movements.'

Gardener stood at his lathe with his back to Powers, concentrating as he guided the tungsten tip tool down the steel barrel belonging to one of the Baikal pistols. The visitor to the shed perched on a tall wooden stool, holding a stained mug of strong instant coffee. 'So, you've never heard of this, Ray Cole?' It fascinated him to watch Gardener work. There was a time, back in the day, when Powers himself wouldn't have minded getting his hands on converting a pistol or two, after all he did have the skills taught him by Her Majesty's Army.

'Nope, you know as well as I do, just because we've never come across him it's not to say he's not on the level.'

'Yeah, but what's bugging me is how did he get my number? More to the point, which arsehole gave him it?'

'I take it you're going to meet him?'

He put his mug down on the workbench and took out his cigarettes. 'Not sure on that, I've got someone running a check on him, depends what they come back with.'

Gardener turned the lathe's wheel, easing back the cutting tool and pressed the stop button. He picked up an oily rag and wiped his hands as he turned to face Powers. 'Did you ever find out where Scabby Dave got a hold of the gun that blew his hand off?' he asked, as he picked up his battered tobacco tin to roll himself a cigarette.

Powers reached over with his lighter and lit Gardener's roll-up. A blue haze hung from the low ceiling like a noxious cloud.

'From what the lads tell me it was converted over here in the UK, they reckon it was some numpty from around here.'

'Makes you wonder what sort of Muppet did the conversion, or tried to.' Gardener picked up his mug. 'Cold,' he said, pouring the liquid down the sink drain. 'You want another?'

Powers shook his head. 'Muppet or not, it's bad for business.'

'Then put them out of business or bring them onboard.'

'The thought had crossed my mind. Any guesses who's likely to be in the frame for it?'

Gardener stood with his back against the lathe resting on the hard metal. 'Been giving it some thought since your last visit and drawn a blank,' he said, as he dunked his tea bag up and down in his mug, giving it an extra squeeze between finger and thumb. 'If it is someone local, it'll only take a few quid to get a name.' He dropped the used tea bag on the bench and poured milk into the mug.

Powers picked up one of the converted guns and admired Gardener's workmanship. 'Nice. I'll take these two with me.' He wrapped both weapons in a clean cloth and placed them in his briefcase. 'If anybody does come to mind give me a bell, okay?'

Gardener nodded and turned back to the lathe and pressed the power button. 'Aye, and you let me know how it goes with this Cole, fella.'

Powers left his old army mate to get on with what he did best. He'd parked his vehicle further along Hendon Street. He always parked a discreet distance away from number 56, there was nothing to be gained by drawing attention to the house. A dog walker stood by his car whilst the mutt pissed up his nearside front wheel, Powers glared, the man dragged the dog away mid pee and marched away at double time. Powers smiled, the glare always worked. He clicked the key fob, opened the door and dropped into the driving seat of his brand-new BMW 7 Series saloon, he put his mobile into the hands-free cradle and made a call. 'It's me,' he said out loud, 'got anything for me?' A very brief conversation took place. 'That's it? You sure? Okay, thanks.' He ended the call. Powers had many people he could count on to supply information, including serving police officers - as long as the price was right.

The search of the Police National Computer revealed what had always been intended. Raymond Cole's back story had stood up to scrutiny. To anyone carrying out a PNC check, he was who he claimed to be. Cole was a player with a reputation to match. Drug importation, robbery, with an unhealthy interest in the arms trade and more importantly a very violent man. A man still on the run from the authorities for murder. Powers informant had summed him up as a "respected" member of the north eastern criminal fraternity, and one who should be regarded as dangerous - a man to be wary of.

'You know where Jimbo is?' Before Trish had a chance to answer Jimbo opened the door and walked in. 'And where have you been?' Warren asked.

'Can't a bloke go for a pee without asking your permission?' Jimbo pulled out his chair and sat down.

'Don't get stroppy, only asking. I thought you'd like to know my mate in BTP has come up with something on Conway's daughter.'

'Then don't keep it to yourself,' Trish said impatiently.

Warren turned to face her, he smiled. 'You mean, "please don't keep it to yourself, sergeant?"'

'Whatever,' she sighed. 'You know you're so full of sh ...'

Jimbo cut her off before she had a chance to finish.

'Now, now, don't go upsetting him, Trish, he'll only get a sulk on.'

Warren tried to keep a serious look on his face. 'Have you two finished taking the piss out of your senior officer?' The comment was followed by a snigger or two. 'Right, according to my mate, Rachell did indeed get on the 6.50am train from Kings Cross to Hull, she was seen waving bye to her relatives and getting on the train.'

'Then how come she wasn't on the train when it arrived in Hull?'

'She got off again, you div.'

Jimbo tutted.

'But what the hell did she get off for?' Trish asked, leaning forward resting her elbows on the desk

'The trains CCTV showed her getting off at Watford. She was met by a young bloke and they left the station together - hand in hand.'

'So, that's it then, problem solved, she'd gone and got herself a bloke - end of.' Jimbo said as he pushed back in his chair.

'Jimbo, can you see Conway leaving it at that? Because I can't.'

'From what I've seen of him - no, the man's too possessive.' Trish added, head down and carried on with her reports, then added. 'More like he'll want the bloke castrated.'

Warren smiled as he answered. 'Ouch, you could be right.'

'So,' said Jimbo, with his serious face on, 'what can we do about it?'

'Call in some more favours, see if they can get an ID on the fella, facial recognition might throw something up if he's got a record. Do whatever I can to try and keep Conway onside.'

Trish lifted her head. 'Costs money, good luck with that. Tea, coffee, anyone?'

Chapter 10

Joey Smale had skipped school - again. Who needed school? He certainly didn't, what good was it learning about equations and adjectives? The fifteen-year-old couldn't remember the last time he had attended for a full day, on the odd day he had turned up, it was only to show his face, then piss off again. According to his teachers, he had reached the stage of "un-teachable" long ago. Arthur Smale, Joey's dad was not around, he didn't need the hassle of a kid in his life and did a disappearing act soon after the lad had been born. Roxy, Joey's mother, she wasn't much better, she didn't give a toss if he went to school or not. As long as Joey was bringing in enough money to help feed her drug habit, she was happy. Any shortfall in cash to feed her addiction was subsidized with prostitution.

The lad grafted hard for his money. He worked as a runner for two or three dealers on a North Hull housing estate, picking up and delivering, topping up his income with a bit of robbing on the side. Overall, he was content with his lot. Most days he managed to earn enough to keep his mum off his back, and at the same time, keep her off hers. He always had spare cash in his pocket to treat himself, even enough to buy a brand new

PS4 console and he rode around the estate on a brand-new bike.

Joey had just completed a drop-off in an alley, behind a Turkish take-away on Beverley Road area. He was on his way to deliver the cash he had collected to his employer. He was in no rush and cycled steadily, he was clean, nothing on him even if the cops did spot him.

Robbo Dooley, the man he was running for, didn't deal in drugs, he ran a semi-legitimate business, carrying out small general engineering repairs from his lock-up workshop in a garage block in North Hull, to say the least, not a very profitable business at that. On the other hand, there was a not so legitimate side to the business - he worked as a contractor carrying out the conversion of illegal firearms.

As soon as Joey cycled into the communal garage block he could hear the sound of metal scraping against metal, it was coming from the other side of the steel garage door at the far end. He cycled to the far end and stopped, sitting on his bike, he thumped the door with his fist. The machine noise inside stopped, then a different noise as the door slid on its track, opening just enough for a face to peer out.

'Oh, it's you. Took your time, didn't you?' It was Robbo. Dooley opened the door enough to allow the lad and his bike to squeeze through. Joey just shrugged his shoulders. 'Got the money?' Robbo asked, as he closed the door.

'Wouldn't be here if I didn't, would I?' Joey replied cockily. Robbo often thought about scelping the lad across his head for his cheek, but Joey was growing fast and starting to fill out, it wasn't worth taking the risk.

The lad unzipped his hoody and pulled out the Tesco's carrier bag from the waist of his baggy jeans. The carrier bag was stuffed with cash.

'Cheeky sod. You nicked any?'

'C'mon Robbo, would I do that?'

'Yes, you bloody would.' he replied, as he took the five hundred quid from the bag, then counted off four ten-pound notes and passed them over to Joey. It was easy money - as long as the coppers didn't stop you. All he had to do was pick up a parcel from Robbo, drop it off at a meet down some alley or another and collect the cash. 'You fancy making a bit more?'

'How much more?'

'Sixty quid.'

This sounded good to the lad. 'I'm listening.' Joey was saving up for a new flat screen plasma television for his bedroom.

'I'm expanding the business, going into short term loans. You deliver the goods as usual, the only difference is you pick it up pretty sharpish after it's been used for the job.'

'Sounds a bit risky, riding around with a "hot" pistol in my hoody. Make it eighty and we have a deal.' Robbo had expected the lad to negotiate, he was nobody's fool.

'Good man,' Robbo took out his fags and lit up.

Eighty notes, it would keep his mother in Crack for two, maybe three days. If she was happy, so was he.

'When do I start? Joey asked enthusiastically.

'You just have,' he put his arm around the lad's shoulder. Robbo knew Joey's situation, the need to help feed his mother's habit and in a sort of a way he admired his resilience.

'Here's the deal.' Robbo crossed the untidy floor space, took a key from his pocket and unlocked the top drawer of the metal filing cabinet. From the cabinet, he took out a Baikal automatic. The weapon was identical in looks to those converted by Gardener. 'You take this now, and at half ten tonight you meet a bloke who calls himself Seb, in the underpass on Hall Road. He gives you cash and you give him the goods, no cash - no goods, got it?' Joey nodded. 'Remember get the money first before you hand over. You shove the cash through my letter box. If I don't see you in the meantime, day after tomorrow I'll give you a call, you come by and collect an envelope, then you meet the same bloke, same time, same place. This time he gives you the package, and you give him the envelope, it's his deposit. I'll be here waiting, simple. What could be easier?'

Robbo checked that the weapon's safety catch was on then, he wrapped the weapon in a clean cloth, stuffed into the same Tesco carrier bag and handed it over. 'You okay with this?'

'Done it before remember?' Joey put the package inside his hoody.

'So, you have. But listen, from what they tell me this Seb has a bit of a reputation, if he tries to pull a fast one, hold on tight to the goods and get the fuck out of there. Comprendo?'

Joey nodded. 'You worry too much, Robbo, I can handle myself. What about my money?'

'Half now, the rest when you bring the goods back, okay?'

'Cool,' said Joey, holding out his hand for the cash. Robbo peeled off another four, ten-pound notes and handed them over. 'Cheers.' Eighty quid, not a bad mornings work the lad thought.

'Don't let me down now,' Robbo called out as he closed the workshop door.

Robbo had been a little worried about his own workmanship since he'd heard about what happened to Dave "Scabby" Scabies. He went over and over it in his head, he was sure he'd done everything right with the conversion, this was the second time something had gone wrong - but what? He didn't know. The one good thing to come out of it was that the pistol had blown up, and the police wouldn't be able to trace it back - as long as Scabies kept his gob shut, which he would.

In a previous life, Robbo had been a skilled engineer in one of Hull's large engineering companies until the company went bust and he lost his job - along with his pension. So, out of necessity he'd become self-employed doing small jobs for several of his old employer's customers. The converting of firearms was something he'd fallen into, a favour for a dubious friend. A favour that had now turned into a very lucrative side-line, dealing directly with his friend's, associate. As far as bringing the guns into the country was concerned it was easy, it was his associates responsibility. The weapons, concealed inside pre-marked crates were smuggled into the country on one of the North Sea Ferries from Bruges, Belgium.

Robbo's friend was responsible for making sure that minor engine parts that needed attention were crated up and transferred from the ship to shore, to whichever repairer in the city was to be used. Dooley was illicitly on the preferred supplier list. He wasn't in the same league of converters used by Powers, not by any means, he only ever used qualified armourers. Strangely, his contact had never mentioned Powers, perhaps there was method in the madness, no doubt if he had heard, he would have taken up some other occupation.

With the goods tucked well away inside his hoody, Joey cycled home through the alleys, keeping well away from the main roads, checking all the time for coppers, over time he had even been able to recognise the undercover cops who operated in the area. Cycle fast and keep your eyes skinned was his motto, the last thing he wanted was for some nosey copper to do an impromptu stop and search.

Joey and his mother lived two floors up in the last remaining tower-block on the estate. He manhandled his bike up the stairwell with no problem - he'd done it hundreds of times. Joey opened the front door to the three-bed roomed flat he shared with his mum.

'That you, Joey?' his mother called out from the living room.

'No, it's the Boston Strangler. Who else was you expecting?' He called back, as he propped his bike against the wall in the hallway.

'Cheeky sod. You got my cigs?'

Joey, still with the goods inside his hoody stuck his head around the living room doorway. A small square room with furniture that had seen better days, the television fixed to the wall. His mum sat on the settee with her legs tucked beneath her, eyes glued to the crappy daytime reality show.

'Can't see why you couldn't go to the shop yourself. Not as if your legs don't work anymore?' He threw the cigarettes across the room and tutted, he didn't know what her "friends" saw in her, with her bleached blonde hair, thickly applied makeup, and she was as thin as a rake.

'Less of your cheek,' she said as she ripped off the cellophane. 'You going out again?'

'Only just come in,' he grumbled.

'Got someone coming around later, that's all.' Referring to one of her regular "friends".

'Whatever.' Joey left her to her smokes and disappeared into his bedroom.

Joey's room was his private space, a room his mother never entered. It was the cleanest and tidiest room in the flat. He made sure the bedroom door was firmly closed, opened the Ikea type, touch me and I'll fall to bits wardrobe, then pulled out a bundle of clothes that lay on the base. Inside the wardrobe was a false bottom made of plywood. He eased the plywood free and placed the Tesco carrier bag in the void. Next, he took out a biscuit tin where he kept his earnings, well hidden from his mother. He removed the lid and stuffed in the cash Robbo had given him earlier, then replaced the tin and its contents inside the void, and everything back as it was.

Joey went through to the lounge; his mum was still sat in the same place still watching the boring reality show on the television. 'What's for tea?' he asked.

'Whatever you want, as long as you make it yourself,' she replied, not taking her eyes off the screen. For some reason, she was enthralled with the rubbish.

'Right, I'm off out then.'

'What about our tea?'

'You can get your own, I'll get something out.' She was a rubbish cook anyway, he was better off with a McDonalds. He just hoped her 'friend', left before he returned to collect his package.

After catching up with some of his mates and enjoying his double cheese burger and fries from McDonalds, Joey headed home to the flat. It was almost time. Being in a hurry he didn't carry his bike up two floors, he locked it to the radiator in the foyer and took the stairs two at a time. He listened outside the door, for the tell-tale signs of whether his mum had company or not before letting himself in. All silent, his mum's visitor had already left, still, he tried to be as quiet as he could. He stuck his head around the living room door frame, with her clothing in disarray, she lay full length on the settee, comatose. Her drug paraphernalia laid out on the coffee table, her "friend" had obviously brought her a present. Joey shook his head and closed the door - he'd seen it all before.

In his bedroom, he retrieved the Tesco carrier bag, tucked it inside his hoody and left. Joey was a tough kid, still, riding around North Hull at night could be tricky, especially on your own. He constantly glanced over his shoulder, always on the lookout; this was the reason he'd managed to evade arrest. As he approached the Hall Road underpass, he was doubly cautious, arriving early and hanging back in the shadows between two industrial wheelie bins. From his vantage point he had a good view of both the underpass entrances on either side of the road, not that he expected to see many use it. At night, it was a no-go area to decent people, the only people who used it after dark were those up to no good, another hour and the gangs would begin to gather. The lad checked his watch, it was almost time. He'd seen no one enter or come out of the underpass, he reckoned there was a good chance that this Seb bloke hadn't turned up.

Joey had a cautious look around, no strangers hanging around, no cop cars - nothing. Another last look around, then took a scarf from his pocket and wrapped it around the lower half of his face - like he'd seen them do on the telly. With the hood of his hoody over his head, he cycled into the gloom. He moved out of the shadows and cycled towards the underpass and paused at the entrance. Not surprisingly, only half of the underpass lights were working, people who made use of the underpass at night preferred the darkness. Joey peered into the gloom, midway in the tunnel, a figure stood leaning against the graffiti covered wall. It had to be this Seb fella, scruffy looking, he stood in the gloom, smoking. The lad braked and pulled up short, one foot on the floor and the other still on the pedal ready for a quick exit, the last thing he wanted was to be mugged.

'You, Joey?' The scruffy bloke asked.

'Who's asking?'

'Seb.' He reached inside his own jacket. Joey watched, eagle eyed, ready for a quick spin around and away. A brown padded envelope was produced and he opened the flap enough for Joey to look inside. 'And you got something for me?' Joey came closer, reached inside his own hoody and took out the carrier bag, simultaneously they swapped goods. Seb opened the bag and un-wrapped the Baikal. 'Cool, same time in forty-eight hours - right?' Joey nodded, staring into the rat like face.

Seb tucked the gun out of sight in the back waistband of his jeans and swaggered off. Tosser thought Joey, his heart beating hard, he was glad the deal had been done. He'd done the same thing a dozen times before, this time it was different though. There was something about the bloke, he didn't know what, but was glad it was done.

He cycled through the alleys and cut throughs, as fast as he could, constantly looking over his shoulder. He was sweating, his t-shirt beneath the hoody clung to him, he wasn't stopping until he reached Robbo's house. The lights were on, but he didn't knock on the door, just did as he was told. He cycled right up to the front door, stuffed the money through his letter box and was away home.

Today was just another day for Robbo. The first job every morning was filling and switching on the kettle for his caffeine fix, he always started the day with a coffee and a fag. Inside his jacket, was the bundle of cash Joey had pushed through his letter-box the previous evening. He made his brew of supermarket instant, then tipped the cash onto the workbench and counted; it was all there - all twelve hundred quid. Not a bad turn around. His contact, the wholesaler let Dooley have the Baikal for a round "ton", one of the perks. The plan was to give Seb his deposit of five hundred notes back when the pistol was returned, after the job was completed. Even after giving Joey his cut he would clear five hundred quid for an hour or two's work and still have the pistol to rent out again. He was getting faster at converting, but he was a long way from being in Gardener's league in both skill and speed.

He was opening the bottom drawer of the metal filing cabinet, to hide the stash with the rest when there was a banging on the door. Quietly he edged towards the door and looked through the spy hole he'd made. It was Joey.

Robbo slid open the door, just enough for the lad and his bike to get in.

Joey always looked forward to his visits to the workshop; he loved the smell of oil and machined metal.

'How did it go?'

'No problems,' said Joey as he propped his bike against the workbench. 'Do you know this bloke, Seb?'

'No, not personally, I was recommended. Did it all through a contact. You know how I work.'

'Who?'

'C'mon, Joey, you know I can't tell you that, why?'

'Cos he's seriously weird.'

'Define weird.' He picked up his mug.

'I don't know, just something about him, your regular customers are bad enough, but this bloke was in a different league altogether. On top of that he was a right ugly fucker, face like a rabid rat.'

Robbo laughed. 'Don't care what he looks like, as long as his money's good. Anyway, you up for another drop?'

'So soon?'

'Supply and demand, apparently. If there's a demand, I'll supply,' he laughed out loud. 'Seriously, this is the last one for a while. Don't want to attract too much attention.'

It was easy money for Joey. 'Yeah, but not for too long?'

'No, but I've got to keep my head down, don't want to overdo a good thing, just do the odd contract work.'

'So, how are you going to fill the time?'

'I'm going to spend a bit of time doing up an old motor bike I got my hands on.' At the rear of the workshop was what looked like a pile of junk covered with an old sheet. Robbo, pulled off the cover. 'It's a 1960s, 250cc Triumph.'

'Can I help?' Joey asked, enthusiastically.

'Don't see why not,' Robbo replied, as he put the cover back in place.

'Cool, when are we starting?'

'Let's get this job over with first,' he said laughing. He was surprised and pleased that the lad was showing some interest, interest in a job that was actually legal. He went over to the filing cabinet in the corner. He took a key from his pocket, unlocked a drawer and took out a Baikal pistol. He wrapped the pistol in a clean rag and passed it to the lad.

'No problem, Robbo. Where's the drop?' He took the package and concealed it inside his hoody.

'Ingelmire Lane,' he scribbled down the address on a scrap of paper and handed it to the lad. 'The blokes kosher, but as always, cash first before you hand it over.'

'You want me to count the dosh?'

'No need, he's cool, but like I said, cash first. Then straight back here and through my letter-box. Okay?'

'No probs, Robbo. Tonight?'

'Between 10pm and 10.30pm, right? Right, bugger off and I'll see you later.'

Joey dutifully did as he was told. He'd always fancied having a motorbike and was a little excited at the prospect. Maybe Robbo would let him ride it when they'd rebuilt it? He was feeling quite pleased as he cycled home, as ever he was aware of everything and everyone around him, always on the lookout for coppers.

Back home, he left his bike in the hallway and went through to the kitchen. 'That you, Joey?' His mum called out when she heard the door opening. As usual she was sprawled on the settee watching daytime television.

'No, it's the Boston Strangler.' Same greeting whenever he came home and the same response, but she never ever realised.

'Don't be clever, be a love and make me a cuppa.'

She never called him love. He thought it must be something she'd taken.

'In a bit,' he opened the fridge door and looked inside, empty as usual. He grabbed a can of cola and went through to his bedroom. Joey made sure the door was closed firmly. He reached inside his hoody and took out the Baikal, placed it on the bed and carefully unwrapped the weapon. Sitting on the edge of the bed, he picked up the can and pulled back the tab. He took a sip of cola and put the can down on his bedside table.

'My tea ready?' his mum called out.

'Two minutes,' he called back. Two minutes turned into twenty. He picked up the Baikal and stood in front of the mirror fixed to his wardrobe door. He stood legs apart, arms out straight, gripping the pistol with two hands. Cool, he thought, as he admired his reflection. Then he changed stance. Standing sideways facing the mirror, he held the weapon with one hand, the pistol tipped sideways gangsta style, just like he'd seen Robbo's customers do when they checked the goods. He tucked the pistol in the back waistband of his jeans and dropped his arm by his side. 'You dead, man,' he snarled at his reflection in the mirror, swiftly reaching for the Baikal and bringing up his arm outstretched, pointing towards his image. His finger, ever so lightly brushed against the trigger - that's when the Baikal exploded. His screams could be heard throughout the block of flats, if not all of North Hull. But in the living room, not ten feet away, the screams fell on deaf ears, his mum lay sprawled out on the floor by the coffee table. She had given up on waiting for the coffee, and decided a shot of "H" was a better option.

Chapter 11

Warren sat at his desk deliberating as to whether he should pre-empt things and give Powers a call, the twenty-four hours he had stated had already been and gone. He sat tearing his plastic coffee cup in shreds. 'Have you heard how the boss is?'

Trish looked up from her computer monitor. 'He's doing alright, but it's going to be a long job.'

'So, we'd better get sorted with our replacement.' He went back to the shredding. 'The McDonalds shooting, has there been any progress?'

Trish rifled through the increasing pile of folders on her desk. She found the one she wanted and opened it. 'Not a great deal, the witness checked out okay, in his interview he said he was too far away to get any details other than he was sure it was an Audi, no description of the occupants - it's a blank. See for yourself,' she pushed the folder across the desk to Warren.

He threw his artwork into the bin and spread the folder open and began reading. 'Alan Browning, 19 years old and a bit of a pusher. Probably stood on someone's toes, dealing where he shouldn't have been.'

'Harsh, not so long ago he would have been given a kicking and spent a couple of days in hospital, but now?' Trish shook her head. 'You think it could be gang related?'

'Always a possibility,' said Warren with his head down reading the file.

'Say's here the bullet that killed him was a 9mm.'

'Hmm, ballistics think it could have been fired from one of these Eastern European pistols. A distinct possibility it was a Baikal.'

Warren closed the folder and passed it back. 'We're not getting very far are we?'

'Early days, Greg, early days.'

Warren's mobile rang, it was the call he'd been waiting for. Warren looked across at Trish and gave the thumbs up and mouthed the name Powers.

'Mr Powers, it's good of you to call me back. I trust I come up to scratch?'

'Just doing my homework you understand, have to be careful with who you're dealing with,' the voice said.

'You do indeed, as it happens I've carried out a bit of research myself and I'm even more convinced we can do business together.'

'We're a long way from that scenario. There's a café at the Humber Bridge viewing area, 10am in the morning. Please come alone, Mr Cole. Goodbye.' He hung up.

'And it was very nice talking to you, Mr Powers,' Warren said, as he placed his mobile down on the desk. 'Well he sounds like a nice bloke, he wants to buy me a cup of tea.' Warren paused. 'I wonder if he'll stretch to a toasted tea-cake?'

'You're crackers,' Trish told him.'

'C'mon, you know as well as I do this job's not for anyone sane.'

Powers often conducted his business meetings at the Humber View café, it was respectable and at certain times of the day quiet. It was a place where travelling businessmen regularly carried out meetings, often hundreds of miles away from the offices. Today, Powers sat alone, he'd paid a visit to Gardener earlier in the day and needed a little time out without any interruptions, the café was a place he could sit in peace without being constantly interrupted. He'd needed to decide if he would return the call to Raymond Cole. If as the information given to him was correct, he would be foolish not to make the call, after all it looked as if it could turn out to be financially lucrative.

The call duly made, Powers placed his mobile on the table, he was staring through the window when the waitress brought across a second pot of tea. 'Thanks, love,' he said as she placed it down. Then his mobile vibrated and skidded about the table. He picked it up, looked at the screen, recognising the caller ID he accepted the call.

'Neil, it's me.' It was Powers' police contact.

'What can I do for you?' Powers asked.

'Got a lead on where that dodgy pistol might have come from.'

'Share,' he said in a low voice into the phone.

'This isn't official, as far as I know it could be a load of cobblers, right?'

'Okay, I'm listening.'

'I've heard a whisper the bloke you are looking for works out of a lockup workshop in north Hull.'

'Got a name for me?'

'Robert Dooley, goes by the name of Robbo. Now you have to understand, Neil, this isn't a cert, just a name one of my snouts came up with. Like I say, it's only a whisper.' The voice sounded nervous, as if he didn't want any repercussions from Powers if the information turned out to be useless.

'Does anyone else know about this?'

'No, not as far as I'm aware.'

'Keep it that way.' He ended the call, and keyed in another number. The call was picked up almost immediately.

'Boss, what can I do for you?' It was the newly named Sebastian.

'You sound like shit,' Powers told him.

'Yeah well, got a bad tooth haven't I?' replied Seb, referring to the teeth loosened by Warren.

'You heard of anyone called Robert Dooley?'

'Can't say as I have, why?'

'Just interested, this bloke lives somewhere in north Hull, find him and I want to know everything about him - right?

'No probs boss, get back to you soon.'

The call was disconnected, Powers returned to staring out of the window.

The north bank towers of the Humber Bridge stood tall and proud as Warren drove beneath the bridge along the A63, Clive Sullivan Way. He thought how murky the Humber looked when the tide was out, a series of mud flats covered in white specks, feeding gulls. He turned off the A63, drove past the Humber Bridge viewing area and headed for the overflow parking area. He arrived before the arranged time, arriving early was a habit that had proved to be a good one - always get to the rendezvous well before time, it was essential to check things out, it was more imperative to find a quick exit should one be needed.

Warren parked the Escort out of direct view between two heavy goods vehicles, climbed out and clicked the key fob. He stood looking around taking stock of his surroundings. The car park was larger than he had anticipated, with high sloping grassy banks and thick privet hedges, ideal if anyone wanted to conceal themselves. Warren walked the perimeter; everything appeared kosher, nothing untoward. Jimbo was getting good at the undercover lark, Warren never spotted him.

Jimbo had arrived separately, and, like Warren, well in advance and carried out his own recce of the area, finding himself a concealed hiding place amongst vegetation with a good view of the café and its approaches. By the time Warren arrived back at his vehicle it was almost time for the meet. He opened up the Escort, climbed in and then drove through to the main visitor parking area, this time pulling up in clear view of the café. For appearance sake, should anyone be watching, he sat a while, making the pretence of talking on his mobile, all the while he was scanning the area.

Once satisfied that things looked okay, not that there was much he could do about it at this stage of the game,

117

Warren walked across the open space of the car park. If there were anyone concealed with a weapon it would be now he used it.

Nothing.

Pushing open the café door he looked around. Two guys sat close to the counter having a late breakfast meeting, towards the far end sat a family enjoying their bacon rolls before venturing down onto the riverside foreshore. One solitary figure sat towards the rear of the café, like Warren, he liked a good view of the exits. Warren gave his walk an exaggerated swagger, the Raymond Cole bluster. He approached the table and stood before the solitary figure.

'Mr Powers?' he said, reaching across the table holding out his arm. Powers ignored the hand. Warren shrugged. 'May I?' he asked inclining his head to a vacant chair. 'I'll take that as a yes,' he said when he still didn't receive an answer, just an intimidating stare. So, you *are* a hard-man, thought Warren, there was something about Powers that made him come to the conclusion so quickly. 'Tea, please, love,' Warren called over to the young woman behind the counter as he sat down. Still no response from Powers. Warren sat, arms folded across his chest, the well-practised stare hadn't worked, he'd seen it all before.

Then Powers moved, his hands came up from his lap, he placed them palm down on the table, arms outstretched. 'Who are you?'

'Raymond Cole, but you can call me Ray.'

'Who are you really?' All the time he tried to stare Warren out.

118

'I'm the man who's giving you five hundred notes for ten minutes of your time.' The waitress brought over Warren's tea and put the tray down on the table. 'Thanks, love.'

'Then you've already wasted three minutes. What do you want?'

'I have a colleague in Newcastle who requires information. See, it's been brought to our attention someone in this area has been supplying defective firearms. Not good for business.'

'What makes you think that I can help?'

'I've been told that you're the man in the know, shall we say the man with his finger on the trigger, so to speak.' Warren gave a short faux laugh at his own joke.

'Before we go any further, who gave you my number?'

'Ha, that would be telling,' he said touching the side of his nose knowingly.

'Then good morning to you, Mr Cole.' Powers stood up to leave.

'You know someone who goes by the name of Mouse?' Warren said quickly before Powers had chance to move from the table.

Powers promptly resumed his seat. 'The name rings a bell.'

'You might want to have a word with him, it only cost me a ton for your number.'

'Noted, Mr Cole. Yes, there has been some defective Eastern European pistols, I didn't realise they'd reached your neck of the woods?'

'Oh yes, bad merchandise rubs off on all of us. We want it ended.'

'Well, I can assure you the matter is already in hand, it's being dealt with. So, now if you will excuse me I have a business to attend to.'

'Before you leave,' Warren reached inside his jacket and took out a bulging envelope and placed it on the table. 'Five hundred, as agreed.'

'Keep it, not necessary.

'Call it a goodwill gesture,' Warren told him. 'Of course, there's plenty more where this came from.' Warren held onto the envelope momentarily. 'My colleagues and I are looking to find a new, more dependable supplier, someone who can supply reliable goods.'

'As I said, I have a business to run. You have my number, use it sparingly.' Powers brushed aside Warren's hand and picked up the envelope and put it in his own pocket, 'I'll look forward to hearing from you,' and left.

Warren watched through the café window as Powers headed towards a new BMW. There was no guessing what the business Powers had to attend to was, he didn't want to be in Mouse's shoes any time soon.

Powers hadn't realised how wide spread the problem had become, he thought it a local problem, not one which had repercussions in other parts of the country. Obviously, this Dooley had been spreading his wings. The matter needed dealing with sooner rather than later. As for Mouse, Powers did have plans to deal with him, but first there was one more thing he needed the rodent to do.

Chapter 12

Trish came into the office waving a sheet of paper, her face like thunder, she was fuming. 'Don't suppose you've seen this?' She slapped the sheet down with the palm of her hand. Neither Warren nor Jimbo had seen her so worked up, they sat in awe and let her finish her rant. 'Well, say something?'

Warren was the first to respond. 'Trish, calm down, what's got you rattled?' he said as he reached across the desk and slid the sheet toward him.

'Fifteen year old lad got his bloody hand blown off, that's what's rattling me. This is getting bloody ridiculous, kids getting maimed.'

Warren sat forward in his seat. 'When was this?'

'Late yesterday afternoon. And where was his mother? Out of her head on Heroin, she wants bloody locking up.'

'Okay Trish, you've got the lad's details?' She nodded. 'Grab your jacket and we'll check it out, then we'll go see the lad in the infirmary.'

Trish continued to put the world to rights as they drove to the North Hull address. 'Not very appealing, is it?' Trish remarked as they walked across the parking area. Warren was non-committal. He'd seen worse places in north London. A uniformed officer stood by the entrance to the flats. The detectives flashed their warrant cards, and were directed to the flat the lad shared with his mother. Another uniform stood by the door, wrote their names into the log and allowed them access.

'Where's the mother?' Trish asked the uniform.

'Living room,' was all he said, shaking his head in disgust.

Trish stepped over the threshold, Warren close behind, followed her through the short hallway. There was nothing remarkable about the place, small basic kitchen - not the most hygienic room in the house, about on par with the bathroom and toilet that could have benefitted from a splash of bleach and a good clean through.

Warren entered the living room. 'Mrs Smale?' he said as he looked around and saw a woman with bottle blonde hair, sprawled legs akimbo on the settee. She didn't respond, still half cut from her fix. He looked towards Trish and wrinkled his nose, convinced she must have pissed herself while she was out of it. 'Mrs Smale?' he repeated. He was wasting his breath, he turned his back on her. 'Must have been some fix if she's still out of it,' he said as they left the room.

'The lad's room,' Trish told him, as she gently pushed open the door with the toe of her boot. 'Best put these on,' she passed him a pair of protective nitrile gloves.

The room was not typical for a fifteen-year-old boy - it was clean and tidy, apart from the blood and mess left by the Paramedics. A made up single bed was pushed against one wall, again, untypical for a boy of his age was the expensive television fixed high on the wall facing the bed. Next to the bed was a melamine bedside cabinet with a lamp, a couple of mountain biking magazines lay on the floor next to the bed. The wardrobe wobbled as Warren opened the door, the false bottom still open, inside Warren saw the biscuit tin, the type usually seen in the shops around Christmas time, carefully he lifted it out and placed it on the bed.

'What have you got there?' asked Trish.

'Let's have a look shall we?' The festive snow scene lid was a loose fit and came away easily. 'Wow,' he was amazed. 'This is a serious amount of cash, you don't get this much for doing a paper round.'

'Do lads still do that - paper rounds?' Trish asked seriously.

'Buggered if I know.'

'I'm not surprised he kept it hidden away from her,' Trish inclined her head toward the living room.

Warren shouted to the uniform on the door. 'Have the CSIs been yet?'

'Not yet, Sarge, they've been held up.'

'Give us a minute will you,' asked Warren.

The uniform left his post at the door and joined them in the bedroom. 'Sarge,' he said to Warren, still searching in the wardrobe.

Trish responded. 'Keep this safe until the CSIs get here,' she said putting the lid back on the tin.

'What's in it?' She lifted the corner slightly allowing him to see the contents. If she hadn't she knew curiosity would overcome him and he'd look inside, possibly interfering with any trace evidence. 'Jesus, how much is in there?'

'A lot, we'll let the CSI's count it, just keep your eye on it.' Again, Trish gestured towards the living room where Joey's mum sat, still high as a kite.

'Bloody hell, yes, if she gets her hands on it she'll be stoned from now until Christmas.'

'Now where, the Infirmary?'

'Yep,' Warren replied.

Trying to find a parking place at the Hull Royal Infirmary was nigh on impossible. 'I'm not driving around this bloody car park any longer,' grumbled Warren, as he pulled the pool car into a restricted area on the hospital concourse and stopped directly in front of the thirteen-storey hospital.

'Oi, you can't park there,' a security guard shouted and marched across as Warren and Trish climbed out of the vehicle. Warren flashed his ID at the guard. 'Makes no difference, mate, you can't leave it there,' he said in his 'jobs worth voice'.

'If you don't want it there - you move it,' Warren replied sternly, as he tossed the vehicle keys to the man who nearly fell arse over tit to catch them. 'And don't scratch it.' Not that it would have made much difference to the battered vehicle - maybe even enhanced it a little.

'Bloody coppers,' the man mutter behind Warren's back as he walked back to his security cabin.

The detectives made their way across the hospital lobby and walked across the large open foyer.

'Excuse me.' Warren said, again, holding his warrant card high to the girl behind the booking-in desk. 'Can you tell me which ward Joey Smale is on?'

She looked up from the computer screen, glanced at the ID and started to tap tap on the keyboard. 'He's over in the Women and Children's building, just across the way, turn left out of the main doors, you can't miss it.'

'Thanks.'

'No problem, just press the buzzer on the door and they'll give you access.'

Warren and Trish were duly admitted into the Women and Children's building, a modern purpose-built unit. It was a much friendlier environment than the main building. A charge nurse once again checked their identification then escorted them along brightly painted corridors with cartoon characters and posters on the walls. Joey was recovering in a private side ward following the operation on his damaged hand.

'He's not long out of surgery,' the nurse told them.

'Is he conscious?' asked Trish.

'Not really, on and off, more off than on. I doubt you'll get any sense out of him until the anaesthetic wears off, of course then there's the pain killers to contend with. Poor lad's in a terrible state.'

'In here,' the nurse opened the door, a second nurse sat on a chair by his side. She smiled at the officers and continued to monitor the machines. The room was bright and cheerful, not that Joey was taking any pleasure from his surroundings. The lad lay on the bed, wired up to the heart monitors and fluid drips and goodness knows what else. 'He's stable,' she said, 'keeps drifting in and out. It'll be a while before you can speak to him.'

Trish was visibly upset. Joey looked so small. She'd seen it all during her career, but the sight of the lad minus his hand and half of his right arm touched a nerve. 'How is he really?' she asked.

'The operation went well, he'll make full recovery. Once the wounds healed he'll be fitted with a prosthetic limb. What he'll need when he wakes is his mum.'

Trish walked to the bedside and placed a hand on his forehead. 'Fat chance of that happening.' The nurse raised her eyebrows, gave an enquiring look. 'She's a junkie, she was out of her head when it happened.'

'Who rang for the Paramedics?'

'A neighbour, his mum was high on Heroin when they arrived, didn't have a clue what happened or what was going on. Doubt she still does.'

'Takes all sorts,' the nurse replied, 'we've alerted Social Services about what's happened.'

'Let's hope they can sort something for him.' Warren turned to Trish, 'not much point hanging about,' he said, taking a business card from his wallet. 'Do me a favour,' he asked the nurse, 'will you give me a call when you think he'll be able to talk to us?'

'Of course,' she replied taking the card.

'No pressure, but the sooner the better you understand, the faster we find out what happened we can try and stop it happening again.'

'As soon as he's able to talk I'll be in touch.'

'Thanks,' said Warren as they left, closing the door on the bleeping machines.

Chapter 13

It wasn't long before the news of what happened to Joey reached Powers, via the power of local radio. He was scathing, how the hell had a lad of that age got himself involved with a dodgy weapon and who the hell had been the supplier? If truth was known, he had very little doubt that it was none other than Robert Dooley, who else? The matter needed dealing with ASAP.

Powers needed a drink. He went through to the kitchen and selected an expensive bottle of red wine from the rack. Settled in his leather Chesterfield chair with a large glass of red, he took out his mobile and dialled. The recipient of the call recognised the ID and answered almost immediately.

'Yes, boss?' Sebastian said into the handset.

'Dooley, did you do a deal with him?'

'Yep, met a young lad for the handover.'

'Thought as much. Have you heard the local news recently?'

'Can't say I have, never listen to that crap, why?'

'Seems the lad you did the deal with, might have had his hand blown off by a dodgy one.'

127

'For fuck's sake, still if he was working with Dooley ...'

Powers cut him short. 'He was a kid for fuck's sake, I want him taken care of sooner rather than later, Dooley that is, just in case it's not clear.' Bloody moron, Powers thought to himself.

'No probs boss, I'm on it.' Then the line went dead. Sebastian immediately dialled another number.

'Yo, Mouse what can I do for you?' Albert Drury was an old pal from Mouse's school days, between them they had caused the teachers untold grief right until the day they were excluded.

'I've told you before you moron, call me Sebastian or Seb. Listen, the boss wants a special job doing. You up for it?'

'How special?'

'Very, know what I mean? I reckon there will be a bonus if we play our cards right.' Mouse knew the boss would be willing to pay a little over the odds for a quick result. 'I'll be in touch soon, so lay off the gear, know what I mean?'

Ever since Robbo heard on local radio about Joey, he'd gone into a depressive mood and started hitting the bottle a lot more than he usually did. He genuinely liked the lad, and to say he felt sorry for him would be an understatement. Time and time again he went over the conversion process in his head, he couldn't fathom what the hell he was doing wrong? He couldn't talk about it - who *could* he talk to?

Several times Dooley tried telephoning the hospital to see how Joey was doing, but some jobs worth at the other end of the line wouldn't tell him anything unless he was a relative.

He swore to himself he'd never, ever convert another pistol, but he knew it was only the booze talking, who was he kidding? Nobody but himself, the money was too good. But he was worried, very worried - he hoped to Christ, Joey would keep his mouth shut?

He had a steady day planned, he was going to spend a few hours on his restoration project, the Triumph motorcycle. Then back home for lunch and then he was going to try and con his way in to visit Joey in hospital. 'Bye, love, see you later,' Robbo shouted over his shoulder as he stepped out into the street, shutting the door behind him. Head down he trudged toward his workshop, unaware of the Ford Focus, parked up just down the road from his house.

'That him?' The Focus' passenger asked.

'Yep.'

'Don't look owt special.'

'He isn't, he's a shit brain.'

Robbo walked, it wasn't far, only a couple of hundred metres to the garage block. The driver of the Ford Focus watched Robbo turn the corner, then he eased the car away from the kerbside - slowly they followed, the occupants watching Robbo's every move.

Parked up at the entrance to the communal garage block, they watched him unlock the garage folding door, slide it open and go inside, closing the door behind him.

In the Focus the passenger opened the window to let out a plume of stale, blue tobacco smoke. 'We doing this now?' He asked as he took a pull on his fag.

'Na.'

'Why not, it's perfect, no one hanging around?'

'We've just been parked up practically outside his house for the past hour, you plank. Don't you think some busybody has clocked us already?'

'Suppose. When then?'

'Soon, very soon.'

Chapter 14

For the next twenty-four hours, Mouse, who now kept trying in vain to revert to his given name of Sebastian, pulled in every favour he could to find out everything there was to be known about Robert Dooley.

The sun had long gone down, but the heat of the day was trapped beneath the now dark clouds, threatening a storm. Every now and then heavy drops of rain splashed onto the windscreen and spread like spider's webs along the glass. The Focus was parked up by the kerbside, giving the occupants an uninterrupted view of Robbo's house and the approaching side roads. The curtains were drawn closed on the pebble-dashed council houses. Homes arranged in blocks where the occupants sat glued to the latest reality show or enthralled in their latest soap episode.

The council described the layout of the housing estate as courts, but the further you went into the estate, the more akin they were to 'rat runs'. The estate had been built in the 1960s to house the families affected by the west Hull slum clearance. The council in their wisdom had thought it wise to move the residents of the tight knit fishing communities to a sprawling estate on the northern edge of the city. Progress came during the Thatcher era when many took the advantage and sought the opportunity to buy their homes, and the legacy lived on, with many descendants of the original families still living there. These were the lucky ones, facing onto open fields with views toward Cottingham.

Inside the car Sebastian, AKA Mouse and Albie sat waiting patiently, smoking and listening to music. It was quiet. This was after all, the time of evening when most people were indoors settled in front of the box after a busy day at work.

Mouse, sitting in the driving seat of the Ford, took out his pack of smuggled duty-free cigarettes, placed one between his lips and lit up. He didn't offer one to his companion. 'Tonight's bingo night,' he said as he opened the car window to let the smoke escape. He glanced at his watch. 'His missus will be home any time now.'

'How come you know so much?'

'Been asking around, haven't I?'

The amateur gunsmith had a predictable routine, it soon became clear his schedule was a simple one. Altogether he led a very mundane ordinary life, work, home, bed, and an occasional visit to the betting shop. Saturday, was shopping with his wife, with the week broken up with a visit to the pub on Saturday evening, not forgetting bingo night.

'And him, this Robbo?'

'Pub, always goes for a pint while the missus is at bingo. He usually comes home shortly after her, brings fish and chips with him.'

'So, we're really doing this tonight Mou...' Albie quickly corrected himself, 'Seb?'

'Yep, that's what the boss wants.' He put his arm through the open window and pointed with his fingers, gun like. 'Boom.'

'Here she comes now, bang on time.'

'*Bang* on time, yeah, I like that.'

'Grow up, this is serious shit, man.'

In the distance Mrs Robbo was walking toward them. She wasn't alone, she walked arms linked with her sister and bingo partner.

Mouse and Albie sunk down in their seats out of view, watching. The two women reached the corner of the street, and stood chatting for a few minutes more before saying their goodnights and going their separate ways.

'Why is it that women still have something to natter about, even when they've been together for the last couple of hours?'

Mouse ignored him.

'Won't be long now. Remember do it exactly as I told you.'

'Yeah, yeah, I've got it.'

He reached under the seat and produced a Baikal, the very same gun he'd hired from Robbo. His boss thought it was symbolic, poetic justice that he should be cut down with his own pistol, regardless of how much he had to pay for it.

'Then tell me one more time,' he demanded.

'Hell, you're as bad as the boss. He's walking towards us, I have the gun, we drive towards him, you slow down almost stopping, I poke me arm out the window, I point and put two in his chest. Okay?'

'You sure you're definitely up for this? We can't afford any cock-ups.'

'I'm as ready as I'll ever be.' He was, and showing no sign of backing out.

'It'll be a piece of piss, first one is always the hardest. Now we wait.' Mouse removed the magazine from the pistol and made pretence of checking it was okay and wiping his prints clean with a rag before sliding it back into position. Still holding the weapon in the rag he then passed the weapon over to a nervous Albie, who was keeping his apprehension well hidden.

The wait wasn't a long one. Ten minutes later Robbo came into view walking on the opposite side of the road. With a couple or three pints inside of him, he didn't have a care in the world. Dooley sauntered on, a plastic carrier bag containing their fish and chip supper in his right hand. Albie sat fidgeting nervously, keeping his finger well away from the trigger of the Baikal. This was to be Albie's first kill, and he was determined not to bottle it, he needed to prove himself. He was a thug, breaking legs and heads didn't bother him one iota, but this was the big one - and he was ready.

The field was clear. Curtains were still closed and no dog walkers, no possible witnesses that Mouse would need to take care of later. He turned the key in the ignition and the engine purred. Gently, he eased his foot down on the accelerator pedal. 'Ready?' Albie didn't speak, just nodded and wound down the window. Mouse smoothly put pressure on the accelerator pedal and the Focus moved steadily away from the kerb. Robbo came closer and closer, oblivious until an outstretched arm thrust through window. There was no time to react, a quick burst of two bullets ripped into his chest, bang, bang, from almost point-blank range. As Robbo fell to the concrete in a heap, the Focus accelerated, took a left turn at the end of the road and was away.

Lights in the neighbouring houses came on, curtains twitched and front doors opened. Robbo lay on the pavement, legs twisted beneath him - hands clutching his chest as a dark pool of blood spread through his fingers, pooling beneath and around him. The fish and chip supper spread over the roadside. Albie put the weapon in the foot-well and closed the car window. Sitting back in his seat he laughed like he'd gone crazy - he was wired, hyper with the adrenaline rush.

'Man, oh man, that was so fucking cool,' Albie shouted out loud, as the Focus joined a line of vehicles on Orchard Park Road. 'You see him go down? Bang, bang,' he gestured with his fingers. 'Fucking hell, he went down like a bag of shit.'

'Calm down, man,' Mouse urged.

'Yeah but ...' Albie started to protest.

'Yeah but, nowt. Just get back in your box and pull yourself together. If the cops see you acting like a loon we'll be pulled over, know what I mean?'

Albie took heed of Mouse's warning. He was right. Getting pulled over was the last thing they wanted.

The evening traffic along Beverley Road was light and all the traffic signals were in their favour. Beverley Road had changed over recent years, this was a time when all the shops would normally have been closed for the evening, but now there was an abundance of early opening – late closing Eastern European convenience stores and supermarkets. Mouse took the journey at a steady rate, making sure he drove within the speed limit and pulled the Focus down by the side of the Rose.

Albie was still hyper but managing to hold it together. 'Right,' Mouse took his mobile out of his jeans pocket, 'time to let the boss know it's done.' He sent a very brief text message, one word. *Done*.

'What about the gun?'

Mouse looked him in the face. 'You keep it.'

'Thanks, man.'

Albie thought all his birthdays had come at once, but there was method in Mouse's action. Should there be any comeback, anything at all that would lead the police to the weapon, it would be in the possession of Albie and the only prints they would find would be his. If Mouse should be implicated, all he had to do was to hold it together, deny everything and let Albie take the fall.

'No problem, mate, you can buy me a pint.'

Chapter 15

It had been a long day, Warren hadn't left the station until 9.30 p.m. He hadn't eaten since breakfast and his stomach was grumbling for England, there was only one thing for it, he stopped at the local take-away and bought himself a very predictable pepperoni pizza.

Home for Greg Warren was a large three bed-roomed terraced house along Alliance Avenue, he'd bought the house shortly after moving to Hull, after a brief period of living in rented accommodation. With the pizza box on his lap, he sat on the sofa, feet up on the coffee table, watching the evening news. He reached down to the floor for his bottle of imported lager, noticed the pale bleached patch in the carpet pile and shook his head, remembering, not one of his finest moments. That was the exact spot where he had put a bullet through Bob's foot, Bob being one of his ex-masters at Gemmell Stratergies. As it turned out Bob was one of the good guys. Still balancing the pizza box on his knee he retrieved the bottle and sipped. That was when his mobile scurried across the table top. He swapped the bottle for the phone and recognising the caller ID he pressed the accept key.

'Yep,' he said into the handset.

'Greg, you busy?' said a voice down the phone line, it was the Duty Inspector at the nick.

Warren knew it wouldn't matter if he was busy or not. 'Nope, what can I do for you?'

'There's been another drive by shooting in North Hull.'

'Christ, what's going on? It's getting more and more like London and Manchester by the day.'

'Yeah, well this one's still alive, just. He took two bullets to the chest and by some bloody miracle they didn't damage any vital organs. My lads on the scene thought he was a gonna but the Paramedics found a pulse - just.'

'Anyone we know?'

'Robert Dooley, not on our radar.'

'Okay, I'll get myself down there.'

Warren looked at the empty lager bottles, should he call a taxi? Na, he'd only had the two, there was no way he'd be over the drink drive limit. He pulled on his trainers, grabbed his jacket and left the house, not before giving Trish a call and spoiling her evening. The pizza would have to wait.

The journey from Warren's home to the Hull Royal Infirmary was a short one, just a couple or three miles away. At least at the late hour parking at the Hull Royal Infirmary would be no problem, or so he thought. He gave up looking and parked up on double yellows and placed a police sticker on the dashboard.

The three story apartment building on the Victoria Dock was built on a premium plot, with direct views

138

overlooking the River Humber. The exclusiveness of this imposing block with magnificent location had been reflected in the buying price when the Victoria Dock complex was completed.

The third floor was even more special with only four apartments, each occupying a corner location, one of which was owned by Neil Powers. Powers was pleased to call the apartment home, many times he reflected on his past, who would have thought a rag tag kid from the slums would ever be in a position to own such a place. Every time he thought about it, he had to smile to himself - he'd made it.

This was a place he could escape to, a place where his business dealings didn't encroach on his private life. Yes, once the door was closed on his Victoria Dock home he could turn off the worries and woes of the day - most of the time. This particular fine evening the French windows were wide open, a gentle salty breeze blew along the Humber. He sat on a bistro chair, bottle of expensive craft beer in hand, and let his thoughts wander as he enjoyed the view from the narrow balcony. The setting sun over the river reminded him of the time he was stationed in Kenya, a far cry from Victoria Dock.

He sipped his beer and deliberated as to whether he should enter business discussions with the man he knew as Raymond Cole. His credentials were good but first impressions hadn't been favourable, Cole seemed so sure of himself, cocky to the point of being arrogant, but then again, so was he, it was the only way to be in their business.

He put down his bottle on the bistro table and picked up his mobile, the untraceable Pay-As-You-Go. Warren's number was still in the call log, he was just about to dial, faltered and put the phone back on the table and picked up his beer. Unsure, he stared out over the river, the tide was turning, a coaster was heading out to the North Sea. In for a penny he thought and picked up the mobile once again, after all if things turned pear shaped, well - he was, after all an arms dealer.

Trish was already waiting outside the Infirmary Intensive Care Unit when Warren arrived. 'You look how I feel,' she said as Warren walked up.

'Yeah well,' he replied, 'just got sat in front of the telly with my pizza and half way through my second lager then the phone rings, I was in half a mind to ignore it.'

'Nature of the job, can't expect to have a private life.'

'You're telling me. That the wife?' Warren asked, nodding towards the woman sitting on a tubular framed chair outside of the ITU department.

Mrs Dooley looked to be in complete shock. A slim woman, pale faced with short dark hair cut in a bob, she looked as if she'd rushed out in a hurry, she was still wearing her slippers.

'I take it you've had a word already?'

'She can't tell us anything of use, she was at bingo with her sister, came home around 10pm. The husband always goes for a couple of pints and comes home with fish and chips. She put the kettle on and buttered some bread ready for when he arrived. Next thing she knew there was a knocking on her door, one of her neighbours coming to give her the bad news.'

'So, what's the position with the husband?' Warren cupped his hands on the glass as he tried to peer through the blinds into the ITU.

Trish opened her notebook. 'Robert Dooley, walking home from the pub, around 10 p.m. last night, neighbours heard two loud bangs, of course they ignored it, saying they thought a car was back firing.'

'When was the last time you heard a car back fire?' Trish shrugged her shoulders, 'modern cars don't back fire, fact.'

'Anyway, nobody saw anything, one of the curtain twitchers saw him lying there, called the emergency services then went to see if she could help.'

'Nice that, at least one person not afraid to get involved.'

'Yeah, considering she's eighty-two. Two bullets to the chest and he's lived to tell the tale.'

'Shall we?' Warren asked, as he squirted antibacterial hand wash onto his hands, then held his warrant card against the glass and rattled on the door to be admitted. The charge nurse gave him a stern look through the glass. 'That's me told,' he mumbled as she opened the door and allowed them to enter. It was all too familiar, first it was the antiseptic smell, then the bleeping of the monitors, IV lines hanging from stands ran into the backs of his hands, all with one purpose - keeping Dooley in the land of the living.

'I'm afraid he's in no condition to answer any questions, he's not long out of surgery,' the nurse who'd given Warren the stern look told them.

'This is getting to be a bit too frequent,' said the nurse, inclining her head towards the patient.

'Tell us about it,' was the reply from Warren.

'He is going to be alright?' Trish asked.

'Oh yes, he had two bullet wounds to the chest but fortunately they missed all the vital organs. To be honest I'm amazed,' she replied, as she checked the monitor. 'He's still got a long way to go yet, but he'll live.'

'Don't suppose you know anything about the bullets they took out of him?'

'Not a clue, way above my level of expertise,' she said, jotting down notes on Dooley's chart.

'His belongings?' asked Warren.

'His wife asked for them. I told her we had to keep them for the police to examine.' She went over to the bedside locker and retrieved a green polythene bag with the NHS logo all over it and passed it across. 'That's everything.'

'Thanks.' He checked his watch, looked toward Trish and then back to the nurse. 'Don't suppose there would be any chance of us seeing another patient, in the Children's section?'

'Look out the window,' she said.

Warren crossed the room, lifted the blind and looked outside. 'What am I looking for?'

'Flying pigs,' she relied humorously.

'Point taken,' he dropped the blind back in place. Although he'd checked the time two minutes ago subconsciously Warren checked his watch again. 'It's getting late, we'll give the wife a visit first thing in the morning and then come back and see if we can have a word with the lad.' Warren thanked the nurse once more and left her tending Dooley. Back in the corridor, Mrs Dooley still sat in the same position, head in her hands clutching a paper tissue. 'Do you know what he does to earn a crust?' he asked Trish.

She referred to her notes. 'Self-employed, some kind of engineer.'

'Interesting.' The word engineer triggered Warren's thoughts. 'Don't suppose you got the address for his workshop?'

'Funnily enough the word engineer struck a chord with me, so I asked the question. It's a lock-up garage, five minutes walk from his home,' she scribbled the address down and passed it over. 'According to Mrs Dooley, he does anything and everything mechanical that people want fixing.'

'Fancy taking a look?' he asked.

'We can hardly ask his missus for the keys, can we? Look at the state she's in,' she said nodding over her shoulder.

Warren gave her a quick glance. 'Maybe not, but I know a man who can open it up for us,' he took out his mobile and dialled.

Trish shook her head as she listened to the short telephone conversation.

'Right, Jimbo, what you up to, mate?' Warren asked when the call was answered.

'Watching telly, why?'

'We could do with your expertise.'

'This is more like it, the 'A Team' on the case.'

Warren had to smile at the comment, he could sense Jimbo's excitement. He gave him the address and added. 'Don't forget your lock picks.'

'Lock picks?' said Trish, 'I don't think I should be involved in this - no, I'm positive ...'

'C'mon Trish, this is what it's all about, live a little.'

'Breaking and entering?' Warren was half way down the corridor before she finished the sentence. 'Hang on, wait for me.' She was up for it, Warren knew she would be, just needed a little encouragement.

Jimbo was already at the location when they arrived. 'Didn't expect to see you here Trish?'

'I didn't expect to be here, but someone's got to keep you two in check.'

The garage block housed sixteen prefabricated adjoined garages arranged in a courtyard style with only one entrance and exit.

'Which one?' asked Jimbo, taking the picks from his pocket.

'This one,' said Warren as he walked across the block and placed his hand on the door. Jimbo stepped forward, in less than two minutes he was sliding the door open. The smell of machine oil and cooling fluid attacked their senses immediately the door was opened.

'Bloody hell, Mr Boland,' said Trish, 'I'm impressed.'

Jimbo took a faux bow as he stood aside. 'Easy peasey when you know how, now you should see some of the locks I've opened up for Greg here ...'

'Enough mate,' Warren cut him short, 'save it for another time,' he said as he stepped in the workshop and fumbled for a light switch. 'Hell fire,' said Warren as the room lit up like Blackpool Illuminations. 'Close the door, mate.'

Jimbo stepped inside and slid the door shut behind him.

'For Christ's sake, be careful, don't touch anything, we don't want any cross contamination of possible evidence!'

'Trish,' said Warren, 'I have done this before,' and fished a pair of nitrile gloves from his pocket and snapped them over his hands.

Dooley kept a tidy workshop, it may have been a single lock-up garage but well equipped. There was a small compact high-tec lathe he thought easily capable of firearm conversion, surface grinder, a shiny newish free-standing bench drill and a variety of hand tools. Warren wondered if all the machinery came from his ex-employer, he guessed so, and for rock bottom price at that.

Jimbo and Trish stood aside as Warren rummaged his way through the equipment looking for anything that may have a significance.

'Jimbo, over here mate,' said Warren studying the heavy metal filing cabinet tucked away in a corner next to what looked to be a pile of scrap. The top three drawers didn't warrant being locked, they just contained paperwork, however the large bottom drawer was protected with a heavy security padlock.

'Just make way and let my fingers do the talking,' Jimbo said, as he made a pretence of flexing his knuckles. Warren stepped back while the Civilian Advisor crouched in front of the cabinet and worked his magic, the lock proved to be a little more difficult, taking Jimbo all of three minutes. 'There you go.'

'Don't know what I'd do without you,' said Warren as he put a gloved hand in the drawer. 'What have we here,' he said producing an Eastern European pistol, checking it was safe before showing his colleagues. 'There's another four in here beside this one.' Warren never mentioned the brand-new, Walther PPQ, 9mm automatic. Unseen, he slipped the Walther into his jacket pocket, along with the silencing suppressor and box of ammo. He had a feeling a little further down the line it might come in useful. It wasn't as if Dooley would report it missing to the police.

'So, we can assume it was the opposition that tried to knock him off?' Trish said as she moved in closer for a look.

'That would be my guess. During my meeting with Powers he agreed it was bad for business all round and already had it in hand.'

'Do you think it was Dooley who's responsible for the exploding pistols?'

'Dooley, very likely, but if you're asking are these dodgy, I'm not qualified to answer, but I'm sure we have some expert or another who can. Okay, I'll put this back, and in the morning, it can be done all over again with a search warrant.'

The weapon was returned to the drawer with the others and the cabinet duly locked. 'Everything as we found it?' They both nodded in response. 'Okay Jimbo, sort the locks.' Jimbo only took a matter of seconds to relock the cabinet. Warren took one last look around and turned off the lights. Once outside, Jimbo closed the exterior door and secured the lock. To all intents no one had ever been in the place.

'Now we're aware of the firearms, best get uniform to keep an eye on the place, just to be on the safe side.'

'Couldn't agree more, Trish.'

146

'Do you need a lift home?' Jimbo asked.

'You can drop me at the Infirmary to collect my car if that's okay,' Trish replied, as she fastened her jacket.

'No probs.'

'Right then, I'll see you in the morning.'

'That you will, goodnight.'

Warren settled himself into the low seat of his motor, dropped his mobile onto the passenger seat and was just about to buckle up the seatbelt when his phone sang out. He picked it up and pressed the accept key without checking the caller ID

'Yep,' he said into the receiver, he was surprised, it was Powers.

'That you, Cole?' Powers was the last person he was expecting to call at that hour of the night.

'Good of you to call, Mr Powers, I take it you want to talk business?' Warren spoke confidently as if it was a done deal.

'Talk yes, we'll discuss the other when we meet.'

'When will that be?'

As they were speaking a second call came through on Powers phone, he checked the caller as he spoke. 'Very soon, I have an important call on hold. I'll give you a bell later in the morning.'

'I'll look forward to it.' The call ended and Warren dropped the phone back on the passenger seat. 'Well, well, well,' he said to himself as he drove away from the workshop. Progress was being made.

Powers still had his mobile in his hand when it rang. 'Speak,' he said immediately. It was Mouse.

'Don't like having to tell you this boss...'

'Spit it out, Mouse.'

Mouse wanted to correct Powers, he knew he wanted to be called Seb, but held his tongue. 'Boss, he's still alive.'

Silence followed, Powers wanted to blow his top but managed to keep things civilised. 'Alive, what do you mean he's still alive? You and that dead-headed friend of yours were paid to make sure he was finished, how the hell is he still alive, how many shots did you put into him?'

'Two, right in his chest, he went down like a bag of shit.'

'Did he see you?'

'No boss.'

'Can the pistol be traced back to us?'

No, I made sure of that, if anything does come of it, it won't lead back to us.'

'Well that's one good thing. Listen, what's done is done, but let's not take any chances. I want you to find out all you can, and if you can finish the job I'll give you a bonus.'

'It's as good as done, Mr Powers.'

'One proviso, no tossers, you do the job yourself, right?'

'Right, I'll be in touch...' Powers ended the call before Mouse could go any further.

'Fucking imbeciles,' Powers said, as he dropped his mobile to the floor. 'Fucking imbeciles.'

Chapter 16

'Have you had any dealings with this Robert Dooley,' Trish asked Jimbo, who sat dunking his herbal tea bag up and down in his mug.

'Nope, not until you told me, died has he?'

'No, he was bloody lucky, he's still in a bad way but they said he'll pull through.'

Jimbo dropped the teabag in the bin. 'Any idea who the shooter was?'

'You know as much as I do.'

'Two hits in less than a week, that's high by any standard never mind in Hull.'

The office door opened. 'What are you two chin wagging about?' Warren asked as he set down a tray with three hot drinks on it.

'Dooley. One of those for me?' Trish asked.

'Help yourself.'

'Got one thanks,' Jimbo said as he held up his mug.

'What *about* Dooley, any developments?' questioned Warren.

'Nothing to tell barring he's come around, but still in intensive care.'

'Okay, we'll have our drinks and then see if we can have a word with him.'

'Might be an idea to hear what Joey has to say first,' suggested Trish.

'Jane, the nurse in charge said she would give us a call when he could talk to us.'

'What about Dooley's lock-up?'

'I've given uniform the nod and the CSIs, we know what they're going to find, so no rush there. What have you got planned, Jimbo?'

Before Jimbo had a chance to respond there was a brief knock on the door and a smart looking bloke walked in. 'You want something?' Warren said to the newcomer he didn't recognise.

The stranger was taken aback by the abrupt greeting. He was a good six feet, two inches tall, short cropped blonde hair, built like a brick shit house, wearing jeans, Chelsea boots and a casual jacket over his collarless granddad shirt. 'PC Philips,' he said as he walked toward Warren with an outstretched hand.

At that moment, Trish turned around. 'Bernie, prompt as usual.'

'Ah, I get it, this is Elvis,' Warren said.

'Excuse me?'

'Wrong,' said Trish.

'Nothing mate, my mistake, no quiff.' Philips looked puzzled.

Warren accepted the hand and shook. 'DS Warren - Greg, good to meet you.'

'Don't worry about him, Bernie, he might be a DS but he's as daft as a brush.'

Warren shot her a look. 'Thank you for that, DC James, keep your opinions to yourself. Now, Bernie tell me, have you done a stint in CID before?'

'Yes, Sarge, three months on secondment when they were shorthanded at the Hessle station.'

'And?'

'And what?'

'Did you enjoy it? They sling you out on your arse? How did you find it?' Warren asked, genuinely interested, he needed to be sure now not a couple of months down the road.

Bernie was put on the defensive by Warren's questions. 'First off, Sarge, no I *didn't* get turfed out - as far as I know they were pleased with my work. The secondment came to an end, and if you can call long hours and challenging work enjoyable, then yes I did enjoy my time in CID.'

'Bernie, pull up a chair,' Warren told him. 'What do you know about us?'

'Only what Trish said, a new sort of independent team.'

'Well that's one way to describe us I suppose.'

Before Warren had a chance to elaborate further, there was another knock at the door and a tall slim casually dressed chap walked in. This one did have a quiff.

He nodded to Trish and smiled. 'Trish'. She responded by inclining her head towards Warren. 'DS Warren,' he said, holding out a hand. 'DC Edward Dixon ...'

'Don't tell me, Elvis?'

'Uh huh,' he replied jokingly to everyone's amusement.

'Good to meet you, first off a couple of questions, how long have you been a DC and what's your current role?'

'Right, straight to the point, I've been a DC for nearly two years now and been working with the Neighbourhood Community Team for the past three months.'

'And?'

'And I'm ready for a change, Trish told me a bit about your team and it sounded right up my street.'

'Glad to hear it, park your arse over there.' DC Dixon sat at the DIs desk. 'Okay, first off we do need a new team member - maybe two, so, this is - what shall we say a trial period to see how we all get along? Are you both okay with that? If not this is the time to say so.' No response. 'I'll take it that you agree?' They both nodded.

Warren carried on. 'The guy who was previously running the team was DI Bill Grimes, unfortunately Bill suffered a stroke, there's no telling when or if he'll be coming back to work. Although a lowly DS, I've been put in charge. Now, what we're all about is undercover, well, not strictly undercover work but if the job warrants it, we'll do it. You might be involved in what shall I say, things that are a little unorthodox, working outside of normal police procedures. Is that something you're prepared to do?'

Elvis smiled his acceptance.

'Don't see why not,' Bernie said, with a slight trepidation in his voice.

'What's said in this office goes no further, it stays within the team, right?'

'This could suit me down to the ground,' Elvis replied.

'Good, I hoped you'd say that. Okay, interview over, welcome to the team. I'll give both your bosses a call and get it sorted.'

'That's it?'

'What can I say? You both came highly recommended,' Warren looked toward Trish and smiled, then offered his hand to each in turn.

'So, when do we start with the team?' asked Elvis.

'You just have.'

'Great.'

'Oh, and that fella over there is the fifth team member, our Civilian Advisor, James Boland.'

'Jimbo, everybody calls me Jimbo,' Boland corrected, as he stood up and shook hands.

'Don't let appearances put you off,' Trish added, 'he doesn't usually dress like a dosser.'

'I'm doing a bit of undercover work,' Jimbo said proudly, touching the side of his nose and winking as if it was a secret gesture.

'One more thing,' said Warren, 'is it Edward, Eddie or Elvis?'

'Whatever you want, you're the boss.'

'Uh huh,' Warren replied with a smile, attempting an Elvis impression.

'Trish, will you bring Bernie and Elvis up to date on where we're at?' said Warren, as he shuffled a pile of files around his desk for no particular reason.

'For now, you'll have to share the DI's desk, until we get a bit more organised,' Trish nodded towards the desk where Elvis had already established himself. Then her desk phone rang out. 'DC James,' she said into the receiver.

'Hi, it's Jane, the Charge Nurse at the HRI, you wanted to know when Joey Smale could talk?'

'How's he doing?'

'Pretty good, for a lad with half an arm. He's still a bit drowsy but I think he's up to a few questions now.'

'Great, Jane, thanks, we'll see you shortly.' The DC turned toward Warren. 'You get the gist of that? Seems we can have a word with Joey.'

'No time like the present.' Files shuffled and restacked in no particular order, Warren stood, put on his jacket and picked up his mobile. 'You ready?'

Trish already beat him to it, jacket on and bag over her shoulder. 'Ready when you are.'

Sitting on the edge of his seat, Bernie asked. 'What about us, what do you need us to do?'

'For now, not a lot, get acquainted with Jimbo here,' he turned to Jimbo. 'Jimbo's not a copper, but he is an important part of the team and I'm sure he will do his best to try to fill any gaps you're not sure about. You okay with that, Jimbo?'

Jimbo had a proud look on his face. 'I'm in charge?'

'Sort of,' Warren replied, immediately regretting the words.

'Great.'

'You'll regret telling him that,' Trish said as they headed out of the door.

Warren laughed. 'I already have.'

The hospital car park was a damn sight busier than it had been the previous evening. Warren gave up looking for a space and manoeuvred the pool car into the taxi parking area. 'I don't know why the hell they can't put up a multi-storey, it's not rocket science.'

'Oi,' the parking attendant called out, pointing to markings on the road, 'says taxis only.' Warren took out his warrant card for the man to see. 'Oh, that's okay then,' and turned about looking for someone else to harass.

'At least that one has a few brain cells.'

'What's with the pool car anyway?' Trish asked.

'Thought I'd better keep the Escort for 'Cole' business.'

'Joey first?'

'Yeah it'll be interesting to hear what he has to say.'

Outside the main doors of Women's and Children's Department, patients and visitors alike, gathered 'vaping', it seemed e-cigarettes had taken over big-time.

'Now don't take offence, but let me take the lead with Joey,' Trish said. Warren gave her a questioning look. 'You can come over as a bit scary at times.'

'Me, scary?'

'Yep you, especially to a frightened kid.'

'That's twice someone has told me that I'm scary. Okay, you do the talking,' he said as they entered the building. Trish had been expecting more resistance.

'Can I help?' asked the young lady sat behind the reception desk. The pair held their identification for the girl to check out.

'We're here about Joey Smale?' Warren said, giving the girl a big smile.

Always the flirt, thought Trish, never stops.

'Oh yes, just a mo,' she picked up the phone and spoke quietly into the handset. 'There's two police officers here asking about one of your patients, Joey Smale ... Okay, will do.' She replaced the phone on the cradle. 'If you'd like to take a seat someone will be with you in a minute or two.'

'Thanks, love.' Warren said as they moved towards the waiting area. 'Why do they always say that?'

'Say what?'

'Take a seat, they would go barmy if you picked up a seat and walked out.'

'Just take a ... sit down, Greg.'

They had no sooner sat down on the uncomfortable tubular framed plastic chairs when a nurse came through and stood before them. 'Officers?'

'Didn't think we looked so obvious,' Warren said as he stood up.

'Believe me, when you've been doing the job as long as I have ... this way please.' They followed the nurse through a series of brightly painted corridors.

'It's a lot different to across the way,' Trish said.

'The main building does leave a lot to be desired, but saying that, it's much better than it used to be. Here we are.' Stopping outside of a small side ward, she nodded towards the antiseptic hand cleaning gel in its stand by the door. They all applied the gel before entering the room. 'Police officers,' she told the nurse sat beside Joey's bed. She stood up, smiled and moved aside.

Joey lay propped up atop of the bed, still wired up to monitors and saline drips, his damaged arm hung from some sort of contraption. His dark fringe had been

156

brushed away from his face, making him look even younger than his fifteen years.

The nurse stood by Joey's bedside, a hand placed on his shoulder. 'Joey, here are two police officers, they want to ask you some questions, are you feeling up to it?' He nodded, no smile just the nod. 'Try not to be too long,' she said, turning to Trish.

'Hi Joey, my name is Trish, this is my colleague Greg.' Greg held a hand up. 'Hi,' he was going along with Trish's softly, softly, approach, remaining standing unimposing by the door.

'So, Joey, how are you feeling?' Trish asked as she sat by his bedside.

'I'm cool,' he said trying to be brave. He looked to be far from 'cool'.

'Are you up to answering a few questions?'

He shrugged, his face twinged with pain as he changed his upper body position. 'Suppose.'

'Can you tell me how come you came to be in possession of a firearm?'

'Where's my mam? She hasn't been to see me,' Joey asked, his voice low and small, eyes looking tearful.

'She's not feeling too good herself, Joey.'

'She high again?'

You know her so well, thought Trish. 'She'll be visiting as soon as she's well enough,' she lied. She knew Joey knew the truth behind her answer. 'The firearm?' she asked again.

'Found it on some waste land near the flats.' The last thing he wanted to do was drop Robbo in it.

'You don't really expect us to believe that do you?'

'Told you I found it.'

'Okay, just for now, let's say for now you found the gun, took it back to your room, then what happened?'

'I stood in front of the mirror, just holding it, you know like they do on the telly?'

'That's when it happened?'

Tears began to swell in Joey's eyes. 'Shit, it ...it ...just ...like exploded, didn't think I'd touched the trigger.'

Trish let him settle a while. 'Do you know Robert Dooley?'

'Yeah, he's a mate.'

'How do you mean - mate?'

'I do some odd jobs for him, errands and stuff.'

'Stuff? What sort of stuff?'

'Just stuff.'

Trish let the lad think for a minute then took a gamble. 'Your friend Robert Dooley told us you did a bit more than just 'stuff'.'

Joey looked a little sheepish, he didn't know if she was telling the truth or not. 'What did Robbo tell you?'

'Why don't *you* tell us about the *stuff* you do for him?' Silence. The lad was thinking. Warren watched on as Trish let the silence linger. 'By the way, your friend Robert, he was shot last night in a drive-by.'

'No shit, Robbo shot? He dead?' Joey said, trying his hardest to sit forward.

'No, Joey, he survived, he's not too good but he'll live.'

He lay back on his pillows. 'Do you know who did it?'

'I was about to ask you the same question,' Warren said from his position near the door. So, stuff?'

'I do deliveries and collections for him,' he said, as he looked towards the window.

'Such as?'

'Shooters,' he said sheepishly. 'When he gets an order, he pays me to deliver.'

That went a long way to explain the flat screen television and PS4 in the lad's room, Warren thought.

'So, the one that exploded, you didn't really find it, did you?' Warren asked.

Joey looked across and shook his head. 'No, got it from Robbo, I was supposed to deliver it.'

Trish looked to Warren, he said. 'Do you know any of the people you deliver to?'

'Na, always someone different.'

'Doesn't it scare you?'

'I can handle myself, mind you, there was this one bloke on the last delivery I made, there was something about him.'

'Like what?' asked Trish?'

'Don't know really, just something.'

'Can you describe him?'

Joey struggled, trying to reach over to the bedside cabinet for his plastic cup, Trish stepped in and picked up the cup and passed it over. The lad sipped through a plastic straw before carrying on. 'He was skinny, not much taller than me, he had a face like a rat, think he had a tat on the side of his neck, couldn't see what though just the ink. He looked well hard, but reckon I could have taken him if he'd kicked off,' he said, remembering how shit scared he really was.

Warren inwardly smiled at the lad's bravado, and thanked God the deal had gone well, or Joey may not have been here now to answer their questions.

'Can you remember his name?'

'Robbo only ever told me first names, it was Seb, something like that.'

Result, thought Trish, she caught Warren in the corner of her eyes, smiling.

'I think that's enough for now,' said the nurse as she proceeded to make a pretence of checking the monitors.

'Think we're done for now anyway. Joey you've been very helpful,' Trish said, as she rested a hand on the lad's good arm.

'Yeah, cheers for that, mate,' said Warren. 'Now you get better soon. Okay?' Joey nodded and lay his head on the pillows and closed his eyes.

They thanked the nurse for her cooperation and left Joey to get some rest.

'Poor lad, his life changed forever and having to go through all this on his own.'

'No doubt Social Services will sort him out.'

'Yeah, I know, Greg, but not the same as having his mam by his bedside, is it?'

Warren didn't have an answer.

'So, Seb - face like a rat, got to be Sebastian London, can't be anyone else. Once we've been across to the main building and seen Dooley, we'll see about having London brought in.'

Warren and Trish walked across the hospital complex to the main building, compared to the Women's and Children's Building the main Infirmary appeared austere.

'You should have seen the place a few years back before the renovations,' Trish said to him.

'It's been renovated?' Warren replied sarcastically. 'I'd never have guessed.'

Taking the super-fast over crowded lift, they stepped out on the fifth floor. On reaching the reception area of the intensive care department they were greeted by a staff nurse with a friendly face. 'Good morning, can I help.'

Warren stepped forward. 'I'm DS Warren and this is my colleague DC Trish James,' they both held the warrant cards for inspection. 'We're making enquiries about Robert Dooley, he was brought in with gunshot wounds.'

The nurse tapped the computer keyboard, bringing up Dooley's details. 'Ah, yes, Mr Dooley, he's in a side room.'

'Is he awake?' asked Trish as she slipped her ID back in her shoulder bag.

'I'll check, won't be a minute.' She disappeared down the corridor to reappear less than a minute later. 'He is awake, but ...'

Warren casually leaned on the reception desk, trying his flirting approach. 'Just a quick word, that's all we need,' his pale blue eyes looked directly into hers, then he added, 'please.'

'You'll have to be quick, the doctor said he needs to rest.'

'You're an angel,' said Warren as she led them to Dooley's room. Trish, walking along side of him shook her head in disbelief at the sheer nerve of the man.

As the door opened they were greeted with the familiar sound of the medical equipment. Dooley didn't look too good, he lay back slightly supported by pillows, the obligatory saline drip was inserted into the back of his hand. Wires connected him to the heart monitor which constantly bleeped, not to mention the drain tubes from his chest cavity that disappeared down the side of the bed into glass bottles.

'I'll have to stay,' said the nurse standing by the door.

'No problem,' said Warren, as he crossed the room and stood next to the bed.

Sensing Warren's approach, Dooley opened his eyes. 'Police?' he asked in low voice.

'Got it in one. Won't keep you long, Mr Dooley, just a couple of questions.' Warren didn't pull his punches and went straight in before Dooley had time to think. 'Do you know who shot you?'

A slight shake of the head in response.

'Do you know *why* you were shot?'

Dooley answered with his own question. 'I take it you've been to my lock-up?'

'The CSIs are going through the place as we speak.'

Dooley raised his eyebrows. 'There you have your answer.'

'Okay, I'll take that as a yes. Now, as I see it, whoever is responsible for shooting you appears to be taking out the competition, who do you think it is Mr Dooley?'

Another shake of the head, but Warren saw Dooley's eyes react to the question.

'Have you heard of a Neil Powers?'

'No, should I have?'

'What about somebody called Seb? According to young Joey Smale, you know *Joey*, the lad who's laid across the way with his hand blown off, he seems to think you did some business with him.'

'No comment.'

'Come on now, you're not under arrest - at least not yet, let's keep this amiable. Seb, real name, Sebastian London, have you, or have you not, done any business with him?'

'Now that you mention it, I do recognise the name, let me think on it.' He lay back on the pillows and closed his eyes.

'Don't think on it too long, Mr Dooley,' said Trish.

'I think that's enough for now,' said the nurse, 'if the doctor comes in you'll get me shot.' The officers turned to face her, even Dooley opened his eyes. She looked guilty. 'Sorry.'

The nurse ushered them out of the room closing the door behind them.

'Well that was a waste of time and effort,' said Trish.

'I think we'll have to keep a close eye on Dooley, my guess is, whoever tried to top him is likely to try again, sooner rather than later. When we get back to the nick, I'll have a word with uniform and see if they can spare anybody for a bit of babysitting.'

Alone in his room, Dooley regretted the day he ever did that first conversion. What a bloody mess.

Bernie moved and sat at Trish's desk, feet up. 'So, Jimbo how long have you been a Civilian Advisor?'

163

'Officially, a couple of months, mind you I've known Greg - DS Warren long before I took the job.'

'That how you got the job?'

'No, that was the DI's idea, I'd done work for them both in the past.'

'You know a bit about police procedures then?'

'That's a tricky one, let's say I know a bit more about what it's like on the other side of the law.'

'So, what sort of work have you done for them?'

'Cool stuff,' Jimbo answered proudly.

'Sounds interesting, tell me more.'

Elvis said nothing, he simply sat taking it all in.

Jimbo went on the defensive. 'Sorry, mate, that's something you'll have to ask the Sarge and the DI.'

Bernie tried probing a little deeper. 'C'mon, you can tell us. We're interested aren't we, Eddie?'

Non-committal, Elvis shrugged his shoulders.

'Soz,' the younger man said, 'my lips are sealed.'

'I *will* find out you know.'

'That's as maybe, but you'll get fuck all out of me, now leave it alone.'

'Sorry, Jimbo, I didn't mean anything by it, just curious that's all.'

'It's okay, forget it.'

But it had set the cogs working in Bernie's head, he was determined to somehow find out what the true relationship was between Jimbo and Warren. 'Going for a piss,' he said, standing up and walking out of the office letting the door slam behind him.

'Seem to have hit a nerve there,' said Jimbo. Elvis shrugged once more. 'Don't say much do you, Eddie?'

'Only when I have something to say,' he replied running his hand through the quiff.

'How come you know Trish?'

'We did our probation together at Tower Grange. How about you?'

'Just mates really, maybe a bit more than mates, if you know what I mean?' Jimbo said giving a wink.

Elvis gave a 'whatever' shrug like he recognised bullshit when he heard it, and Jimbo just knew it was going to be a struggle to get on with the bloke.

'Trish, when uniform locate London and bring him in, I want you to take the interview, keep Jimbo well out of the way. We don't want him getting any inkling about Jimbo.'

'No problem, I'll take Bernie in with me.'

'Talking about Bernie ...'

'What about him?'

'You know him well?'

'I wouldn't say that, we've worked together on quite a few occasions, had a couple of drinks, that sort of thing.'

'The occasional drink, nothing more?'

'If he'd had his way it would have been, but he's not my type. Why do you ask?'

'Just curious, what I really want to know is, can he keep his mouth shut? You know how we - I work, I wouldn't like to think he'll go running off and telling the Super as soon as he gets wind of anything untoward.'

'I'll sound him out, if I don't think he's right for us I'll let you know.'

'Fair enough - then you can sack him.'

'Above my pay grade, Greg, you can do your own dirty work.' They both laughed as the tension eased.

'In the meantime, I have a meeting with Powers.'

'Good luck with that.'

Mouse had work to do, he had yet to carry out Powers previous request, no, not request - order. Robbo was still alive, and how was he going to do it? He knew one thing, Powers wouldn't stand for him cocking it up again, best to get it done with, it was time he made a visit to the Infirmary.

Mouse lived in a flat above *The Rose*, the same place Jimbo and Warren had visited not so long ago. The licensee was a brash woman who even scared Mouse at times, not that she ever made an appearance, licensee in name only. The pub was owned by a London Holding Company, a director of which was Neil Powers. The entrance to the upstairs flat was via a private door, adjacent to the front door of the pub. Mouse locked the flat door, bounded down the narrow staircase two at a time, opened the front door and almost ran straight into the arms of two very large uniformed officers. 'Whoa, steady up, pal, where are you rushing off to?' PC Speck asked, as he held his hands up and took a step back.

Mouse froze when he saw the two coppers standing on his doorstep.

'I take it you are Sebastian London?' asked Speck's oppo. Mouse had been taken by surprise and nodded, he didn't have time to try and be sarcastic. 'We'd like you to come down the station and answer a few questions.'

'Questions about what, I ain't done anything?' He spat out as he regained his composure.

'Did we say you have?' said Speck.'

'You arresting me?'

'Nope.'

'Then I ain't coming,' he said reaching behind him to close the door before they had a chance to enter.

Speck, built like a brick shipyard, took a step close, emphasising his height and stature over the shorter man. 'I *will* arrest you if that's what you want?' he said looking down on Mouse.

'Don't suppose there's any harm in me coming with you, just make it quick I've got things to do.'

'Not our problem, mate, it takes as long as it takes,' he said, as he held Mouse by the bicep and led him to the patrol car.

Chapter 17

Jimbo was once more taking up his position of 'watcher'. The team's Civilian Advisor, scrabbled through the bushes at the Humber Bridge Country Park, seeking out a suitable viewing point over the parking area approaches and the Humber View Café exits.

'Oh, for fucks sake,' Jimbo swore out loud as he felt his hand sink into a pile of fresh dog shit. He almost retched as he lifted his hand clear of the ground. 'It's your bleedin fault, Greg, why can't you have meetings in offices like normal people?' he said into the covert microphone attached to his denim jacket. Silence. 'Don't ignore me Greg, I know you can hear me.'

'What the hell are you whinging about now?' a voice replied in his ear piece.

'Bloody dog shit, that's what, and I've just put my hand in a bloody great turd.' Jimbo said, as he tried to scrape his hand through the long grass to clean off the mess. He could hear laughter at the other end. 'Not funny.'

'Just stop pissing about. Are you in position yet?'

'Give us a minute,' keeping himself concealed, he stuck his head through the foliage and did a sweep of the car park and around the café. 'Yep, got you,' he said, as he still tried to clean his hand on an empty crisp packet he'd found in the grass

'Never mind me, anything suspicious, or anybody hanging around?'

'Nope and nope. Ahh, this shit stinks!'

Warren smiled to himself. 'Okay, keep your eyes peeled,' he said into the concealed microphone. Warren locked the car and walked across to the café, his eyes scanning constantly. So far so good, he pushed open the café door. A few tables in the café were occupied, as before, mostly families enjoying a snack before or after venturing into the country park. He looked around; Powers was already there, sitting at the same table as before. 'Tea, please love,' he said to the waitress, as he walked over doing the 'Cole' swagger.

Warren offered his hand across the table, this time Powers did respond and shook the offered hand. Warren sat down, looked expressionlessly into Powers eyes, then smiled a beaming smile. The waitress brought over Warren's tea and placed it on the table. 'Thanks, love.'

Powers as ever, was dressed in a well-tailored business suit, hand-made shirt and matching tie. The arms trade pays well, thought Warren.

The Civilian Advisor had devised a plan of his own. Despite still being blathered in dog shit, he double checked that nothing looked untoward in the car park, then he moved quickly through the shrubs until he was a comfortable distance away, making sure he wouldn't be seen he then slid down the grass bank into the carpark. He sauntered casually towards Powers motor, paused as if he was fastening his shoe lace, reached into his pocket and took out a metallic rectangle smaller than a match box, a tracker, and swiftly attached it under the wheel arch of the BMW. Job done he retraced his footsteps back to his watching position.

'So, Cole, how can we make this work?' Powers asked, as he watched Warren add a dash of milk into his cup of tea.

Warren smiled again. 'So, we *are* going to do some business?'

'Let's say this is a kind of get to know each other meeting.'

'Not into the bonding thing myself,' he gave a short laugh, then put the serious face back on. 'Look, let's not piss about, are we doing business or not?'

'As I asked, how can we make this work?

'The way I see it, it's simple, a straight forward transaction. You have what I need and I've got the money, simple as that.'

Powers sat back in his seat, arms outstretched he placed his hands on the table palm down. 'In principle, it sounds easy, but before we actually do any business I want the details ironed out. I need guarantees.'

'Guarantees? You know as well as I do there are no guarantees in this job? I'm sure you must be happy with my credentials otherwise you wouldn't be here now.' He picked up his cup and sipped.

Powers smiled. 'Fair enough, I need to know what it is you need, quantities and how the payments will be made.'

'Look, Neil,' Powers didn't object to Warren using his Christian name. He took that as a good sign. 'I think we should start small, see how things go between us, stick to something simple. If I was to ask for say, a dozen hand held. What could you let me have and how soon?'

'Cash on delivery?'

'Of course - if we can agree on the price.'

'Would 9mm Baikals complete with suppressors be any good to you? If so delivery could be...' he checked his watch, 'this time tomorrow?'

Warren poured himself another cup, added a dash if milk. 'Sounds interesting and the price?'

'£650 each.'

Warren shook his head. He pushed his cup and saucer into the middle of the table and stood up. 'Nice meeting you, Neil, but no thanks, maybe another time.' He made a pretence of leaving.

'Sit down, Ray, don't be hasty, just testing the water, we have to start somewhere.'

Warren once again took his seat and called over to the waitress. 'Excuse me, love, can we have another couple of teas, please.' Things were going as he hoped.

'You do realise the Baikal can demand a price of a grand, even more?'

'That's as maybe, but you forget I'm in the business and represent people who can make you rich, and I mean seriously rich, Neil.' Warren could almost see the pound signs in Powers' eyes.

Powers appeared to do some quick calculations, as if he didn't want to lose an opportunity or appear too eager. 'Look, I'll tell you what I'll do, as a goodwill gesture I'll let you have the first dozen for say, £500 per unit.'

Warren smiled. 'How about £200?' He knew he was pushing it.

'Ray, Ray, I'll barely make beer money out of a deal like that. The way I see it you're wasting my time.'

'Let's not turn this into a pissing contest, Neil, last time offer £250, if things all go according to plan with no hitches on either side, this could be the start of a very lucrative opportunity for you, and my backers. I tell you what, no need to commit to anything now, sleep on it before you decide. Give me a bell tomorrow. Can't be any fairer than that, can I?'

Powers didn't answer. He pushed back his chair and stood up, reached across the table and offered his hand. Warren smiled as he shook the offered hand. Powers took a ten-pound note from his wallet and dropped it on the table. Warren took it as a good sign.

'Call you tomorrow,' he said and left.

Warren was pleased with the way things had turned out, he'd been sure Powers would tell him to piss off. But if things went according to plan, where the hell was he going to get the money to pay for the firearms, without bankrupting his new boss's budget? Warren remained sitting at the table and finished his cuppa as he watched Powers drive away in his BMW. Then he saw a figure appear from the bushes and walk towards the café.

'Jimbo, you can't be serious coming in here, I could smell you as soon as you opened the door,' Warren lied.

'It's not that bad, is it?' The lad said as he sat down.

'Worse, mate, worse.'

Jimbo, detoured to the gents, returning five minutes holding his hands to his face sniffing. Warren sat smiling to himself.

'Well?' he said as he sat down.

'Better, Jimbo, much better.'

'I don't mean the smell; how did the meet go?'

'Got you a brew, one of your herbal teas,' gesturing to the additional cup and saucer. 'Spicy Lemon, okay?'

'Thanks,' he said and started dunking the tea bag up and down. 'How did it go?'

'Couldn't have gone any better.'

'You haven't committed to anything, have you?'

'Me?'

'You have been known in the past to commit to something that's gonna cost us money.' He dropped the tea bag on the saucer, picked up his cup, 'Cheers,' and sipped.

'The price I negotiated just stopped short of Powers thinking he'd been mugged off.'

'By the way,' said Jimbo, 'while you were enjoying your cup of tea I used a bit of initiative.'

'You did?' Warren replied in faux surprise. 'And just exactly what was this initiative you showed?'

'Only put a tracker on the BMW, didn't I,' he grinned from ear to ear.

'Bloody hell, Jimbo, you don't get paid enough to take risks - but a bloody good idea all the same.'

'Had a good teacher, didn't I? Give us your mobile and I'll put the App on.'

'This could be good, might lead us to whoever does his conversions.'

'That's what I was thinking.'

'Good move mate, good move.'

Chapter 18

Trish stood deep in thought, with her back to the window, hands behind her resting on the sill. 'Has your mate in BTP come up with anything on Conway's daughter?' she asked Warren, who stood beside the whiteboard adding details.

'Not the result we hoped for,' he replied turning to face her. 'As we know already, the Liverpool Street Station CCTV cameras picked up her and the lad going through the exit, they got on a bus to Earls Court. The bus CCTV shows them getting off one stop from the exhibition centre and that's where it gets a bit iffy ...' Greg replied

'Define iffy?'

'They lose them.'

'Oh, bloody hell, Greg, that's all we need,' Jimbo chipped in. 'Conway isn't going to be very chuffed when you tell him.'

'Calm down, Jimbo, it's not as bad as it sounds.'

'Why's that then, oh wise one?" he asked sarcastically.

'It means my mate *also* called in a favour and she was spotted with the lad leaving a flat not far from the bus stop. Turns out the kid is a music student and plays lead guitar in a band.'

'You have an address?'

'I do indeed.'

'So, looks like she's fallen for a musician, can't see Conway being too pleased about that either. You going to tell him?'

'All in good time.'

'Who's for a coffee?' asked Trish.

'If you're buying I'll have a fruit tea,' Jimbo replied.

'No thanks,' Warren smiled to himself at the transformation in Jimbo, who, at one time would have preferred a can of lager.

'Greg,' said Jimbo as Trish left and closed the door behind her. 'About the money, have you given it anymore thought?'

'Nope.'

'You mean you've bottled it?'

'You could say that,' he said as he walked across the squad room and sat facing Jimbo. 'I was thinking maybe we could self-finance the operation.'

Jimbo pushed back in his seat. 'Oh no, definitely not, you're not getting your hands on any of my cash.'

'You tight fisted git, I was thinking maybe I could finance the deal with the money I made from Conway.'

'You got enough?'

'I reckon so, just. And let's face it, if push does come to shove we can always move them on.'

'Seriously Greg, you are kidding?'

''Course I bloody am you div, if, and I say if, we have to actually buy them, we can always rob the money back, with a little interest of course. What do you reckon?'

'Sounds like a plan to me, a bloody good one. I like to keep my hand in. Not that I have been you understand?'

'Of course, Jimbo - as if.'

Chapter 19

London wasn't best pleased, the last thing he had expected was to be accosted on his own front doorstep by two burly coppers. Speck and his mate had been instructed to inform Trish as soon as they arrived back at the station, and to keep Sebastian 'Mouse' London in the custody area.

'Jimbo, under no circumstances are you to leave the office until Mouse is back on the street,' Trish warned him.

'And what if I need a pee?' he asked sarcastically.

Trish threw him a paper cup. 'Make do with this and stop moaning. You ready, Bernie?'

'When you are, boss,' he said as he stood up, smiling at Jimbo.

Trish raised an eyebrow. 'Do *not* leave the office,' she cautioned as they left.

London had been put in a side room in the booking in area, he waited patiently flicking through a magazine while he waited, confident they were only fishing, nothing could be traced back to him, or so he hoped.

'Mr London, thanks very much for coming in,' Trish said as she held open the reception door, and led him to an interview room.

Trish smiled at the rat face as she opened the door to room one. 'Please, take a seat.'

'Didn't have much choice did I,' London grumbled as he was directed to a seat and slunk down, arms folded across his chest.

'I'm Detective Constable James, this is my colleague Detective Constable Philips.'

Trish lifted her eyes from the folder that lay opened before her on the table. Your mug shot doesn't do you justice she thought, as she looked across the table, suppressing a smile.

'What's this about?' asked London, looking from one to the other.

'What's your occupation, Mr London?'

'Please, call me Sebastian.'

'So, Sebastian what do you do to earn a crust?'

'Anything really, buying and selling.'

'Like what, drugs, counterfeit cigarettes and stolen goods?' Trish said as she read from his file. 'And that's only the tip of it.'

'That's all in my past, I've changed.'

Yeah, like hell you have, Trish thought, as she looked at the prison tats on his hands.

'So, what do you really do?' Bernie asked as he leaned forward resting his elbows on the desk.

'Anything I can to make a few quid on, I buy and sell the odd car on eBay, like I said, anything.'

'And where does Neil Powers fit into this?'

'Mr Powers, I do the odd job for him don't I?'

'Like what?'

'Usually it's a bit of decorating around his flat, that's what I am a decorator by trade, a bit of diy, anything really.'

'Does the delivering and collecting of firearms fall in the remit?'

'WHAT? You're having a laugh surely?' he replied with a brimming smile on his face. 'Firearms, don't know anything about that.'

'How do you know Robert Dooley?'

'I don't.'

'Really? What about a young lad by the name of Joey Smale?'

London rocked back on his chair. 'Same, never heard of him.'

'Maybe you recognise him from this photograph.' Trish took an 8inch by 10inch colour photograph from the folder. The picture was taken on the lad's arrival at the hospital, his face contorted with pain - the remains of his hand hanging in shreds.

With no trace of emotion whatsoever, London denied ever meeting the lad. 'Looks in a bad way, what happened to him?'

The comment wasn't worth responding to. 'So, you've never seen him before?'

'Not that I can remember.' London was confident, he knew they had nothing on him or he would have been charged before now. He was right, so far, they only had Joey's word.

The interview was over before it had hardly begun. 'That it, can I go now?'

'For now, we will probably need to speak with you further,' Trish told him as she closed her folder and stood.

London followed her lead. 'Anytime,' he pushed back his chair, stood up and started towards the door.

'Just one more question before you go, what kind of car do you drive?'

He turned and smiled. 'I don't, ain't got one.'

Bernie held open the door. 'I'll show you out,' he said, moving aside to let London pass.

'Be seeing ya,' London sneered as he left the station.

'Cocky little bugger,' said Trish when Bernie returned.

'Tell me about it.'

Sebastian London walked away from the police station with a spring in his step. They had bugger all on him, however, he did have one worry, Albie, had they got wind of him? Na, he decided, otherwise he was sure he would have been given a tug. A little further down the road, away from the nick, he took out his mobile and dialled.

'Boss, it's me,' he said, when the call was picked up. 'Me, Seb, thought I'd best let you know the cops have just had me in asking about Dooley ...na, they don't know fuck all ...just fishing ...yeah, I'll keep you in the loop.'

Chapter 20

The lunch time trade was starting to die off, but *The Halfway Hotel* public house could always rely on its hardcore regulars. The flat capped former fishermen, who sat playing dominoes, their pints lasting as long as possible. It was the company they craved more than alcohol. Then there was the out of workers gathered in groups at the bar, staring up occasionally at the television high on the wall, in-between nipping back and forward to the nearby betting shop. At the far end of the long bar two men sat in a semi-private booth.

'So, why am I here? You'd better not be wasting my bloody time,' Powers told the man sitting opposite.

'Oh, I think you'll be interested in what I've got to tell you.'

'Well you'd better get the drinks in then, mine's a malt.' The man gave a reluctant smile, shook his head and headed towards the bar. 'Make it a double,' he called out.

Neil Powers watched as Police Constable Bernard Philips went to the bar. When all was said and done, Philips was nothing more than a glorified confidential informant, a snout. Powers didn't like snouts. Once upon a time, in what seemed a lifetime ago, in desperation, Philips had borrowed two grand from a money lender, a debt that he never had a hope of paying back, due to the constant rises in the interest charges. Eventually the two-grand escalated into five and showed no sign of decreasing anytime soon. That was when the money-lender made a deal and sold the debt to Powers. PC Bernie Philips had no other choice than becoming the copper in Powers 'pocket'. The debt was put on hold in return for information. Philips even made money from the situation. Philips duly returned from the bar, placed the drinks on the solid wood table top and sat down facing Powers.

'So, Bernie, what have you got that's so interesting?'

Philips edged forward in his seat, resting his elbows on the table as he moved closer.

'I've been assigned to a new team ...'

'What do you want? Congratulations?' Powers asked sarcastically.

'Hear me out, you heard about Scabies getting his hand blown off, and that young lad in hospital.' Now he had Powers attention. 'I've been assigned to the team looking into it.'

'Have you now,' Powers picked up his glass and sipped at the single malt, 'tell me more.'

'The team's been headed up by a DS, goes by the name of Greg Warren.'

'Never heard of him, carry on.'

'Not much more to say really, just thought you'd better know, cos, from what I can make out they're going hell for leather to find out where these dodgy pistols are coming from.'

'Explain?'

'It seems they're looking in to arms suppliers in the Hull area.'

'So, what's this got to do with me?'

'Someone I think you know was pulled in. I was in on the interview.'

'Who would that be?'

'Sebastian London.'

'Not one of my lads, never heard of him,' denied Powers.

'What's more your name has been mentioned, more than once.'

'It has, has it?'

Philips looked like the cat who got the cream.

'And there's more. Pat Conway, did you know he has a daughter?'

'So, he has a daughter. Look Bernie, where's all this leading?' For once it looked like he had the upper hand. Powers again picked up his drink and sipped.

'I have it on good authority his daughter has gone missing, well not really missing, just gone to ground.'

'And?'

'Reading between the lines, Conway is just about pulling his hair out.'

'How do you know this?'

'One of my colleagues is interested in finding her.'

'Your colleague's name?'

'Same bloke, DS Warren, but not official, it's all on the Q.T.'

'Then how do you know about it if it's all hush, hush?'

'Picked up his phone and took a message from someone in the Met, saying she'd been spotted but gone to ground again.'

'So why does he have an interest in this?'

'No idea, but if it's all on the quiet, well, there's something going on, don't you think? Like, I mean it seems a bit strange to me, a copper and a villain ...'

'That scenario seems to ring a bell,' Powers said, smiling for the first time. "Why are you bringing this to me?'

'I made some enquiries of my own, seems Conway won't accept the fact that she could have done a runner, he reckons that she must have been abducted, when all along she's shacked up with a musician. So, I got to thinking you might find the info useful, even use it as a leverage without having to do anything seriously illegal, just advocate the outcome.' Philips smiled, and sat back in his chair. 'That's about the gist of it. The only thing is we don't really know how long this will go on for, she might get pissed off and want to see her old man sooner, rather than later.'

The cogs in Powers head were already ticking over, it could be useful, then again maybe not. He sat back in his chair, took out his wallet and removed two fifty-pound notes and passed them across the table. Philips did a quick skeg around then quickly accepted the money and put it in his pocket.

'Conway's daughter, you hear anything, anything at all, you get back to me, okay?'

Philips gave a nod and left the pub, his drink untouched on the table.

Chapter 21

It was something Warren had been putting off, but it was time for the inevitable, a face to face meeting with Conway. He was thinking that maybe, he could assure his 'friend' there was really nothing untoward going on with Rachell.

'Pat,' Warren said into the car's hands free, 'you at the flat?'

'Yeah, have you found her?' he asked, his voice agitated.

'I've told you, she's okay.'

Jimbo sat in the passenger seat, making mouthing gestures with his hands.

'Yeah, according to you.'

'Listen, that's what I want to talk to you about. Okay if I come around?'

'No, tell me over the phone.'

'Better in person, Pat, I'm not far away, see you in a few minutes,' he hung the call up.

Jimbo shook his head. 'I don't think I'm going to like this.'

'Oh, give over, it'll be fine. A very reasonable man is Pat.'

'We are talking about the same bloke, the bloke who let you beat one of his team into a pulp.'

'It'll be fine,' he repeated, not believing a word of it. True, he did get along with Conway, but the man could be a right arse when he wanted to.

'Changed my mind,' said Jimbo. 'I think I'll give it a miss, you don't need me tagging along.'

'You've got to kiss and make up some time,' Warren said, as they pulled up at the Argyle Street traffic lights near the Hull Royal Infirmary.

'Maybe, but not this time.' Not waiting for Warren's reply, Jimbo opened the car door and stepped out of the stationary vehicle, nearly knocking a bloke off his bike as he did.

'Wanker,' the wavering cyclist shouted as Jimbo reached the pavement. Jimbo turned and gave both the cyclist and Warren the finger.

'Chicken,' Warren called out, as the car door slammed shut. He didn't really blame him, Conway had been the one who looked out for him in the rough times, and during the young man's life he'd had more than his share, but Warren had been the one responsible for him shifting allegiance.

Jimbo was only a matter of minutes away from his old mate Lee Etherington's place and thought he may as well pay him a visit. He was adamant there was no possible way he was going to make amends with Pat Conway, at least not yet. Warren was right, he was chicken.

Breaking the news that Rachell was shacked up with a musician wasn't something Warren was looking forward to. It could go either way, he either accepted his little girl was growing up, or, more likely he would blow his fucking top.

Things hadn't changed near the Ice House Road flat, same old, same old. He drove into the parking area and duly parked up in front of the high-rise block. He looked around the car's interior, making sure he hadn't left anything of value on view as he knew it wouldn't be there when he came back if he had. He eased himself from the car, locked it, checked again, then walked across the litter strewn concrete.

As he entered the foyer, a group of wannabes stood blocking the stairwell.

'Well, are you going to shift?' he asked, making eye contact with the youth he took to be the gang leader.

'You gonna make us?'

'Don't even think about it,' he took a step closer. 'Does Mr Conway know you're making a nuisance of yourselves?' Warren asked. 'Because if he doesn't, he will in a couple of minutes, so move your arses.' The young guy tried to stand his ground. Warren took another threatening step forward – 'NOW.' He moved. The others followed. 'Thanks.'

'Whatever,' the youth replied and led his small gang out of the building.

Warren didn't fancy the lift and took the concrete stairs to the third floor. Took a breath and then hammered on the Conway's steel plated door. He could sense Conway checking him out through the door viewer. Then the locks turned and bolts slid open.

'So, Rachell ...' Conway started to demand before the door was even fully opened.

'C'mon Pat, give me a chance to get through the door.'

'Hmm,' he muttered under his breath as he let Warren pass and relocked the door. 'You'd better have something worthwhile,' he said as he followed Warren into the living room.

'Not quite that straight forward, mate,' said Warren, dropping down onto the settee.

'What's that supposed to mean?'

'What I can tell you is that she's safe,' at least Warren hoped to Christ she was. 'Like my mate in the Smoke said, she's staying at a flat in Earls Court with a music student.'

'Like hell she is, I want her here, not arsing about with a loser.'

'There's not much I can do about it, Pat, she'll get in touch when she's ready.'

'You got an address? Cos, you need to drag her up here.'

Warren stood up and put his arms out in protest. 'Whoa, hold your horses, Pat, I said I'd try and find her and find her I did.' Warren took a piece of paper from his pocket and passed it over. 'You're on your own on this one, I'm not in the abduction business, not any more. Don't you think I've had more than my share of bother with the law?'

Conway read the address. 'This is where she is?' A nod in response. 'Ray, she's just a kid, she shouldn't be arsing about in a city she doesn't know with a bleedin student.'

Warren was all set to head for the door, then out of some misguided loyalty he said. 'Look, Pat, let's give it a couple of days or so, and if she hasn't been in touch give me a call. Okay?'

'Don't have much bleedin choice do I. You want a drink?' A subdued Conway asked.

'No thanks Pat, I'd better be making a move.'

Warren felt a twinge of guilt as he left Conway alone with his whiskey. He really did hope Rachell would contact her old man soon - for both their sakes. As for Warren, he had enough on his plate.

Jimbo walked a little way along Anlaby Road, judged a gap in the traffic and dodged across the road to the sound of blaring car horns.

'How are you doing, matey?' Jimbo asked his pal as the door to the flat opened. Just like Ice House Road, same old, same old. The place was still damp and smelling of piss and decay. It would eventually change - for the worse.

'I'm not so bad, Jimbo,' Lee Etherington said just after coughing up a lump of phlegm and swallowing it again.

Jimbo was no medic, but it was clearly obvious Lee sounded considerably worse since his last visit. 'You been to see the Quack about that?'

'Yeah, yeah, got some antibiotics but they don't seem to be doing much good.' Lee dropped into his chair and immediately started to skin up a roach.

'They won't be doing much good either,' Jimbo told him, as Lee lit his Jamaican rollie and immediately started to cough his lungs up.

'Anyway, how come you've come around so soon, never see you for months, now twice in a week. Reckon it's not just to ask about my health?'

'Worried about you, mate, no law saying you can't call on a mate for chat is there?'

He sat in his chair and shrugged his shoulders. 'Suppose not. You got any weed, not got much left?'

'I have, but not on me, don't carry since the cops gave me a tug.'

'Just asking.' Another coughing fit as he took a deep draw on his fag. 'I heard that a mate of yours gave Mouse a hiding?'

'Yeah well, only got what he was asking for. My mate was looking to do some business, Mouse took the piss out of the wrong bloke that time. He mentioned a bloke named Powers, you reckon he could be the 'face' he told you about?'

'Dunno, maybe, like I told you before it could all be a load of crap, you know Mouse - full of shit. There's a couple of cans in the fridge if you fancy one.'

'Cheers,' Jimbo went through to the kitchen, opened the fridge door, took out one can of lager. 'Changed my mind mate,' he said when he returned to the living room and passed over the can to Lee. Jimbo doubted very much if there were much less bacteria in the wheelie bin than there was in the interior of the refrigerator. Jimbo hesitated and then thought he would chance his hand. 'So, you hear about the young lad who had his hand blown off, like Scabby Dave?'

'What is it with you and guns, its unhealthy, man'

'Just asking, mean like, I wouldn't mind getting my hands on a shooter, never know when it could come in

191

handy.' he said, taking out his own tobacco tin and rolling a thin smoke.

'Not my scene, but I heard there's some gadger in north Hull does a bit of dealing.'

This was good, heading the way Jimbo wanted without being too obvious. 'You got a name and number?'

'Na, but leave it with me and I'll see what I can do. Can't lend me a tenner can you?' Another one thought Jimbo, he took out his wallet, slipped out a couple of fivers and passed them over. He knew he'd never see the money again. 'Cheers, pay you back.' Lee grabbed his chest as the coughing started again.

'Right, I'm off mate. Keep taking the meds,' he said as he stood up to leave, 'and try and lay off the fags.' The door closed. He could hear Lee coughing and retching on the other side.

Jimbo was glad to be outside in the relatively fresh air, even the fishy odour on the breeze coming from Albert Dock was more welcome than the atmospheric despair emitting from Lee's flat.

Lee's brain might have been drug puddled, but he knew there was something different about Jimbo. As soon as the coughing fit subsided, he reached for his mobile, scrolled through the contacts and dialled. 'Mouse ...sorry, Seb, I've had Jimbo around again ...asking a shit load of questions, thought I'd give you the heads up.'

'Cheers mate, thanks for that.'

Mouse was curious. He wanted some answers of his own, namely who was this guy Ray, and why the sudden interest in shooters, besides he needed to get even and he would, if not with the black guy, Jimbo would make a good substitute.

Warren closed the open folder in front of him. He had spent the past hour reading up on the illegal firearms trade. He rubbed his eyes with his knuckles. Sat back in his chair and folded his hands behind his head.

Jimbo sat head in his hands studying his iPad. 'Have you checked out the App I put on your phone?' he asked Warren.

'Not recently, problem?'

'Not so much a problem but Powers seems to make regular visits to a property in Hendon Street.'

Warren pushed back in his wheeled chair, stood up and stretched. He walked over to Jimbo's desk.

'See?' Jimbo tapped the screen with his finger. The flashing blip that representing Power's BMW, it was stationary. 'Been there three times in the past two days. Could be worth checking out?'

'On the other hand, it could be completely innocent, maybe visiting his mum?' Warren replied as he stared at the screen.

'Or there could be something dodgy?'

Warren gave it some thought, it was quite a possibility. 'Tell you what mate, why don't you take some time out of the office and follow it up. But not in your bloody bright red SmartCar, you'll stand out like - well, a bright red SmartCar. I'll sort you a pool car.'

'Will it have comms?'

'Of course.'

'Cool,' Jimbo beamed.

'But the comms are strictly hands-off. I'll get shot if they know a civilian is driving around in an unmarked police vehicle.'

'Suppose,' he replied, hiding his disappointment.

The next morning, Jimbo sat in the driving seat of the pool car, a dark blue Ford Focus, he took out his tobacco tin and rolled himself a skinny smoke, and, going against all laws and regulations he lit up – after all he was undercover, all par for the cause. He opened the car window, blue smoke curled through the gap. He could hardly believe how his life had changed in a few short months. Jimbo, the ex-scally driving around the city in a police vehicle and not cuffed and sat in the back.

In anticipation of what lay ahead he had been up early, eager to make a start. Sat at the kitchen table nursing a mug of instant coffee he'd watched the tracking screen on his iPad. The BMW was still parked up outside Powers apartment block where it had been since 11.30pm the previous evening. Then the blip moved.

Now, two hours later with the BMW in view, parked outside of a solicitor's office in the old town, boredom was taking over. After half an hour and two rollups, Powers emerged, climbed in the BMW and pulled away from the kerb.

Jimbo kept his distance, and discreetly followed the blip on his iPad. Powers crossed the busy Castle Street junction at the traffic lights. The BMW followed the road around and turned onto the A63, heading towards the west, away from the city centre. Jimbo followed.

Eventually the BMW turned off at the Liverpool Street junction onto Hessle Road, and over the flyover towards Gypsyville. Jimbo had no need to guess at Powers destination, he was heading for Hendon Street.

He was proved to be correct. Powers signalled and turned left into Hendon Street, a narrow street comprising of post war housing, some terraced and others semi-detached. Powers pulled into the kerb, Jimbo was close and drove straight past the BMW. At the end of the street he did a turn in the road, facing towards the way he had just come.

He took out his mobile, went into the contact list and tapped Warren's number.

'Jimbo, where are you?'

'Keeping tabs on Powers aren't I?'

'Yes, I know that but where the hell are you?'

'Calm down, Greg, I've been on his tail for bloody ages, he eventually found his way to Hendon Street, same place he's been before, he's on his mobile. Hang on, he's getting out, I'll call you back.' The line went dead before Warren had a chance to respond.

'Oh bugger,' Warren dropped his mobile on the desk.

'Problem?' asked Trish.

'Who bloody knows? Jimbo, he's only following Powers.'

Trish shook her head. 'You know what the trouble is don't you?'

'Enlighten me,' Warren replied leaning forward resting on his elbows.

'He thinks he's a copper, that's what,' she said, smiling.

'You know what? I think you're right, I'll have to keep him right when he eventually turns up, if he turns up.'

Jimbo pulled up the hood of his jacket and walked around the back of the Ford, popped the boot and made as if looking inside, all the while keeping an eye on Powers.

'Shit,' he said under his breath, Powers was walking toward him, he was carrying a silver aluminium briefcase. He'd been rumbled, his heart skipped a beat or two, then all change, Powers turned into the drive of a semi-detached house. He didn't ring the front door bell, instead, he walked down the path beside the house, heading towards the backway.

Jimbo slammed the boot shut, and walked briskly toward the house, he could see Powers at the far end of the garden, he was knocking on the door of a workshop. The door opened. Jimbo did a quick side step out of view, as Powers did a quick look over his shoulder. He watched as the door fully opened, Powers went inside and the door closed behind him.

The street was quiet, Jimbo was standing out like a spare prick at a wedding, he couldn't risk watching any longer and walked back to the vehicle. He sighed a sigh of relief, as he dropped into the driving seat. Once more he took out his mobile and dialled.

'It's me,' he said into his mobile.

'What the hell do you think you're doing following on foot ...'

'Greg, hang on, I think I've found his 'converter', looks like a workshop in a bleedin garden shed.'

'What makes you think that?'

'Powers, he was carrying one of those metal briefcases, what else could be in it but firearms?'

'Sounds likely. Leave things be and get back here.' Warren couldn't help but smile to himself, Jimbo never ceased to surprise him.

'Well done, Jimbo, good call, you've played a blinder. A little praise now and again wouldn't do any harm,' Jimbo said into the mobile, even though there was no one at the other end to hear him. He put the mobile on the passenger seat, fastened his seatbelt, turned on the ignition and drove away.

It was lunch time by the time Jimbo got back to the station. He found Warren in the canteen tucking into an All Day Full English breakfast. 'That looks good,' said Jimbo, dropping down into the chair opposite.
'It is,' Warren speared a piece of sausage, 'so, you reckon we could be on to something?' waving the fork in front of Jimbo.

'Yep,' then, quick as a flash Jimbo reached across and grabbed the sausage off Warren's fork and stuffed it in his mouth. 'That'll teach you.'

'So, you saw Powers go to this house, then what?'

'Like I said, he went down the side of the house, there was this pre-fab type building, he knocked and went in.'

'Then what?'

'Didn't stop to find out, too conspicuous, so I came back here. Mind you the case he was carrying looked kinda heavy.' Jimbo stole a piece of Warren's toast, reached across the table and dipped it in his fried egg.

'You're on dangerous ground, mate, keep off,' Warren continued eating. 'So, I think we should take a closer look at this place. What do you reckon, you up for it?'

'Do you need to ask?'

'Tonight then.' Jimbo was about to reach across when Warren stabbed the back of his hand with his fork. 'Warned you, dangerous ground.'

Back in the office Trish was busy uploading the latest events into the online system. 'How's Bernie doing?' asked Warren.

'So far so good.'

'He's a nosey bastard, if you ask me,' Jimbo said, as he sat down.

'Explain?' Warren told him.

'Just wanted to know the far end of a fart, how come I know you, how long, that sort of stuff.'

'That all? It's only natural, isn't it?' Trish chipped in.

'Can't help it, just something about the bloke I don't trust.' He sat down at his own desk and turned on his iPad, put the earphones on then looked up. 'Where is he anyway?'

'Like you, he's entitled to a lunch break,' Trish said protectively, if truth were known she didn't have any idea where the hell he was.

Warren was quiet, listening. Jimbo was a good judge of character, he'd had to be in his previous career, you had to trust your mates one hundred percent, it was the only way if you didn't want a tug from the law. Maybe there was something in what Jimbo said, he'd keep an open mind for now, and at the same time keep an eye on PC Philips.

'Trish, don't take this the wrong way, me and Jimbo are going on a bit of a nocturnal outing, let's just keep it between the three of us for now. You okay with that?'

'Course, as long as you don't expect me to come along.' Warren looked across and smiled. 'Oh no, you're not expecting me to, are you?'

'Na, you can sit this one out.'

'Thank Christ for that, the less I know about your escapades the better.' Trish carried on inputting information. Warren sat and waited. 'What are you two up to anyway?'

'I knew you wouldn't last, thought it would be a bit longer before your curiosity got the better of you though.'

'So, I'm predictable, tell me.'

'We're going to pay a visit to the place on Hendon Street, looks like it could be a conversion workshop.'

'Okay that'll do, don't tell me anymore.'

Warren laughed, tapped his keyboard and did a search of the property in Hendon Street. 'Interesting,' he said, 'seems number 56 is owned by a Bill Gardener, and guess what?' Trish and Jimbo both looked up. 'He was an Armourer with the Royal Logistic Regiment.'

'Wasn't expecting that,' Trish replied, surprised.

'It's win, win,' Jimbo said.

'Let's hope so mate,' said Warren, eyes fixed on the screen. Now they had a name he could check the National Computer database for any previous criminal activity.

Chapter 22

Jimbo had taken Warren's instructions to wear dark clothing to the extreme. Making an excuse he had left the office early, and visited an army surplus store to kit himself out with a black jump suit, not unlike police issue. 'I'm sweating bloody cobs,' Jimbo said as he scratched his head beneath the ski mask and then pulled it down over his face, just holes for his eyes and mouth.

Warren wanted to laugh, but held it back. 'You look like a Ninja, I can hardly see you myself,' he said as he faked feeling about in the dark. 'Where you gone, oh, there you are,' he said, as he poked Jimbo in the ribs.

'Piss off. You're only jealous cos I've got the right gear.'

'If you say so, mate.'

They'd parked the Escort two streets away from Hendon Street, in the shadows of a disused metal box manufacturing company. In the darkness, they'd managed to scale the loose shale railway embankment without too much effort. Luckily the sky remained overcast and the moon didn't make an appearance. They continued following the railway track until they were at the back of number 59.

Standing on the disused railway embankment, they had an unobstructed view into the armourer's garden. Warren took out the night vision binoculars from Jimbo's rucksack and scanned the area below them.

'Looks quiet, no light on in the house. You ready for this?' asked Warren, as he handed back the binoculars.

'Always am,' Jimbo replied, as he put them in the pack and hung it over his shoulder.

'Right then, matey, let's go.'

Warren went first, Jimbo close behind. Slipping and sliding down the muddy ridge they reached the boundary fence between the embankment and Gardener's property. The six-foot wooden lap timber fence looked as if it had seen better days. Jimbo held the fence panel rigid. Warren hoisted himself over, then roles reversed, Jimbo slipped over like a cat - this had been his game in a previous life as a burglar.

'Still got it,' he said as he dropped to the ground behind the bramble bushes and crouched next to Warren.

'You hang on here, I'll check out the back of the house.'

'Okay, keemosabi.'

Warren shook his head at the comment and moved off. Crouching low he moved along the garden path keeping to the shadows. Things looked good, no noise from the house no lights suddenly flicking on. He waved an arm to Jimbo. Stealthily, they moved through the darkness towards the workshop. Jimbo knelt by his side, took the rucksack from his shoulder and placed it on the floor beside them and took his picks from the side pocket.

The workshop was constructed from pre-cast concrete panels, no windows and only one entrance and exit, a solid hardwood door was secured with two heavy security locks. Carefully Jimbo ran his fingers around the door edges, everything seemed okay, no sign of an alarm. He nodded to Warren and started work with his pick.

Gardener rubbed his eyes with the back of his hands, checked the time, it was 2. 15a.m, the room was in darkness. He'd fallen asleep on the settee. A cold mug of tea was on the floor by his side. His wife had already climbed the stairs to bed long ago. He reached down, picked up the mug and placed it on the coffee table, careful to put it on a coaster. He yawned, stretched his arms behind his head. Out the corner of his eye, he noticed the red light flashing on the security control panel. He wasn't duly worried, it had happened before, it wasn't unusual for a visit from the odd urban fox to trigger the infra-red alarm system. All the same, he thought it best to make sure. He switched on the laptop to check out what his concealed CCTV system had spotted. There was no fox - on the screen two grainy black and white figures knelt by the workshop door.

'Little sods,' He watched, they seemed to be having trouble opening the lock, he wasn't surprised, the locks were the best that money could buy. Not turning the lights on, Gardener went through to the kitchen and put on his boots. He had no intention of letting the little bastards get away with it, they weren't leaving without a beating. Before he opened the door to the garden, he took the aluminium baseball bat from the corner. Silently he opened the door and gently closed it behind him. Keeping to the shadow of the kitchen extension he edged his way around the back of the house.

'How much longer?' Warren asked his burglar colleague.

'Nearly there, it's a tricky one,' Jimbo replied, concentrating on the lock.

Then all hell broke loose as Gardener left the shadows. Yelling like a Banshee he ran down the garden path, the baseball bat held in both hands, high above his head. 'C'mon ya fuckers,' he yelled, 'let's see how hard you are.'

'That's fucked it,' said Warren, turning just in time to avoid the swinging aluminium bat.

Jimbo didn't even turn his head, he stuffed his picks in his pocket and grabbed his rucksack. Gardener swung the bat, Warren sidestepped the aluminium weapon, unfortunately Jimbo, now on his feet didn't. The momentum swung Gardener around, the bat connected solidly with Jimbo's ribs. Warren instinctively reacted, he managed to land a good solid punch in Gardener's kidneys, followed by a kick to his thigh, he dropped to his knees. No words, just grunts from both Gardener and Jimbo, both nursing their wounds. Again, more by instinct than anything else, Warren grabbed Jimbo by the arm, half running and half dragging Jimbo, they made their escape and scarpered down the side of the house towards the street.

'Thieving ...scum,' Gardener called after them as he knelt on the concrete path winded, panting for breath.

'Take off the balaclava and don't stop running until we're well clear,' said Warren, as they rounded the front corner of the house and ran into the darkened street. Their luck was holding, no late-night dog walkers, no one, not a person in sight. They kept running until they reached the ten-foot at the bottom of the street. Jimbo almost collapsed. He lay back against a parked car panting, wincing in pain as he caught his breath. Warren wasn't in much better shape, he bent forward, hands resting on his knees while he gathered his breath. 'That was bloody close,' he said between gasps. 'You okay, mate?'

Jimbo wrapped his arms around his chest. 'I think the sods gone and broke a couple of my bleedin ribs.'

'That was something I wasn't expecting, a baseball bat wielding psychopath. It does prove there's something in the workshop worth protecting.'

'Greg ...I don't feel so good ...think I'm going to be sick ...' Jimbo dropped to the floor.

'Shit, you'll be alright,' he said as he helped Jimbo in the sitting position, back against a brick wall with his legs stretched out before him. 'Just hang on.' Warren didn't want to risk dragging Jimbo up and over the embankment to the car. 'You should be alright here, I'll go and get the car. Don't go anywhere,' he said as he moved off.

'Ha, beedin ha,' Jimbo said through gritted teeth.

'What's going on down there?' Gardener's missus shouted down the stairs.

'Nothing, go back to bed,' he called back. Sitting at the kitchen table he remembered a time when he could have taken both of the intruders with one arm tied behind his back. Who the hell were they? not a couple of lads on the rob that's for sure. And that big bugger who gave him a pasting, he was no street fighter – he was a professional. He checked the time, it was getting on for 3am, there was no point in calling Powers, there was bugger all he could do about it anyway, morning would do.

'You want me to take you to get checked out?'

Jimbo sat low in the passenger seat, holding his seat belt clear, so as not to let it over tighten.

'Na, just get me home, I'll pop a couple of pills and I'll be right.' Warren very much doubted this.

'Jimbo, you look like shit, you need an x-ray.'

'Look, Greg, just take me home to my bed. Please.'

'If that's what you want, home it is.' Jimbo was duly delivered home. 'Look, mate, if you need anything call me - right?'

Jimbo groaned as he climbed out of the low sprung Escort. 'Yeah, will do, see you later.' The car door slammed shut as the black clad Ninja headed for his bed.

By the time, Warren reached home he was still wired, the adrenaline was still pumping. He kicked off his shoes, threw his jacket over the back of a chair and headed for the kitchen, his old friend Jim Beam was calling. With a generous measure poured into his glass, he returned to the living room and collapsed onto the settee.

He was furious with himself for allowing them to get in such a situation. There was no doubt it was all down to lack of preparation, he should have known there would have been an alarm system, of course he bloody should. It was a mistake even a rookie wouldn't have made. None too pleased with himself, he finished the drink and headed off to his bed.

Jimbo on the other hand, had found himself some Paracetomols, downed a couple and then fallen asleep on his sofa.

Chapter 23

Gardener's wife had gone off to her part-time job at a nearby care home. The morning was damp and miserable, pretty much the way Gardener himself was feeling, as he nursed a bruised ego and face. A close inspection of his workshop showed it none the worse for the attempted break-in. He was glad he'd invested the extra cash in the heavy-duty security locks. Inside the workshop, he sat on a high stool with a brew in front of him. He mulled over the previous night's events, then picked up his mobile and made a call.

At the other end of the line, Powers recognised the caller ID. 'And what can I do for you this miserable morning.'

'Had a couple of visitors last night, two tow-rags tried to get in the workshop.'

'Kids?' asked Powers.

'Yeah, well, that's what I thought, until I got out there with the bat.' Powers was intrigued. 'I'd put my money on them being pros.'

'Not seen them hanging around before?'

'No way, the big black guy would have stood out.'

'Black guy you say?'

'Yeah, about five ten - six feet tall, cropped hair, built like a brick shithouse.'

'What about the other one?'

'Skinny fucker, five sevenish, dressed from head to toe in black, looked like a bloody commando. He's the one I clobbered, got a good swing in with the bat. The little shit.'

'Okay, mate, thanks for letting me know I'll put the word out, someone might know who they are. Beef up your security to be on the safe side.'

'No worries, Neil, I'm on it.' The call ended.

A big black guy, could it be Ray Cole? Powers didn't believe in coincidences. Cole was a virtual stranger, an unknown quantity wanting to do business, now this? He would put things on hold, whether Cole would like it or not. Before any business took place between them Powers needed to be doubly sure Cole was kosher.

'I don't give two fucks, I don't want your excuses, when I tell you to do something, you do it. Right?' Pat Conway yelled, into his mobile phone. 'Just get the job done.' He ended the call. 'Wanker.' When Conway told someone to do something he wanted it done without question, he wasn't interested in excuses, he didn't give a toss if the blokes mother *had* just died.

He was about to put the mobile in his shirt pocket when it rang once more. Conway checked the screen, no caller ID, he disconnected, he had no intention of answering a call from a stranger.

The caller was persistent, it rang a further three times, each time he disconnected. Then he received a text message. "PICK UP THE PHONE". His patience was wearing thin, Conway wasn't the sort of man who expected to be told what to do, that was his job. Whoever was calling was going to get the sharp side of his tongue. The next time it rang he accepted. 'Who the hell are you and how did you get this number?'

'No need for that, let's keep it civil, Patrick,' Powers replied. Although they hadn't done business together, they were aware of each other's existence.

Conway didn't recognise the voice at the other end. 'I won't ask again, who the fuck is this?' again on the verge of hanging up.

'Neil Powers, now, Patrick, or may I call you Pat?'

'You can call me what you want, as long as it doesn't rhyme with hunt. What do you want?'

'I want to ask you about someone, someone I believe worked for you a while back?'

'So, ask, it doesn't mean you'll get an answer,' this was one gangster even Conway didn't want to do business with, all the same he wasn't going to let Powers walk all over him.

'Ray Cole, I believe he worked for you?'

Ray Cole, was also someone Conway didn't want to get on the wrong side of. They may be friends, but friendship only extended so far, but he wasn't the sort to piss up your back as soon as it was turned.

'Cole, we go way back. What's it to you?'

'I'm interested, a business opportunity has arisen and I like to know who I'm dealing with. Would you say he was trustworthy?'

'He's a crim for fuck's sake, how can he be trustworthy?'

209

'But do *you* trust him, that's my question?'

'The answer to that is yes, I did and I do, Cole has done the type of jobs that I wouldn't have trusted to anyone else. If an opportunity to work with him comes up I'd have no problem with it, that's if our paths should cross again.'

'That's all I wanted to know, thanks for sharing.'

'No problem, anytime,' Conway lied into the mobile.

Powers thought he'd give Conway something to think about. 'Give my regards to Rachell,' he hung up, not giving Conway a chance to respond.

The remark sent shivers down Conway's spine. What did Powers know about his daughter? He hoped to Christ that it didn't have anything to do with her disappearance. He sat back in his chair, passing the mobile from hand to hand - then sent a text message. "Call me."

Neil Powers went through to the kitchen, filled the kettle and turned it on, spooned fresh coffee into the cafetiere then poured in the scalding water. He thought things over while he waited a couple of minutes then depressed the plunger. Then he made another call.

'Mouse, or are you Seb today?' he asked, sarcastically when the call was answered.

'Told you, boss, it's Seb, now.'

Powers wasn't interested one way or the other. He switched the mobile to loud speaker while he sorted his coffee. 'Listen, whoever the fuck you are, did you get that job sorted?' Powers was referring to Dooley, who still lay in his hospital bed. No response. 'I'll take that as a no, never mind, he'll keep,' he said, before Mouse had chance to make an excuse. Mouse was relieved when he heard the words. Powers needed to know the things about Raymond Cole, that others didn't. 'Got another job that needs sorting. I want you to find out what you can about a fella called Ray Cole, who his associates are, colour of his socks, anything and everything.' Mouse was quiet, these things he wanted to know himself. 'You hear me?'

'I hear you, boss, leave it with me.' He hated it when Powers talked to him that way, as if he was nothing better than dog shit. Then again the money was good.

Jimbo didn't rush to get into work, he couldn't have if he tried. The previous night's encounter with a baseball bat wielding maniac had taken it out of him, what's more he still refused to go to the hospital.

'Bloody hell, Jimbo, you look in a right state,' Trish said as he walked into the office and dropped into his seat.

Warren looked up. 'You should have stayed in bed.'

'Okay, so what happened?' Trish asked. 'I take it this has something to do with last night's escapade.'

Jimbo looked to Warren, he nodded. 'The others about?'

'Canteen,' she told him.

'Best be quick then.' He didn't want the new team members to know he'd been twatted. 'Me and our leader,' nodding towards Warren, 'went on a late-night jaunt to check out Gardener's workshop, it was going okay until the crazy twat came running down the garden

211

path screaming like a madman. Guess who got clobbered with a baseball bat? Yep, me.'

'Ouch.'

'Yeah, bloody ouch, my ribs are killing me.'

'To be fair, we didn't stand a chance, he caught us by surprise, Jimbo copped it in the ribs and I managed to get a couple of good hits into Gardener,' Warren told her.

'Then we legged it.'

'The workshop, did you get inside?'

'Never got a sniff. I think it best if we keep this to ourselves, Trish.'

'No problem. You sure you don't want to go to the Infirmary, Jimbo?'

'Na, I'll be okay.'

'Greg, he shouldn't be here,' Trish said with genuine concern.

Warren had to agree with her, he did look rough. 'Jimbo, get yourself off home and have a kip, I'll meet you for a pint tonight if you're up to it.'

'Think I will, didn't sleep too good last night. Thanks, see you later.'

'You know, Greg, you have double standards,' Trish said getting all uppity.

'Why?' he asked as he sat forward, resting his elbows on the desk.

'You had a go at Bill about putting Jimbo in dangerous situations, and what do you do? You do exactly that, the lad could have been seriously injured.'

'C'mon, Trish, it wasn't exactly planned. It turned out Gardener had some sophisticated security we didn't know about.' He protested.

'Just saying that's all.'

Chapter 24

When Warren first took on the role of his alter ego Raymond Cole, *The Eagle* had become his local, he had grown to like the place, it was much like the boozers in North London or was it perhaps down to Kirsty, the attractive young woman who worked behind the bar? Warren, in the guise of Cole nodded to a couple of the regulars as he walked across to the bar.

'Alright, pal?' asked an old codger, whose name Warren could never remember.

'Not so bad, mate, and you?'

The man shrugged his shoulders. 'Same old, same old.'

Kirsty gave a warm smile, and automatically pulled two pints of lager before they even ordered.

'I'm impressed,' said Warren.

'I know my regulars,' she put their drinks on the bar top.

'Take one for yourself, my mate's paying.'

She looked to Jimbo for confirmation. 'Suppose.'

'Thanks, I'll just take for a half.'

'See you in a bit,' said Warren as he and Jimbo picked up their drinks and found a vacant table.

Warren's head turned, he winked over at Kirsty as he sat down.

'I just don't know how you do it?'

'Can't help it if the ladies find me appealing,' Warren said with a broad smile on his face.

'Not that you're a vain sod, I mean the accent. Here you are, a southerner who speaks 'ull with a southern twang, and as soon as Cole comes onto the scene, you speak like a Wessie,' Jimbo said, referring to Warren's ability to change to a West Yorkshire accent at will.

'Never thought about it, been doing it so long its automatic,' he said as he turned towards the bar.

'C'mon Greg, give it a rest, you're not going to sit ogling Kirsty all night, are you?'

Warren smiled. 'You have my undivided attention, mate.'

'Glad to hear it. Have you heard anymore from Conway?'

'Nope, not that I'm grumbling.'

'Let's hope it keeps that way.' Jimbo picked up his pint and sipped through the frothy head. He could see that there was only one thing on Warren's mind, and it wasn't Pat Conway. 'You're thinking about bloody Kirsty again, aren't you?'

'Far from it, I was thinking back to the time when we were sat in this very pub, and I told you I was a copper, remember?'

'Remember, are you serious? It nearly blew my bloody mind. What's brought this on?'

'Life, you know, one minute you are okay with things, then wham, all change - changed forever.'

'Sort of like us.'

215

'That's exactly what I mean, just like us.'

Jimbo let the silence hang for a minute or two. 'This is getting a bit too heavy for me. So, what's your thoughts on Bernie?' he asked, attempting to change the subject.

'Seems to be doing okay, competent at the job, Trish seems to rate him. Why do you ask?' Warren sat back in his chair.

'Just something about him, can't put my finger on it.'

Warren folded his arms across his chest, studying the younger man. 'You're serious aren't you?' He trusted Jimbo's instinct, after all, that's what had kept him out of the clink in his previous life.

'Don't trust the bloke, he asks too many questions.'

'Yeah, but he's a copper he's bound to, it's in his nature.'

'Maybe. I feel crap, knew I shouldn't have come, think I might head off.' Jimbo picked up his pint, drank half down and put the glass on the table.

'Can't tempt you to stay for another?'

'No thanks, I'm going for some fish and chips and then back home to watch the telly.'

They both stood up, Warren gave his pal a slap on the back and Jimbo winced.

'Okay, think I'll have another, see you in the morning.'

Jimbo stood up, gave Kirsty a wave and smile. 'I'll leave you to the delectable Kirsty, see ya,' he said as he made a quick exit.

Smiling to himself, Jimbo let the pub door close behind him. His SmartCar was parked a little way down

Coltman Street. He fiddled in his pocket for the keys as he walked.

'Jimbo,' a voice called from behind, 'hang on a minute.'

'Shit,' that was the last voice he wanted to hear. It was Mouse. He put a smile on his face and turned. 'Sorry about what happened the other night. How are you doing, mate?' he asked feigning concern.

'Not your fault that the bloke's a psycho, anyway I'm a lot better than your pal will be when I catch up with him,' he almost spat the words out. 'But he'll keep,' he said as he fell in step with Jimbo, arm around his shoulder in a show of faux friendship.

Jimbo almost cringed.

'So, what can I do for you?'

'It's about your mate that I want a word, what was his name again?'

'Ray, Ray Cole.'

'Ahh, yeah, that's it. What can you tell me about him?'

Jimbo went on the defensive. 'Who wants to know?'

'A bloke I do some work for, seems he's got an interest in the bla ...' then thought better of it, 'this Cole bloke.'

'Can't tell you too much, mate, first met him a while back when I was working for Pat, you know, Pat Conway?'

'Can't say I know him, but heard of him, a piece of work by all accounts.'

'He's alright, if you keep on the right side of him, not the sort of bloke you want to cross, much like Ray.' He

217

hoped the comment might put Mouse off asking too many more questions.

'So, can you tell me anything about him?'

'Gangster, a real one, got a nasty temper on him.'

'No need to tell me.'

'I did a couple of jobs with him when we both worked for Conway. He's done time for topping some bloke and organised an escape from the inside while he was on remand. An Irish team, flew in, did the job and flew out again. Oh yeah, do you remember my cousin, Billybob?'

'Yeah, likes to wave a Stanley knife about.'

'That's him, but not anymore. Cole only went and crippled him - the quacks had to rebuild his leg with scrap iron. He uses a stick to walk now.' Jimbo was silent for a few seconds, hoping he was getting his message across before he continued. 'Seriously, Mouse, he's got connections you don't want to know about, that should tell you all you need to know about him. My advice would be, tell whoever wants to know to stay well fucking clear.'

Jimbo was relieved when they reached his car, all he wanted to do was climb in and drive away.

'I want you pass on a message to Ray Cole, you'll do that?' Before Jimbo had a chance to reply, Mouse kneed him in the groin, as he doubled he brought the knee up into Jimbo's face. 'Tell your pal, I don't care how hard he thinks he is - I'm harder, get it?'

Jimbo was still on his knees as Mouse walked away, laughing. He seriously thought he was a match for Ray Cole. Jimbo managed to get to his feet and leaned back against the car. Wiping his hand across his face, it came away smeared with blood. 'Shit,' he spat into the gutter. His ribs still hurt from the pasting with the baseball bat, now this. The fish and chips would have to wait, he wouldn't have been able to eat them anyway. Pulling himself together, he made his way back to the *Eagle*.

Warren was standing at the bar, chatting with Kirsty and the old bloke whose name he could never remember, when Jimbo opened the pub door. The old man, nosey as ever, turned automatically when he heard the door open.

'Bloody hell, lad, what's happened to you?' he limped across on arthritic legs to help Jimbo. Kirsty and Warren turned to see who he was talking to.

'Bloody hell, what happened to you?

'Mouse.'

'A mouse, you say?' said the old bloke, not understand the significance.

'A long story, gramps,' said Jimbo.

'The little shit. Get him a brandy, please, Kirsty.'

'Make it a double, seeing as though Ray's paying,' Jimbo said through his swelling lips. 'He was asking questions about you.' Kirsty passed a box of tissues across the bar, then turned to the optics. 'Thanks,' he pulled a couple out and wiped his mouth, 'said a bloke he works for wanted info.'

'Powers?'

'Didn't give a name, but I reckon so.'

'What did you tell him?'

'The truth, that you're a short tempered nasty bastard and not to get involved with you at any cost.' Blood continued to dribble from his split lip.

219

'Really?'

'Well, it's the truth,' Jimbo replied, trying to smile as he eased himself onto a bar stool. 'Don't suppose it'll put Powers off, I reckon I've just put your rep up a notch or two.'

Kirsty stood listening, she took it all in, wondering what the hell it was all about. What she'd heard didn't sound a bit like the Ray she thought she knew.

'You okay?' she asked Jimbo. He nodded. 'See you in a bit. Yes love, what can I get you,' she asked a customer waiting to be served at the other end of the bar.

'How long have we been teamed up again?' Jimbo asked seriously. 'No need to answer that one, two fucking minutes that's how long.' Warren looked puzzled. 'Two fucking minutes and I've already got a cracked bloody rib, maybe two, and had my head kicked in!'

'Look, mate, you know the score, you can back off anytime you want.'

'Oh yeah, and what sort of mess would you get into on your own? You're not getting rid of me that easy. Some fucker's got to watch your back.'

'Then what the hell are you griping about?'

'Just trying to make you feel guilty,' he said, with a chuckle.

'I'll tell you one thing for free, Jimbo, that fucking little turd Mouse, he'll wish he never messed with us – you. That's a promise.'

Warren already had Mouse's punishment lined up, and it would be a bit more significant than just a hiding.

'Isn't that your mobile?' Kirsty said, nodding towards the mobile phone vibrating its way along the bar top. In all the commotion, he hadn't noticed his phone heading towards a beer spill.

'Yeah, thanks.' Warren made a grab for the phone before it drowned itself in beer. He checked the display screen, a text message. 'Pat Conway,' he said to Jimbo, who was sat holding a paper tissue to his lips.

'What's he after?'

'Just says, "call me",' He walked to the far end of the bar for privacy and dialled Conway's number. The call was picked up immediately. 'Pat, what can I do for you?'

'Powers, he's been asking questions...'

'What sort of questions?'

'What do you think? About you, who are you, can you be trusted, he wanted to know the far end of a fart.'

'And?'

'I lied, told him you're as sound as a fucking pound, as if ..., but what concerns me, is, before he hung up he asked how Rachell was keeping. How the fuck does he know about her?'

'Search me.'

'Yeah, well, what I want to know is, have you been speaking out of turn? Cos I've not told anyone - only you.'

'Listen to me, Pat, I can tell you for free, I haven't told anyone. Why the hell should I?'

Silence on the line.

'Ray, I'm worried, what the hell does he actually know? You've got to get her back.'

'You know I can't do that,' Warren's voice dropped to whisper, 'I can't take the chance in case I get picked up, technically I am still a wanted man.'

'Then what the hell am I to do?'

'You know where she is, go collect her yourself.'

'ME?'

'Well, let's face it, you *are* her father. Send her a text, tell her how you feel, that you're worried, all the things a dad would say. You never know she might reply this time. Anyway, gotta go.'

Warren hung up the call, he was sure this wouldn't be the last he heard from Conway. He turned, smiled at Kirsty and went back to carry on the conversation with Jimbo.

'What was the fat twat after?' Jimbo asked, hardly legible as he swilled brandy around his mouth, wincing as the alcohol stung the cut in his lip.

'You weren't the only one being quizzed about me. Seems Powers has been sounding out Pat, pretty much along the lines of the conversation you've just had, without the violence.'

'And?'

'And nothing, he was cool about it. Can you believe he gave me a glowing reference? What is strange, is, before Powers hung up he asked how Rachell was keeping. Now, my question is the same as the one Pat just asked me, how the hell does he know about Rachell? And what's the significance?'

'Odd, all this coming about so soon after we tried to turn over the workshop. Could be linked.'

'You're starting to think like a copper. Come on mate, I'll walk to the car with you.'

'I don't need a bleedin babysitter,' he told Warren.

'I know you don't, but I'm walking with you all the same.' Warren very much doubted that Mouse would be hanging around, but still, better to be safe than sorry.

Chapter 25

The more he thought about it, the more he was convinced that doing business with Ray Cole was a bad idea, no matter what his credentials were. He picked up his mobile and dialled. DC Bernie Philips was duly summoned.

Powers sat in the BMW, checking emails on his phone when there was a tap on the widow. He glanced and carried on. Then the door opened and Philips climbed into the passenger seat.

'So, Raymond Cole, what can you tell me?' He didn't look up, still busy checking his emails.

Philips took a sheet of A4 from his pocket. 'Raymond Mathew Cole, age thirty-two, both parents dead and brought up by his grandparent in Leeds. He's been arrested for GBH, aggravated assault, suspected of being involved in a number of contract hits in Holland, Germany and in the UK. Funnily enough he was only convicted the one time. Even then, while he was inside on remand for murder, he arranged to be sprung on the way to his court hearing.'

'What's the score with him now?' asked Powers.

'That's it, he was never recaptured. No one has seen hide nor hair of him since he was sprung. But I believe different.'

'So, explain,' Powers told him.

Philips didn't speak, just took an envelope from his inside jacket pocket and passed it over.

Powers gave his quizzical look, opened the envelope and took out a photograph. 'Why are you showing me mug shots of Ray Cole?'

'You sure about that?'

'Sure about what?' he asked and put the photograph back in the envelope.

'That it *is* Cole?'

'Don't piss me about, I've met him, remember?' he made to reach across Philips to open the passenger door.

'Just hang on Mr Powers, then who is this.' He again reached into his pocket, took out his mobile, selected an image and placed it down on the dashboard.

Powers settled back in his seat and looked him in the eye, without speaking he picked up the mobile, turned it over and looked, Cole again, now he was seriously getting pissed. 'Just what are you getting at?

'That, is a photograph of my boss, Detective Sergeant Greg Warren, Cole and Warren, Warren and Cole, call them what you will, but I'm telling you they are one of the same.'

'Piss off, you really expect me to believe that?'

'Straight up, Mr Powers, I took that photo of Warren myself, he's an undercover cop.'

'Let me look at that picture again.' Philips once again passed over the envelope. 'If, as you're telling me they're both the same bloke, does Cole really exist or is he someone your lot dreamt up?'

'Oh no, Mr Powers, Raymond Cole is real alright - somewhere, everything about him is genuine, but as to where the real Cole actually is, I haven't got a bloody clue, but I'm working on it.'

As before, Powers put his hand in his inside jacket pocket and took out an envelope and handed it over. Powers kept a tight hold onto the envelope. 'You keep me up to speed on everything, okay?'

'No problem, will do.' Philips nodded and pocketed the envelope, took back his mobile and left Powers to do what he willed with the information.

Geez, he couldn't comprehend why the hell this information hadn't been passed onto him. He watched Philips leave then took out his mobile and dialled a number not stored in the mobile's memory.

'Sam, it's me,' he said into the handset, 'something urgent has come up, I need you to give it priority.'

'Trouble?' asked Sam.

'Nothing I can't deal with, it's a case of the usual dick heads not sharing information. I need everything you have on DS Greg Warren, he's working out of the Priory Road nick, here in Hull. Also, see what you can come up with on a Raymond Cole, allegedly he did a runner from Belmarsh.'

'Allegedly?'

'Yeah, well, let's just say I have my doubts about it. I know its short notice, but I need it ASAP, make sure the email is encrypted.'

'I'm on it.'

'Thanks, Sam.' He hung up. 'So, you think you can play me do you?' he said to himself. 'Well two can play at that game, time to have a bit of fun Detective Sergeant Greg Warren.'

Chapter 26

Warren sat forward in his seat, elbows resting on the desk and looked over towards where Jimbo sat fiddling with his iPad. 'Been thinking, Jimbo, I don't suppose ...'

'Oh, no you don't.' He shook his head.

'Don't what?'

'I don't like the way you said that, that tone always means trouble.' He stood up and started to pace around the small room.

'Just listen for a minute, that's all I ask. Before we take care of Mouse, you reckon you'd be willing to have another chat with him?'

'Chat? A fucking chat, are you having a laugh? NO, I bloody well won't, I don't want another fucking beating.'

'I knew you'd be up for it.'

'Are you bleedin listening to me? NO.'

'All I want you to do is sound him out, see if Powers knows anything, just a simple task to do for a mate.'

Jimbo continued pacing, then stopped in front of Warren's desk. He slammed both hands palms down on the surface. 'A proper mate wouldn't even think about it, never mind ask. Oh, for fuck's sake, when would I ask him, before or after I get my head kicked in? Cos, you know as well as I do that's what'll happen ...'

'Not if I'm stood around the corner waiting.'

'Oh, shit. When's this happening?'

In the back of Warren's mind, a plan of sorts was developing. 'Maybe tonight if you're up for it?'

Later that same evening, Warren parked the Escort in the Aldi Supermarket car park, out of view of the *Rose's* entrance. Standing on the opposite side of the road, concealed in a doorway of a closed down shop, Warren watched. Against his better judgement, Jimbo had agreed to have a word with Sebastian London. Standing with his hand poised to push open the pub door he took a deep breath, pushed the door and walked into the pub doing his best to appear confident. No change, the same racist posters on the walls and the same racist thugs occupying the tables. He was pleased to see a different bloke behind the bar, not the one Warren had thrown onto his arse. There was no sign of Mouse, but it was only a matter of time before he turned up, he wasn't welcome in many of the city's pubs. Jimbo ordered a pint of lager, passed over a fiver and pocketed the change. He did his best to appear relaxed and stood with his elbow resting on the bar. With a pint in front of him Jimbo constantly looked around, trying to appear cool, but he was not a happy man. 'Seb been in yet?' he asked the barman, who just shook his head. Ten minutes later, Mouse made an appearance. In the large mirror behind the optics, Jimbo saw him heading towards the bar.

'You're the last person I was expecting to see in here tonight,' he clapped Jimbo on the shoulder. 'No hard feelings?'

'Water under the bridge,' Jimbo lied.

'In that case, giz a pint,' he told the barman, 'my mate's paying.' Jimbo took out a five-pound note from his denim jacket pocket and passed it across the bar. 'So, Jimbo, what the fuck do *you* want?'

As he turned to face him, he could smell the familiar coffin breath coming from Mouse's rotten teeth. 'Thought I'd let you know I passed your message on.'

'And what message was that?' he said laughing.

'Not funny, Seb, not funny at all.'

'So, what did that Rasta pal of yours have to say?'

'Told me to fuck off. Straight up, said I'd served my purpose and he didn't need me anymore.'

'Well, what you expect? Never trust anyone who listens to Reggae, that's what I say.'

'Yeah, well, I've learnt my lesson, played me for a fool he did.' As he eased into the role, the lying came easier. 'What did the fella you work for make of the info I gave you?' Jimbo asked casually, as he picked up his pint and had a swallow.

'You looking to get paid or summat?'

'No, nowt like that, just wondered,' he said as he wiped his mouth with the back of his hand.

'From what I can make out, everything you told me was right, reading between the lines I think this Cole's days are numbered, know what I mean?' he said, making a gun shape with his fingers and holding it to Jimbo's head.

Warren checked his watch. It was twenty minutes since he had seen Mouse go into the pub, it wouldn't be much longer. He left the concealment of the doorway, crossed the road and walked down by the side of the *Rose* and around the back of the pub. The car park, if it could be called that was more akin to a bomb site, with a block of half demolished linked garages strewn with rubble. In the darkness, he carefully made his way through the debris and concealed himself in what was left of a prefabricated garage. From the rear waistband of his jeans he removed the 9mm Walther, took the suppressor from his pocket and attached it.

'So, Seb, can we have a word in private?' Jimbo asked sheepishly. Seb, he thought, the twat would always be Mouse as far as he was concerned.

'There's nothing you can't say right here.'

'Don't think so, mate. Look, let's go around the back, it'll be worth it.'

'You not coming onto me are you, Jimbo?'

'You're not my type, too fucking ugly.' Jimbo picked up his pint and drank it down. 'Well?'

'Better be good, Jimbo, better be good,' he replied, following Jimbo out of the pub.

Jimbo glanced across the road to where Warren had been concealed, he sighed a breath of relief. Warren was in place.

'So, the Rasta fucked you off?' Mouse said, falling in step with Jimbo, as they walked down the dark narrow street.

'Something like that,' he walked into the rubble filled car park, Mouse still by his side.

'So, we're here, what you got to tell me that's so important?'

'Remember I told you I passed the message on to Cole?'

'Y-e-a-h'

'Well he wanted to thank you personally.'

Warren stepped out of his concealment. 'Hello, Mouse man,' he said, taking the thug completely by surprise. Before he had time to react he grabbed Mouse by the bicep.

That was when Jimbo saw the Walther in his right hand. 'For fuck sakes, Ray, where did that come from, for fuck's sake put it away.'

Warren smiled. 'All in good time, Jimbo.'

'Let go of my bleedin arm, you fucker before ...'

'Before what, Mouse man? Before what? Now, I know you like dishing out the pain, but can you take it?'

'You don't scare me,' he tried to shake off the grip.

'You see this?' Warren held the Walther in front of Mouse's face. 'With this I can do some severe damage.'

Mouse's eyes widened, he didn't doubt that he would use it, but all the same he called Warren's bluff. 'You're a fucking pussy, you haven't got the bottle.'

'That so? Now, I want you to lay down on the ground.'

'And you can fuck right off, know what I mean?'

'Just do as you're told.'

'What do you reckon you're gonna do? Give me a massage or summat?' He started to laugh - nervously, keeping up the bravado.

'Let's just call it payback for what you did to Jimbo and all the other poor fuckers who've had the misfortune to come across you.' Then he let go of Mouse's arm and kicked his legs from beneath him.

'Enough, Ray, he's got the message,' Jimbo said, agitated, but he knew there was nothing he could say once Warren had made up his mind.

'But has he? I don't think so. Like I said lay flat.' Mouse turned his eyes upwards to face it out. 'Turn over onto your front.' This time Mouse did as he was told, and lay prostrate among the bricks. 'Where would you like it? Hands, feet, legs? Or maybe all of them.' Mouse lay traumatised, he knew it was going to happen, there was nothing more certain.

'You're nothing more than a Rasta fuck pussy,' he said into the brick dust.

Warren bent over, picked up a plastic carrier bag from the rubbish on the floor. 'Keep still.' Warren put his foot in the centre of Mouse's back. Mouse could feel the muzzle of the silence against the back of his knee. 'Just one more thing, Neil Powers, what can you tell me?'

'Only that you're a dead man walking.'

'That so?' He stuffed the carrier bag in Mouse's mouth.

A second later the first phut from the suppressor blew Mouse's kneecap off.

He writhed in agony, muffled cries barely escaping from his mouth as his knee cap disintegrated. Then another phut, the other knee exploded into a tangled mess of bone and tissue. The crippled man sobbed as the blood became one with the brick dust and lifeless

233

soil. He writhed amongst the debris, he tried to turn, even though his lower legs, contorted, still faced the other way.

Warren dropped to his knees amongst the filth, careful to avoid the free-flowing blood and looked into the tear-filled eyes. Out the corner of his eye, he saw Jimbo throwing up amongst the rubble.

Holding Mouse's head between his hands he told him the score. 'Now, you might walk again, but if I'm honest with you, I very much doubt it, not without sticks anyway. So, now might be an appropriate time to retire from all this racist shit, don't you think? Because if I hear you're still persecuting people I'll be paying you another visit. Know what I mean?' Warren stood up, removed the suppressor from the Walther and put it in his pocket, then replaced the gun in the back waistband of his jeans.

Mouse pulled the plastic carrier bag from his mouth, in shock he was unable to scream, his face, contorted in agony.

Jimbo was struck dumb, he stared from one to the other. He knew Warren's capabilities, he'd witnessed it all before, but the twisted legs ... too much. He took out his mobile and dialled triple nine.

'Ambulance please, there's been a serious incident at the rear of the *Rose* pub, on Beverley Road.' He hung up before they could request any further details. 'Gr ...,' he realised the near slip. 'Ray, time to move.' He turned his attention to Mouse, laying in agony at his feet and shook his head. 'I tried to warn you, I couldn't make it any clearer, but would you listen?'

The two men walked away, the sound of the sobs fading.

'Fucking hell, Greg, that was a bit extreme don't you think?'

'Nope, don't tell me you're feeling sorry for him?'

'No, but ...I thought you were just going to teach him a lesson.'

'I did, Jimbo, a very valuable lesson, let's face it it's going to be a long, long time before he starts any more of that racist shit. Job done I reckon.'

Standing by the car in the Aldi car park, Jimbo asked. 'And where the hell did you get the gun from, I thought you turned yours in?'

Warren smiled and touched the side of his nose, knowingly. 'You don't want to know, mate.'

There had been a time when Warren had never condoned the use of firearms, much preferring his feet and fists to get him out of trouble, or more was the case they had been the things that caused his trouble. During his time with Gemmell Strategies he had undergone firearms training and surprised himself - he loved it. There was no feeling of remorse when he pulled the trigger, not even when he'd topped the hitman sent to kill him. Blowing the man's head off had been easy.

'What do you make of Mouse's comment, was he braving it out or do reckon there's something in it??'

'Hmm, that's the question, Jimbo, if he was being serious, someone has been opening their mouth when they shouldn't.'

'Keep your eyes and ears open, mate, if anyone in the nick has been blabbing, they're the dead man walking.'

Then he lightened the conversation. 'Fancy a pint, mate?'

'Take me home, Greg, just take me home.'

'Hang on a minute,' Warren said as he started the engine, 'what did you get out of rat face?'

'More or less confirms what he told us, he reckons your days are numbered,' making the gun symbol with his fingers.

'That's it?'

'Yep, dead meat, that's what he told me, that's if you can believe a word he says.'

'Best get in first then,' Warren said, as he put the car into gear.

'Thought you'd say that.'

They could hear the blues and twos of the approaching ambulance as they drove away.

Warren sat on his sofa, legs stretched out in front of him, nursing a glass of his newfound friend *Jim Beam.* The television was on, the volume low but it didn't hold his interest. Instead he sat reflecting on the night's events, the violence was a thing of the past, or so he had thought. It was coming easy, way too easy. A few months back, whilst still working in North London the violence had got the better of him, the result of which he was forced to undergo a course of anger management counselling. He was the first to admit it had worked - for a while, until his secondment into undercover work, where it once again reared its ugly head. What frightened him was the fact he no longer cared, he'd killed and maimed with no hesitation, worse, with no feeling of remorse afterwards. He promised himself that when the case was over he would seek professional help - again. In the meantime, *JB* made a pretty good substitute.

The next morning standing beneath the power shower, was it guilt he was feeling? Then he remembered what Mouse really was, a bully and thug who was now out of action and hopefully for a very long time. Warren gave his morning run a miss, along with his usual healthyish breakfast, what he craved was a strong coffee and bacon roll, maybe two from the station canteen. He was already sat at his desk when the team made an appearance.

'Hell, Greg, you been here all night?' Trish asked, as she walked in carrying her own cardboard cup of coffee in one hand and a file in the other and set both down on the desk.

'Can't wind me up to day, Constable,' he replied with a smile on his face.

'Someone must have had a good night, who was she?'

'Nothing like that, Trish, not at all. Just feeling good.'

'Well, let's see if I can wipe the smile from your face, I was handed this when I walked through the main office,' she passed over the file.

Warren reached across and took a hold of the file and opened it. He knew what he would see inside. 'Well, well, well, it couldn't have happened to a nicer bloke,' he said as he opened the file.

'You don't seem surprised?'

'What's to be surprised about? Someone like Sebastian London? It was only a matter of time before someone took a pop at him, it had to happen.'

'Suppose, this comes under our remit?'

'Of course, it's more than likely tied into our investigation, we know he was known to Dooley, along with a strong link to Powers.'

'Don't forget young Joey,' Trish reminded him.

'And Joey. I'll leave this one to you and Bernie,' Warren looked at the clock on the wall. 'When he decides to join us.'

Five minutes later Jimbo and Bernie walked into the office together, laughing. 'Good of you to join us,' he said with a trace of sarcasm.

'Just bumped into Jimbo in the car park, so we called in at the canteen on the way up,' Bernie replied, setting down a tray of drinks and warm croissants on the desk.

'That's okay then.' Warren helped himself. 'Bernie, you're with Trish, apparently, someone put a couple of bullets into Sebastian London last night.'

The expression on Jimbo's face didn't budge.

'Didn't know about this, did you Jimbo?' Trish asked him.

'Me, no, what makes you think I would?' he replied a little sharpish.

'Don't get your knickers in a twist.' The comment brought a smile to Warren's face. 'Just thought, you know, you knowing him, that someone might have been in touch?'

'I might know him, but he's hardly a mate, is he?' Jimbo looked towards Warren for reassurance.

238

'So, Jimbo, me and you are going on a hospital visit, see if we can get any more out of Dooley, he's had a bit of time to stew, we'll pay a visit and see if we can wind him up.'

'Fine by me,' Jimbo said, dunking his herbal tea bag up and down in his cup.

Bernie looked over to Trish and raised his eyebrows, even he could sense the atmosphere change. Warren and Jimbo didn't finish their drinks, just grabbed what they needed and left the office.

'Now, you can't tell me that wasn't weird?' Bernie said to Trish as the door closed. 'Beyond weird. You going to tell me what's with those two?'

'Nothing to tell as far as I know.'

'If you say so.'

'Bernie, you've got to remember Greg sometimes does things that are a little unorthodox at times, just give him space.'

'Hmm, I'll remember that. Right, Mr London,' Bernie said, holding out his hand for the file.

'Not a great deal in it, looks like some sort of punishment to me,' Trish replied as she passed it across.

'Ouch,' Bernie said, as he saw the photographs of London, taken in the hospital. 'Kneecapped, think you could be right about it being a punishment. I suppose this could be termed as unorthodox, don't you think?' he waited for some reaction but didn't get one.

Trish hoped to Christ, Warren and Jimbo didn't have anything to do with the kneecapping of London. But somewhere in the back of her mind something niggled.

'I thought that went out in the 80s with the IRA. Fancy a visit to the *Rose*, see if anyone's talking?'

'Might be worthwhile waiting a couple of hours.'

'Why?' Trish questioned.

'Give us time to go and get matching tattoos so that we can blend in.'

'Now, that would be a novel idea. How about we settle for another coffee instead, then we'll head out?'

Chapter 27

'Jimbo, mate, you really have got to try to keep a grip,' Warren told him as they walked through the station corridors.

'Don't know what you're talking about,' he answered, playing dumb.

'You know perfectly well what I'm talking about - Mouse. You let Trish rattle your cage, just keep it cool that's all I'm saying.'

'So, are we going to the hospital or not?'

'We are, but you'll be going for one of your herbal teas, while I have a word with Dooley.'

'That's fine by me.'

Robert Dooley was still wired up to various machines, but looking a damn sight better than he did the last time Warren had seen him. 'Robbo,' Warren said as he entered the room, 'I can call you Robbo?'

'You again,' was the only response he got back.

'So,' said Warren, as he pulled over a tubular chair and sat down. 'Quite a good set up you have back in your lock-up.'

'I liked it.'

Warren took out his note book and opened it. 'Let's see what we have here. The illegal importation of firearms ...'

'I think you'll find it's not illegal to bring unconverted Baikals into the country, and besides, I'm not the importer,' he replied confidently.

'Ah, now that's where I beg to differ but we can come back to that one, however it *is* illegal to convert them, now you can't deny that one?' Robbo shrugged. 'Have you any idea of how long a sentence it carries?' Robbo was silent. 'Thought not, my best guess is that you're looking at ten - twelve years. On the other hand, if you were to give us something that could help, a reduced sentence might be in order. See, I don't believe you're in this on your own. So, what I say is why take all the responsibility? You know it makes sense, Robbo? You scratch my back and I'll do what I can to help. How does that sound? Because once we get confirmation from the Crown Prosecution Service you'll be arrested, and there will be nothing I can do to try and lessen your sentence, think about it?'

Warren had struck a chord. Robbo was quiet, pensive, he knew he was as deep in the shit as he could possibly be, but give up the guy responsible for supplying him with the Baikals? That was a matter he'd have to give some serious thought to.

Dooley had known the risks right from the beginning, it had been too good an opportunity to miss, it was either carry on making pin money or step things up a little. It was a no-brainer.

'Look, detective, if, and I say if, I was to supply you with information, how would it stand with the charges against me?'

'Robbo, let's face it, there's no conceivable way you can avoid a custodial sentence, possibly a long one, and, to be truthful I really don't know how long.'

'Earlier you said you could help?'

'What I can do to help is let the prosecution know how helpful you've been, as I said before it could go a long way to help getting a reduced sentence, but I can't guarantee it.'

Warren could almost hear the cogs turning in Robbo's head. 'Okay, I'll do it.'

'Good man. Now why don't you start at the beginning?'

What other choice did he have? He settled back as best he could on the pillows. 'When I was made redundant cash was tight, you know, once I'd equipped the workshop I had next to bugger all left, anyway, a mate said he knew someone who was expanding his interests and needed a job doing.'

'And that job was converting automatic weapons?'

'It was just the one at first, a sort of trial, things went on from there.'

'These weapons that - what shall we say, malfunctioned, you carried out the conversion?'

'I can put my hands up to the one Joey had, any others I wouldn't know.'

'This mate of yours, what's his name?'

'Ahh c'mon, I'm not dropping him in it.'

'Then this is going nowhere, seems I'm wasting my time.' Warren makes to stand up.

'Listen, my mate was only involved in introducing me, he never got involved any further. All other dealings were done direct over the phone.'

'You have a name for this contact?'

'No, I never met the guy, just a voice on the other end of the phone.'

'If you weren't responsible for the importation, how did the goods reach you?'

'He'd always phone first and the Baikals would be delivered by taxi.'

'Collection the same?'

'Yeah, I'd ring the number and a taxi came to collect the ones I was contracted to convert at a pre-arranged time and dropped off my cut.'

'Just so I'm clear, you don't know the bloke, you never met him and all arrangements were made over the phone?'

'That's about it.'

'One more question, what's the number?'

Warren passed over his note pad and Robbo scribbled down the number. 'Thanks, Robbo, you will have to make and sign a full statement in due course.'

'Yeah, I gathered that.'

Warren stood up to leave. 'Okay, I'll leave you to get some rest, I'll be in touch.' With his hand on the door handle he turned. 'Out of curiosity, how many weapons have you converted for the man on the phone?' he asked.

'Sixty, give or take. There is one more thing detective.'

'And what would that be?'

'I don't believe I'm the only converter working for him.'

Shit, that was something he'd never given any thought to.

The number given to Warren was for a mobile, but whose? Although he was itching to dial it, he put temptation aside until he got back to the office.

Chapter 28

Lee Etherington was still coughing and barking when he heard a key turning in the door.

'Only me, mate,' Albie Drury called out. The warped wooden door stuck, Albie gave it a boot, shaking the door on its hinges, then slammed it shut behind him. Albie had at one time shared the flat with Lee before moving for pastures new.

'Didn't know you still had a key?' Lee said, between bouts of coughing and then spitting into a dirty handkerchief. He reaches down to the floor and picked up his tobacco tin

'Let you have it back if you want,' he said as he sat down on the settee next to Lee, splitting a four pack of Carlsberg Export Lager and handing one over.

'Cool.'

Albie popped the tab on his own can. 'So, how's it going?'

'You know, mate, same old, same old, nothing ever happens these days,' he said as he popped his own can.

'A bit of excitement, that's what you need, something to get your adrenaline going.'

'Okay, where's this going?' Lee asked, as he put down the can and rolled himself a fag. 'I've known you too long for all this bullshit.' He lit the rollie stuck to his lip and started coughing once again. With the dirty handkerchief, he wiped his lips.

He took the Baikal from beneath his jacket and held it like his prize possession. 'Only gone and got meself one of these bad boys, haven't I?'

'Shit, man, where did that come from?' He asked when the coughing bout stopped.

'Mouse.'

Lee picked up the can and took a swallow. 'Mouse?'

'Yeah, we did a job together and he let me keep it.'

'What job?' he asked knowing he wasn't going to like the answer.

'The Face ...'

'Hang on a minute, Albie, what's with the Martina Cole speak?'

'What you on about?'

'Face – where's that come from?' Albie had been spending too much time with Mouse, the pair of numpties thought they were straight out of a Cole gangland novel.

'Fucked if I know, it's what Mouse calls the bloke we do jobs for.'

'What's his real name?'

'Mr Powers, is all I know him by, anyway, we do some work for him, he wanted someone sorting,' getting animated as he relived the job. 'Man, it was wicked,' he said, holding the weapon 'gangsta style'.

'That bloke up North Hull, it was you and Mouse?'

'None other, it was fucking terrific, boom, boom, he went down like a bag of shit, blood and shit all over the pavement.'

'You *do* know you're supposed to keep this kind of shit to yourself? Mouse will rip your head off if he finds out you've opened your gob.'

'No way, man. Haven't you heard?'

'Told you I don't get out much do I.'

'Someone took him out, kneecapped him, both legs. Gonna be a long time before he's back on the scene.'

'When was this?'

'A couple of nights ago, back of the *Rose*.'

'Shit, any idea who it was?'

'Rumour has it was a mate of Jimbo Boland, some black fella called Cole. Only a rumour like. Cheers,' he said, as they clanked tinnies.

'Cheers.' Lee didn't like the way the conversation was going, Albie was unstable at the best of times, too much substance abuse over the years had left him drug puddled, what brains he had left were nigh on scrambled.

'So, I got to thinking,' he continued, 'now that Mouse is off the scene, why not make use of this beaut?' he said, fondling the Baikal.

Lee took a big swallow of lager, he hoped Albie was only talking the talk. Albie with a gun, fucking hell it couldn't get any worse. 'What did you have in mind?'

'Barclays, the one in the town. Giz another can.'

Albie's face showed he was deadly serious. It took Lee all his time not to burst out laughing.

'Thing is like, the security in banks, mate, it's not like it was back in the 1960s, like you see on telly.'

'How'd you mean?'

Bloody numpty thought Lee. If Albie had one less brain cell he could have been on the reality show, 'Love Island'. 'Cameras, alarms, metal grills, come on, Albie, maybe you should aim a little lower and you might get away with it.'

'Lower, you mean a building society?'

Lee couldn't believe what he was hearing, Albie's brain was definitely scrambled.

'Maybe not, mate, I was thinking more along the lines of a mini-market or a post office.'

'You reckon they keep much money on the premises?'

'If you hit a post-office on pension day you'd be quids in. Okay, they will have CCTV and alarms, but we – you could be in and out in minutes, well before the alarm registers at the cop shop or security company.'

'*We*, are you being serious?' Albie asked getting lively, waving the Baikal. 'You and me, it'll be like Butch and Sundance.'

'Didn't they go down in a hail of bullets?'

'Dunno, never saw the ending, too pissed I fell asleep.'

Oh shit, thought Lee, he'd opened his big gob before thinking it through, but maybe, just maybe... 'Look, put that thing, away will you? Let's give it some serious thought. If we're going to do this, let's do it right.'

Warren sat at his desk with the phone held to his ear. 'Cheers, on our way,' he said, he ended the call and put the handset back on the cradle. 'Elvis, what are you on with?'

'Just doing my homework on the arms trade.'

'Something a bit more interesting has come in, an attempted raid on a sub-post office.'

'Right, ready when you are, boss,' he said, standing up and pushing his chair back. 'Hang on, Sarge' Warren was already out of the office door heading for the car park.

'This bleedin car stinks,' Warren said as he settled into the passenger seat of the pool car.

'Nothing new there, Sarge,' he replied as he pushed back the driving seat to get some extra leg room, turned the ignition key, then slipped the car into gear and drove out of the station car park.

'So, what do you make of our small team?' Warren asked, as Elvis pulled the pool car close to the kerb.

Elvis turned off the ignition, unfastened his seatbelt and turned to face Warren. 'Trish, she's cool, Jimbo, well he's Jimbo what can I say?'

Warren laughed as he shifted in his seat. 'Good enough answer. You've left someone out, what do you make of Bernie?'

He turned to face his senior colleague. 'Hmm, I was hoping I could swerve that one.'

'C'mon, spit it out.'

'Sarge, it's not my place now is it, I hardly know the bloke, what's more it's not as if I'm officially on the team yet,' he took the keys from the ignition and climbed out of the pool car.

'Just interested in your thoughts,' Warren said, as they walked toward the blue and white crime scene tape cordoning off the pavement from the public. 'Between you and me, it'll go no further.'

Elvis knew it was a lie, Trish would be told at the first opportunity. 'Well, if you want my honest answer, he's a total wanker, lazy, full of bullshit and I wouldn't trust him as far as I could throw him.'

'No, tell me what you *really* think?' The tension was relieved and they both laughed.

'There's just something about him, boss, the word wanker comes to mind.'

'Hmm,' he left it at that. 'C'mon, let's go and see what the state of play is, and what the hell are they filming?' Members of the public stood at the road side, mothers with kids in buggies, shoppers, even the grannies and grandads had their mobile phones out videoing anything and everything that was happening.

Warren and Elvis ducked under the tape.

'Oi,' Elvis shouted to a uniformed officer, 'get this lot shifted farther back.'

The officer moved towards the gathering crowd. 'That's it, shows over. Move on please unless you want arresting for obstruction.'

Warren nodded his thanks. 'Just look, I've never seen so many old buggers with Smart phones.'

'Steady up, boss, you'll get done for being 'ageist'.'

The sub-post office was situated on the corner of Gower Avenue on a west Hull housing estate, the estate wasn't one of Hull's finer areas, but then again, not the worst.

A uniformed officer stood by the doorway, preventing anyone leaving or entering without authorisation. 'What's the story?' Warren asked as he held his identification for the officer to see, who then added his name to the incident log.

'One of the counter staff managed to trigger the silent alarm when two blokes came in wearing ski masks. One of them was in possession of a handgun. Me and my partner were first on the scene, we were only a couple of streets away when we responded to the call.'

'What did they get away with?' asked Elvis.

'Bruised egos, they left with nothing.'

'Nobody injured?'

'They're a bit shook up, but no physical injuries.'

'That's what I like to hear, thanks.' Warren said, as he opened the door and stepped inside with Elvis following close behind.

To the right was a tall rack with newspapers and magazines, to the left was the sweet counter and directly in front of them was the post-office section, a long counter with ceiling high glass screen. The staff stood close together, grouped in front of the door to the private quarters.

'Good morning,' Warren said, immediately the small huddle separated. 'The Manager?'

'That's me,' a slim woman stepped forward, she looked to be in her early thirties, about five five tall, black hair styled in a modern lop-sided type bob, oval face with almond coloured eyes. 'Sally Parker,' she said, as she held out her hand.

He took the offered hand and shook. 'Detective Sergeant Greg Warren and this is my colleague Detective Constable Dixon,' he held his warrant card for inspection. 'You okay, Sally?' he asked, noticing the slight tremble in her voice.

'I'm fine, really, just shook up, you know.'

'I'm not surprised, it's a normal reaction in a situation like this. How about cups of tea all round?'

'Good idea,' she turned. 'Do the honours would you please, Sue?' Sue, one of the sales assistants responded with a nod and disappeared through the door marked private.

Notebook in hand, Elvis wandered over to the remaining members of the group to take details.

'So, Sally, are you up to telling me what exactly happened here this morning?' She nodded. 'When you're ready just start at the beginning.' Sally seemed to relax a little.

So much for Trish saying I'm intimidating, Warren thought to himself feeling quite pleased with how he'd settled her down.

'It was only about thirty minutes ago,' she looked up at the wall clock, 'ten fifteenish, the shop was empty, no customers. I was down on my knees behind the post-office counter, looking for some large envelopes. I just happened to glance towards the window and saw the reflection, two men wearing khaki coloured overalls coming through the door, pulling their masks over their faces, you know, the type with just eye and mouth holes. One of them was holding a gun.'

Then what did you do?'

'Well I kept down, crawled to where the emergency alarm button is and pressed. It was only two, maybe three minutes and then I heard the siren.'

'Was anyone else behind the counter?'

'Yes, Graham.' Sally pointed to a middle-aged chap standing with his back to them.

'Call him over please, Sally.'

'Graham, can you come over here?' Graham almost jumped out of his skin when he heard his name, looked as shocked as the rest of the staff. 'This police officer would like a word.'

'Can you get us a copy of the CCTV, please, Sally while I have a word?'

'Of course.' She smiled, then disappeared into the office.

'Hi, Graham, I'm DS Warren, I understand you were behind the post-office counter when the two men came in?'

'Yes, that's right, Sally was searching for something on the shelves under the counter. I was sorting the specials.'

Sue came back from the kitchen with a tray of hot drinks and passed them around, and Warren called Elvis over to take notes.

'Okay, talk me through what happened.'

Graham was still on edge, he was obviously in shock, pale faced and wringing his hands. 'Both men pulled masks down as soon as they came through the door.'

'Did you see their faces before they pulled down their masks?'

'Briefly.' That was something Warren thought.

'Great, carry on, please.'

'The one holding the gun was waving it all over the place, he looked really nervous. The main bloke, he was as jittery as I was, he put a carrier bag on the counter, it was one of those Tesco bags for life. The one with the gun shouted at me to put all the cash in the bag. Well, I just froze, that was when he slapped his left hand down on the counter top and yelled to do it now or he'd blow my head off.'

'Did they wear gloves at all?' asked Elvis, lifting his head up from the note taking.

'No, don't think so. It was all over so fast, I fumbled with the till, not deliberately, my hands just shook. I thought he'd shoot me. Then we heard the sirens.'

'What happened next?'

'The second one grabbed his bag, said something like, '"oh shit, let's go,"' and then started to have a coughing fit. Next thing they were running out the door pulling their ski masks off as they went. The whole thing was over in three, maybe four minutes, can't have been any longer.'

'That's great Graham, thanks, now if you'll give the best description you can to my colleague I'd appreciate it.' Sally came back with a burned copy of the previous twenty four hours of CCTV. 'Thanks,' he said, as she handed him the DVD. 'If you can have everything left as it is I would appreciate it. Also make sure none of your staff touch anything until the Crime Scene Investigators have been and done a complete forensic examination, that would be great.'

'How long do you think it will be before we can open up?'

'That I can't say, sorry. Now is there anything else that comes to mind?'

'Don't think so, I've told you everything,' she replied apologetically.

'Someone will be along later to take everyone's statements.' Warren took a business card from his wallet and gave it to the manager. 'If you or anyone should remember anything give me a call.'

'No problem, officer.'

'How are you doing, Elvis?' Puzzled, Sally looked from Warren to DC Dixon, and back. 'Long story,' he said.

'Be with you in a minute, boss.'

Once outside Elvis took out a packet of cigarettes. 'Do you mind?' he asked Warren.

'Nope, just don't blow the smoke my way.'

He took out a cigarette and lit up, the breeze blowing the smoke directly at Warren, who gave an over emphasised cough.

'I'm thinking amateurs, didn't seem as if they had much idea at all,' Elvis said as he dropped the almost full cigarette down a drain.

'That's what worries me, they're the most dangerous. Let's get back and have a look at this,' he said putting the DVD in his pocket.

'How's it hanging, Jimbo?' Elvis asked, as he and Warren walked into the office.

'Not bad, mate, you?'

'Fine,' he replied. Trish looked up from her keyboard giving them the look and shook her head.

'What?' he laughed.

'If you don't know I'm not telling you.'

'C'mon you two, stop the frivolity,' said Warren.

Jimbo laughed. 'Listen to you.'

'Oi, Jimbo, you may be a civilian but I can still kick your arse.'

'Fair enough. How did you get on?'

'Before we start has anyone seen Bernie?'

'Lunch, I think,' Trish answered.

'Lunch?' Warren said looking at his watch. 'Hardly gone breakfast time. I think me and PC Philips will be having words.'

'About time,' Jimbo muttered under his breath.

'The raid on the Post-Office, turned out to be a fiasco, our two-armed robbers didn't have a bloody clue what they were doing,'

'If you ask me it was doomed from the start,' Elvis told them.

'The good news is we've got them on DVD, and apparently one of them left a nice big hand print on the post-office counter.'

'No gloves?' asked Trish.

'Amateurs, Trish, I'm not saying they're not villains, but not cut out for this kind of job,' he put the CCTV DVD into his computer. Trish and Jimbo stood up from their desks, walked over to view the screen. Warren pressed the fast forward key. 'Here we go, 10.13am this morning.'

They watched as the two men entered the post-office, pulling down ski masks as they did and dropping the latch on the door. 'Everybody, keep where you are, and no one will get hurt,' the gunman yelled, as he waived the hand gun about.

Warren paused the video. 'Anything look familiar?'

'Baikal,' Trish said.

Play button pressed they watched as the gunman's partner put the bag on the counter top. 'The cash, fill the bag,' he told Graham behind the glass screen.

There was something about the voice that sent a shiver down Jimbo's spine.

It was obvious Graham had been scared shitless, he could hardly control his hands as he reached to pull the bag though the opening below the screen. Then the siren of the approaching squad car could be heard. The voice again telling the gunman it was time up, when the man started to cough, Jimbo was certain it was Lee.

'Stop it there and rewind a little.' Jimbo said. Warren stopped the playback and looked at Jimbo.

'What's the problem?' Warren asked.

'Just press play.' Warren did as he asked. He leaned in closer to the screen. 'I know him, the one with the bag, its Lee Etherington.'

'You sure?' Trish asked.

'I wasn't too sure at first, then when he had the coughing fit, I knew it was him.'

'What about the gunman?'

'Sorry, no, nothing ringing a bell.'

'No matter, nice one, Jimbo,' Elvis said, putting a hand on his shoulder.

'Yeah, but all the same, he's a mate of mine,' Jimbo said as he shrugged the hand from his shoulder, and went back to his own desk and sat down.

'That's the nature of the job, Jimbo, you know that,' Warren told him.

'Suppose, all the same, it's like being a grass.'

'You can't look at it like that, Jimbo,' Trish said. 'Think about what would have happened if his crazy mate had lost it and shot someone?'

'Jimbo, do you know where this Etherington bloke lives?' Warren asked his pal.

'He's got a shit hole of a flat on Anlaby Road.'

'Write the address down and we'll pick him up.'

'My name won't come up in any of this, will it?'

'Nope, no need at all, it's not as if you're a copper.'

'It doesn't feel that way at times,' he said as he wrote down Lee's address.

'That's because you do a proper job mate, just like a copper,' Trish told him as a confidence booster. It did the trick, not that she didn't mean it.

'Trish, Elvis, get hold of a couple of uniforms and pick Jimbo's mate up - sorry, ex-mate.'

There was a hush in the interview room. Lee Etherington sat at the interview table, watching the second hands on the wall clock tick by. He didn't know which was louder, the ticking or the pulse banging in his temple. A stern looking uniformed officer sat on a chair in the corner of the room, it was usual practise until the interviewing officers arrived. Etherington nearly jumped out of the chair as the door opened with a flourish.

'Mr Etherington, my name is Detective Constable James, this is my colleague, Detective Constable Dixon,' Trish said by the way of an introduction. She pulled out a tubular chair and sat opposite Etherington. 'Thanks,' she said to the uniform, who nodded, stood up and left the room. To say Etherington was nervous would have been understating the situation, he looked shit scared.

Elvis, picked up a tape cassette, tore off the cellophane and placed it in the recorder, then did the same with a second tape. The lights on the tape machine changed from green to red when the record button was pressed. 'The time is 2.15pm, on the Friday October 20th, present in the room are DC James, DC Dixon and Mr Lee Etherington. Mr Etherington, for your protection and ours, a record of this interview will be recorded on tape. Lee Etherington, you do not have to say anything. But it may harm your defence if you do not mention when questioned something which you may later rely on in court. Anything you do say may be given in evidence.

Mr Etherington, you are charged with being involved in an attempted armed robbery. You have the right to have your legal representation present during the interview, or, if you wish we can appoint someone for you,' Trish told him.

'Yeah, as if ...' catching his breath, 'I have a brief on ...tap,' then he burst into a coughing fit, 'g ...get me one of yours,' he finally managed to get out. 'Till then I'm saying nowt,' he sat back in his chair and folded his arms across his chest.

'In that case, this interview is suspended at 2.22.pm.' Elvis said, as he reached across and stopped the recording. Trish gathered up her folders, stood up and left the room. Elvis took the tapes from the machine, signed and timed them. The same uniformed officer as before entered the room. 'Take Mr Etherington to the cells to wait for his solicitor, and get him some water.'

Etherington stood up and kicked back his chair as the officer walked over and stood beside him. 'How long before he gets here?'

'As long as it takes, in the meantime please enjoy our hospitality.'

'Wankers,' Etherington said and started coughing again, as he was led away to the holding cell.

'Well that was a waste of time,' Elvis said, as he walked into the squad room and dropped his folder down on Trish's desk.

'Just got to be patient,' she told him, 'there's no way he will wriggle out of it.'

'But did you see the state of him? How the hell he managed to leg it when they heard the sirens I'll never know, he can hardly put one foot in front of the other. Jimbo, how come you're mates with a loser like him?'

Jimbo sat up straight. 'I used to go to school with him. I keep thinking, after when my old man topped himself that could have been me if it hadn't been for Pat Conway.'

'Conway?'

'Yeah, that's what I said, Conway.'

Elvis thought it wise not to pursue the conversation.

Chapter 29

Relaxing in his riverside apartment, savouring a glass of Glenfiddich malt whiskey, the question Neil Powers asked himself, was, what was the best way to deal with Ray Cole – AKA Detective Sergeant Greg Warren. Perhaps the simplest way would be the best, just blow him away with a Baikal, the very type of weapon he and his team were investigating. Unfortunately, the information garnered from Sam made this option impossible. Detective Sergeant Greg Warren and Ray Cole were indeed one of the same, Warren's alter ego, had obviously been created by the best, and from what Powers had seen, he had taken to the role like a duck to water.

But, then again, the back story created for Neil Powers was an even better one.

The secret of a good cover story is to base as much as possible on the truth, real life facts and events that can stand up to scrutiny. As far as Neil Powers erroneous past was concerned, much was based on the truth.

True, he had been a sergeant in the Royal Logistics Regiment, a weapons expert.

True, he and Gardener had been close friends while serving in Her Majesty's Forces.

True, he had failed selection on his first attempt to enrol in the Special Air Service, however, on his second attempt, his abilities had not gone unnoticed. Subterfuge proved to be his forte.

As for Sergeant Neil Powers striking a senior officer, it was pure fabrication, along with the myth that he had he served a six-month correction sentence in the 'glasshouse', as was the dishonourable discharge from Her Majesty's Armed Forces. Neil Powers armoury skills, along with his aptitude for subterfuge, had made him the ideal candidate for a new unit born out of the Special Air Services and the National Crime Agency, the Specialist Intelligence Joint Ventures. Powers 'six-month correctional sentence', had been used constructively, intensive training with various law enforcement agencies, at home and abroad. On successful completion of his training Powers was duly promoted to the rank of Lieutenant, the difference being he had the powers of a police officer.

After another whiskey and working his way through assorted options, Powers had come to a decision regarding DS Warren. He couldn't shoot him, although he had liked the idea for a moment or two, things were bad enough, and why complicate matters even more? He would meet his adversary head on, and, in a place he would least expect it.

Chapter 30

Trish had her head down, deep in thought as she updated the daily log book with tasks completed and those yet to be carried out. Eyes sore from staring at his computer monitor, Warren sat back in his chair rubbing them with the knuckles of his hands.

'Don't think it'll be long before I'll be getting two pair of specs for the price of one.'

'Yeah, you are knocking on a bit,' she replied, head still down and chuckling to herself.

'So, who do you think we should make permanent on the team, Elvis or Bernie?'

'Elvis,' a voice said from the open doorway.

Warren recognised the voice immediately, spun around in his chair and stood up. Momentarily he was stuck for words.

'What the ...how the hell did you get in here? Who let you in the place?' Trish looked up, gob smacked. 'This is a restricted area to members of the public, never mind the likes of you.'

Powers stood in the open doorway, an identification card hung around his neck on a lanyard. Holding the

ID in his left hand, he walked towards Warren who was still rooted to the spot.

'S.I.J.P, Specialist Intelligence Joint Projects, Lieutenant Neil Powers,' he said as he held out a hand. He was enjoying the moment. 'I'd definitely keep Elvis; Bernie Philips, he's as bent as nine bob note.'

Warren was dubious as to whether he should shake Powers hand or not, then he did, not before taking a hold of Powers ID and scrutinising it. 'This real?' he asked, as he let the plastic fall back in place.

'No, I bought it off eBay, of course it's bloody real.'

'Lieutenant - S.I.J.P, what the hell is going on here, Powers? You have a lot of bloody explaining to do.'

'You're not the only one who got a bloody shock, when my handler told all the shit about Ray Cole, I wanted to shoot you myself - just kidding. Someone along the way needs a bloody good bollocking for not keeping us in the loop with the correct intel. I think we need a word in private.' He inclined his head towards Trish, who was still trying to comprehend what was happening.

Warren was starting to get himself together, hell, either of them could have topped the other with the blink of an eye and thought no more about it. 'Whatever you've got to say, you can say it in front of DC James.'

So far, Trish had been sat mesmerized with the events unfolding in front of her. 'Can I ask a question?'

'Ask away.'

'When you came in you mentioned Bernie?'

'Like I said, Philips is bent.'

'How do you know this?' asked Warren.

'Because he's my informant, has been for the past three years since I became involved in this operation.' He turned to face Trish. 'Who do you think gave me the information about your boss?'

'Trish, would you mind getting us some coffees, please? And tell whoever is on the desk under no circumstances is Philips allowed upstairs without letting us know first.'

'Does that mean I can sit?'

Warren shrugged, Powers stepped further into the squad room and sat at Jimbo's desk. This will be fun, he thought, Jimbo was due back anytime.

'So, tell me about SIJP or whatever it is, and where you fit into things?' Warren said as he headed to collect his chair from where he'd sent it scooting across the room.

'We're a covert operation, but then again I've no need to tell you how these things work do I? Anyway, we're made up from serving Police and Military personnel, hence my rank of Lieutenant, not that it means much. The firearms market has been on the group's radar for some time now. I've been in deep cover for the past three years, gradually infiltrating various organisations across the country, pretty much like you and Patrick Conway, only on a grander scale.'

That was when the office door burst open. 'You'll never guess whose car I've seen in the car park ...what's he fucking doing in here?' Jimbo stood gobsmacked. 'And sitting in my chair.'

'Bloody hell, it's like 'Goldilocks and the three Bears,' said Powers. 'Lieutenant Neil Powers,' he said standing up and offering an outstretched arm. Warren smiled at the comment, he liked Powers sense of humour. 'Good to meet you, Jimbo.'

'What the fuck's going on here, Greg?' Jimbo was totally confused.

'Seems we've all had our wires crossed, mate ...'

'Yeah, but this is the bloke that had Mouse work me over.'

'As your sergeant said, it was all a mix up, please accept my apologies, Jimbo.'

'Like fuck I will.'

'Jimbo, Neil works for an outfit called Special Intelligence Joint Projects, it's bit like Gemmell Strategies.'

'And what a bleedin outfit that was,' Jimbo said, 'Lieutenant, but you're a cop?'

'Sort of, I'm an Army officer but I could still arrest you,' he told Jimbo with a serious look on his face. Warren was warming to Powers' sense of humour. 'I'm only kidding, Jimbo, I've heard good things about you.'

'What sort of things?'

'If I told you I'd have to kill you.'

'Very bleedin funny – I don't think.'

'Oh, wind your neck in.' Warren told him as Trish returned with the drinks.

'Noticed you drive in so I got you a tea, Jimbo,' she put the tray down and passed Powers a mug. 'Didn't know what you'd want so I got you a coffee, milk and no sugar.'

'Great,' he said as he took the mug from her. 'So, to move things on a little we're all on the same side. Cheers,' he said sipping the hot liquid. 'The question I ask is, can we all work together, at least share information?'

'Sounds like a plan,' Warren picked up his drink, too hot and put it down again. 'Jimbo, remember when you said you wouldn't trust Bernie as far as you could throw him?'

'Too right, the bloke's a wanker.'

'Well that's not all he is, he's bent, Neil has been running him as an informant for three years.'

'I knew the bloke was dodgy, what with all the questions he asks. Lieutenant ...' said Jimbo.

'No need for that, call me Neil.'

'Na, I'll stick with Lieutenant.' Typical Jimbo, thought Warren. 'Did you have somebody try and top Dooley?'

'Ah, I wondered when one of you would mention him. Yes, I did for the greater good, but before you start going all moral on me let me explain a few things.'

'We're listening.'

'First off, Bill Gardener, I believe your paths have crossed already.'

'You could say that, he cracked a couple of Jimbo's ribs,' Warren told him.

'And they still bloody hurt,' Jimbo piped up.

'Will you please stop interrupting,' Trish scolded.

'Gardener and me, we were buddies in the army, top man when it comes to armaments. But in my new role, I had to come on a bit heavy, I had some dirt on him from way back, so it was relatively easy to get him onside. Every weapon he converted for me, went straight into secure storage, not one ever reached the streets.'

'Is he in on this?' Warren wanted to know.

'No, he thinks I'm a bad ass, and he solely works for me. On top of that he's well paid for his services.'

'What's this got to do with trying to take out Dooley? Jimbo, asked as he sipped his herbal tea.

'Nothing really, I thought you should have some background info. Dooley, he was a bad guy, right? The conversions he was carrying out were about as poor as you could get, and, I don't believe he was the only amateur. My logic was, take him out and the others might think twice about what they were doing.'

'Unethical,' Warren said, 'but I can see where you're coming from.'

'Sounds as if you and Greg went to the same training school.' Jimbo sat forward in his seat. 'Who pulled the trigger?'

'It was Sebastian London's hit, he took along some tow rag, Albie – something or other.'

'I only know one Albie,' heads turned to Jimbo. 'I reckon its Albert Drury. You know, Lieutenant, you are a piece of work. What was you thinking employing racist scum? That's as low as it can get.'

'Jimbo, he was expendable. Who would give a toss if anything happened to him? Not me or you that's for sure. And while you're passing the buck, can I ask who blew his kneecaps off?'

'That wasn't me, it was Greg,' he protested.

'Same difference, Jimbo, same difference.'

'What do you know about the shooter they used?' Warren asked.

'One of Dooley's Baikal conversions, I thought it as poetic justice.'

'Man, you really are something else.' Jimbo was making it clear he didn't much care for Powers.

Warren sat back in his chair, a worried look on his face. 'Is the Baikal still out there?'

'London made sure it couldn't be traced back to him, if it should ever be traced back to anyone it will be to this Albie.'

'So, as far as you know he still has it?' asked Trish.

Powers shrugged. 'Seems likely.'

Warren's brain was already one step ahead. 'Don't know if you've heard or not but there was an attempted armed robbery on a Post-Office yesterday morning, we have one of them in custody and it wouldn't surprise me if the other guy was Drury.'

Trish picked up her desk phone. 'I'll check if the CSIs have processed the palm print off the counter top.'

'So, now we've done the introductions and preliminaries, I take it we *are* working together on this?' Powers faced Jimbo. 'What do you think, you prepared to work with me?'

'Not my choice, Lieutenant, I go along with what my sergeant tells me to do, after all I'm just the Civilian Advisor.'

'And will you stop calling me bloody Lieutenant.'

'Jimbo, you can be a right pain in the backside sometimes,' Trish told him.

For the first time since Powers had entered the squad room the atmosphere lightened-up.

Warren had almost forgotten about the scrap of paper Dooley had given him. 'I might have something that can help,' he shifted position and took his wallet from his back trouser pocket and removed the paper with the mobile number written on it. 'Let's see what they have to say,' he picked up the desk phone, dialled and put the phone loud-speaker mode.

It was answered after the third ring. 'Who is this?' the voice boomed out. All eyes turned to Warren. Again, the voice asked the question. 'Who is this?' no response, he hung up.

The room was silent, the three men in the room had recognised the voice immediately. 'Somebody say something,' Trish told them.

Warren was first to speak. 'It was Conway, Pat Conway.'

'This is getting unreal, there's no way Pat can be involved.'

Powers stood up from Jimbo's desk. 'Look, I've got somewhere to be, let's keep this under our hats until we get a chance to talk it through.'

'I agree, we don't go rushing into anything, Jimbo, you okay with that?' He looked towards Warren and nodded. 'Okay, other business.'

'I'm off.' Powers shook hands with each in turn. 'I'll give you a bell, you know where I am if you need me.'

'Fine, but let Trish go ahead, we don't want you bumping into Philips.'

Lee Etherington, didn't feel well at all as he coughed and spat into a dirty handkerchief. His brief gave him a look of disdain.

Elvis pressed the red button on the recorder. 'Lee, I'd like to remind you that you're still under caution, you understand?'

'Course, been arrested before haven't I.'

Yeah, too many bloody times to mention, thought Trish. 'The time is 4.15pm, present are Detective Constable James, Detective Constable Dixon, Mr Lee Etherington and his legal representative Mr Richard McCartney.

Trish lay her open file on the table, Elvis opened his A4 note book ready to record the proceedings. 'Lee, you have been arrested for taking part in an attempted armed robbery on the Post-Office on Gower Road. Is there anything you want to say?'

'Wasn't me,' he said as his right leg tapped nervously.

'Can you tell us where you were on Friday morning?'

'At home.'

'Can anyone verify this?

'Next door's dog?'

This answer even made Elvis give a sly smile.

'For the benefit of the tape, I am now showing the CCTV footage from the morning in question. Have a look at this, Lee, can you tell me, is this you?'

The clip showed a man bending slightly from the waist and having a coughing fit, spraying his germs across the counter top.

'No, already told you I was at home.'

Trish stopped the video and fast forwarded. 'This next screen shows two men leaving the Post-Office, as you can see they are holding the masks they wore in their hands. The man on the left is you, is it not? Trish asked.

Etherington moved in for a closer look. 'Bloody hell,' he knew he was up shit creek., there didn't seem any point it being too evasive. 'Can you prove that I took part in a robbery?'

'Yes, I believe we can. The CCTV footage, the DNA off the counter from your coughing fit and your finger prints on the glass door, oh, and the ski mask we found at your home.'

'Wow, that is some evidence.' He knew there was the point on denying it. 'So, what happens now?'

'I'm going to charge you, but before I do, tell me, who was your accomplice?'

Etherington looked to his brief for some support – he didn't get any, he was about as useful as an ash tray on a motorbike. He gave the matter some thought for a minute or two, okay he accepted that he was going down, but he'd never threatened anyone let alone touched the gun. 'Can we make a deal?'

'No, I don't think that would be appropriate, considering the way the evidence is stacked against you, But, what we could do is tell the CPS how helpful you've been.'

'Tell me, does the name Albert Drury mean anything to you?' Elvis asked.

He gave a sigh. 'You already know, don't you?'

'A team of armed officers are bringing him in as we speak.'

'Yeah, well, it was all Druy's idea, he came to the flat bragging and waving the gun about, if he hadn't brought that bleedin shooter to show me, none of this would have happened.'

'You didn't have to take part, you could have just reported him to the police.'

'Yeah, as if that was ever an option.'

273

'You might be able to assist us on another enquiry; do you know anything regarding the shooting of Robert Dooley?'

'The bloke up North Hull? Yeah, that was Drury and Sebastian London, everyone calls him Mouse.'

The interview was concluded, everyone was happy, even Lee Etherington. At least now he would get proper medical treatment for the cough.

Warren thought it was time to check-in with his fat friend.

'Hey, Pat, how are you doing? Have you made contact with that daughter of yours?'

'Only a text to tell me to stop bothering her. Cheeky cow. I'm glad you rang, I was wondering, while you're down here doing bugger all, if you fancied helping me out, I need someone to oversee some gear that I'm having brought in through Immingham Dock?'

'Meet you at the flat?'

Conway sounded surprised. 'That's it, no arguing?'

'You know me, Pat, anything for a mate.'

Chapter 31

'Must be a darts match on or summat, not usually this packed,' Jimbo said as he elbowed his way towards the *Eagle's* bar. 'You want a pint?' He asked as he waved a five-pound note in the air, trying and failing to catch Kirsty's attention.

'Move over, Jimbo,' Warren said giving him a nudge, 'you haven't got the knack. Two pints of lager when you're ready, Kirsty,' he called out.

The young barmaid recognised the voice, how could she not? She had been infatuated with the enigmatic, tall black guy named Ray Cole, since he'd first appeared on the scene some months ago.

She turned and smiled. 'Give us a minute,' she silently mouthed.

'That's how you do it,' he told Jimbo, as he elbowed more room. 'How come it's so busy?' he asked the old bloke standing next to him at the bar.

'The Wheelhouse - the pub down the road, its gone bust. Gary, the landlord is pulling in all their trade.'

'Alright for some, looks like Kirsty's run off her feet.'

'At least she's got a job,' the old bloke replied, unsympathetically. Warren was going to buy the fella a pint, but changed his mind.

'Thanks, love, take one yourself,' Warren told her when she eventually placed two pints on the bar. 'Take for a pint of Bitter will you doll,' a voice called out over Warrens shoulder.

'Got your timing right there, Lieutenant.' Jimbo joked.

'See you in a bit,' Warren told Kirsty.

'Doesn't look like we're going to get a table anytime soon,' Warren said, leading the way to the quieter end of the bar once Powers had his pint.

'So, have you been with Conway?' Powers asked, when they were out of earshot.

'Would you believe that he wants me on a job?'

'That before, or after, you give Kirsty one?' Jimbo asked. 'What do you reckon to that, Lieutenant? Our Greg here reckons there's nothing going on between him and the delectable Kirsty, but I know different,' he touched the side of his nose knowingly and winked.

Warren gave him a jab in the ribs with his elbow. 'Take no notice of the silly sod, Neil, he's jealous.'

Powers smiled, if all told he was a little envious of the connection the two had. 'So, what's this job?'

'Conway has a shipment coming in from the continent and needs someone to make sure it arrives in Hull safely.'

'What kind of shipment?'

'He wouldn't say, but he wants me tooled up, so, you draw your own conclusions.'

'Jimbo?'

'All the time I worked for him, he never once got involved with firearms, to my knowledge anyway. He knows the score with baccy, booze and of course diamonds, no probs. If you want something brought in through customs he's the bloke, but guns, I don't know.'

'But you wouldn't rule it out?' asked Powers.

'Things change, Lieutenant, people change, look at me? Christ, I'm virtually a copper.'

'Table coming free,' Warren said, inclining his head towards the back corner. A swift move and the table was theirs.

'He never mentioned getting a 'funny phone call'?'

'Not a whisper, wasn't expecting him to.'

'So, Greg, what did you say about the job?'

He sipped the top off his lager. 'Needs an answer by the morning, it's going down in two days.'

'Out of interest, has he heard any more from his daughter?' Powers asked.

'A text, to let him know she's okay and to stop bothering her. Why?'

'I might have an idea, just need to work on it.'

'Not sure I like the sound of that, Lieutenant.'

'Jimbo, for Christ's sake will you stop calling me bloody Lieutenant?'

'Well, that's what you are, right?'

'I give up, call me what the hell you want ... within reason.'

Warren picked up an already soggy beermat and swiped the beer spills off the table onto the floor. 'What's this idea?'

Powers leaned in across the table. 'Maybe we can use his daughter as leverage, let us in on the deal.'

'I'm not sure about using a kid,' Warren told him.

'You trust me?'

'About as far as I could throw you,' Jimbo told him, then he saw the look on Powers' face. 'For fuck's sake, I was only kidding. You've been too long on the dark side, Lieutenant, lost your sense of humour.'

'Sorry, ha ha, very bloody funny. That better?' He leaned in closer across the table fixed his focus on Jimbo's eyes and spoke in a low, serious voice. 'You do realise that I can kill you with one finger?' This time it was Jimbo's turn to look worried. 'Just kidding, Jimbo, just kidding.'

'I'll get the drinks in,' Jimbo said sullenly and headed for the bar.

'He's a good lad, Neil, full of shit at times, but never lets you down once he gets to know you.'

'Don't worry, Greg, I've got him sussed, he's just seeing how far he can go without pushing my button. Tell you what, we could do with more blokes like him.'

'Yeah, you're not wrong there.'

With his mind back on the job, Powers asked. 'How do you think Conway would react to blackmail?'

'Dangerously, very dangerously.'

'The way I see it, is like this, he'd do anything if he thought his daughter was in danger ... right?'

Jimbo came back with the drinks and put them down on the table, he'd obviously been giving Powers' words some thought. 'Lieutenant, you were taking the piss – right?'

'Of course I was, I'd have to use two fingers.'

'Twat,' said Jimbo. They all laughed at Jimbo's misfortune, even Jimbo.

'Listen up, Jimbo, I'm running an idea past Greg and I'd like your input,' he said wanting Jimbo to feel a proper part of things.

'I'm listening.'

'I just asked Greg how he thought Conway would react to blackmail, if he thought his daughter was in danger?'

'He'd go fucking ape shit, bloody mental. All I can say is, I hope he doesn't find out that I'm involved in any of this. Are you thinking of taking him down?'

Powers looked towards Warren and raised his eyebrows. 'That's something Greg and I'll have to discuss?'

'First, let's hear what you have in mind?'

'Kidnap ...'

'Oh, no, you can't kidnap a kid, Lieutenant,' Jimbo protested.

'I'm thinking more along the lines of virtual kidnap.'

Warren smiled. 'Virtual kidnap, now I could cope with that.'

Jimbo sat shaking his head. 'Well, I haven't got a fucking idea what the hell you're on about,' he sat back in his seat, arms folded across his chest. 'Go on then, explain.'

Warren was also keen to hear more.

'It's simple, Jimbo, as long as he *thinks* she's been kidnapped, that's all the ammunition we'd need.'

'Ah, I get you, she's already incommunicado ...' Warren and Powers looked at each other. 'I do know some big words you know. So, as long as things stay that way he thinks the worst.'

'Got it.'

'Your round I think, Lieutenant?' Jimbo pushed his empty glass across the table.

'You really are pissing him off, mate,' Warren told him when Powers went to the bar.

'Yeah, I know, I just want him to know I'm not one of his lackeys, I've no intention of ending up dead down some back alley.'

'I get where you're coming from, from what I've found out he really is kosher, so, just wind you neck in, because I can see us doing a lot more business with him and his organisation. You'll do that?'

'Greg, if you trust him I'll give it my best shot, not literally of course.'

'Good to hear it.'

'Still heaving round the bar,' said Powers when he returned doing a balancing act with three pints of lager between his big hands. 'That Kirsty, she seems like a nice kid,' he said as he sat down.

'Whoa, best keep your eyes off her, Neil, not wise to step on Greg's toes.'

'Neil,' Powers repeated, throwing his arms in the air, 'wow, have we made a breakthrough?'

'Maybe,' said Jimbo, picking up his pint. 'Cheers,' Jimbo desperately wanted to add Lieutenant.

Chapter 32

Warren hammered on the scarred steel plated door of the Ice House Road flat. He heard the numerous locks being opened on the inside. Conway was security conscious, he had made more than a few enemies over the years.

'Morning, Pat,' Warren said when the fat man eventually opened the door.

'Morning,' he grunted back.

'Had a bad night?' Warren asked.

'Just got a lot on my mind,' he said, as he led the way through to the living room.

'Anything I can help with?' Warren asked as he sat down on the settee, picking up one of Conway's boxing magazines and flicking through the pages.

'That daughter of mine, she won't answer any of my bloody texts, the one she did reply to she told me to stop bothering her.'

'While we're on the subject, we had a deal, remember? I helped you with Rachell and you find out about the firearms in return?'

'I'll be honest with you, Ray, with all this shit going on with Rachell I haven't give it much thought.'

'Yeah, I can understand that, but all the same ...'

'For fuck's sake give over, I'll put the word out, okay?'

'Don't have any option do I?'

Conway dropped down onto his leather armchair. 'Well, you decided, are you in or not?'

'What's my percentage?'

'Fuck off, Ray, you'll be on wages. Don't worry you'll be due a bonus if things go to plan.'

'Bit presumptuous, Pat, I haven't said I'm in yet?'

'Just make your fucking mind up, Ray, I can't be arsed to play your games today.'

Conway was truly worried and Warren hadn't heard from Powers, had it begun?

'Okay, but I use my man.'

It would be a two-man job as far as Conway was concerned, he wouldn't be aware of Jimbo, lurking in the background.

Little did Elvis know, but he was to be the other half of the team.

'Whatever.'

This, Warren was not expecting, Conway usually supplied the line-up, it was more confirmation on just how worried he was about Rachell.

'Okay, Pat, now that's sorted, details.'

'There's a container coming in through Immingham docks, customs are fixed ...'

'What's that mean?'

'Don't worry about it, no problems there. The container is a mixed load of motor bike spares, re-con engines and general engineering parts. I've got two crates amongst the legit gear. The driver will drop them off at a lock-up on the South Bank. All you have to do is transfer them to a tranny van and deliver safely, don't worry, they're manageable for a couple of blokes. Piece of piss.'

'Now the million-dollar question, what's in the crates?'

Conway didn't answer the question. 'You don't need to worry about that, just get them back here.' He passed over a sealed envelope. 'Details are in here.' It was then that Conway's 'other' mobile vibrated across the coffee table. He seemed undecided about answering the call in front of Warren, then mumbled-'sod it,' and picked up. He didn't recognise the number. 'Fuck off, whoever you are,' he said into the handset without giving the caller a chance to speak.

'Nice telephone manners you have, Pat,' said Warren.

'You still here?' He said to Warren as he hung up the call.

Then a text message came through. Conway opened the message, it was an MMS, a picture of Rachell. He jumped up from his chair. He held the phone allowing Warren to see the picture.

'What the fuck's going on, Ray?' The picture didn't show much, just a head and shoulders shot, on a white background.

Before Warren had a chance to respond the phone rang once more.

'Nice picture, don't you think, Patrick?' The voice down the line asked, as the call was accepted. 'Have you had contact with Rachell lately?'

It was obvious that Conway recognised the voice, so did Warren, it belonged to Powers. 'What's that supposed to mean?'

'Like I asked, have you spoken to her lately?' Silence. 'No, I didn't think so.'

'Where is she? You'd better not have harmed her or I'll rip your fucking head off and spit down your neck.'

'Calm down, Patrick ...'

'You have her?'

'Don't worry, Rachell is fine ...for now.'

'For now? How much do you want, Powers? Name your price.'

'I don't want your money ...'

Conway was quick to cut in. 'Then what the fuck DO you want, name it and it's yours,' Conway yelled down the phone. 'I just want my girl back.'

'Very kind of you to offer, I'll be in touch very soon.' Powers hung up.

Conway started pacing up and down the small lounge, face red and sweating.

'What was all that about?' Warren asked. 'Pat, you listening to me? I said, what was that about?' Conway was hyperventilating. 'For Christ's sake, sit down before you have a coronary.'

Conway shot him a look and dropped down heavily into his chair. 'That bastard, Powers, he's got Rachell ...if he harms a hair on her head, he's dead I tell you, fucking dead.'

I hope to hell that Neil knows what he's doing, Warren thought, as he watched the effect the phone call was having on Conway.

'Listen, what can I do to help?'

Conway lifted his head and looked Warren directly in the eye. 'Find her and then kill him.'

Chapter 33

According to Neil Powers, Rachell was safe and unharmed. Conway was relieved, after all what reason did Neil Powers have to lie? He was holding all the cards, he had something Powers wanted, there would be no advantage to be gained from hurting the girl. This was Conway's logic.

Their telephone conversations did nothing but create a stalemate, therefore there was only one logical option available, face to face negotiations if they wanted to come to an amicable solution. At least that was the way Neil Powers saw things, for Conway on the other hand there was only one acceptable outcome, Rachell back and Powers dead.

Conway arranged to meet Powers on neutral ground. It was agreed they would meet at the river front Victoria Pier, but first he had to make himself ready. Patrick Conway was calm, he went upstairs to his study, and behind his desk he pulled back the carpet to get access to his safe. It was double locked it required a key and a combination code inputting. The lid clicked open. Inside was a large amount of cash – a very large amount and the small bag of 'Blood' diamonds he'd acquired from Cole some months previous. He ignored both, today he was only interested in one item, a Smith & Wesson M&P Shield, a compact 9mm handgun. He took out the gun, placed it aside while he relocked the safe.

He sat at his waxed solid oak desk, passing the pistol from hand to hand. Conway then removed the magazine, holding the 9mm weapon in his right hand he pointed straight visualising Powers standing before him. BANG, he shouted, as he pulled the trigger. Sitting back in his chair he replaced the nine-shot mag and contemplated on the outcome of his meeting with Powers. Rachell by his side and double tap from the S&W to Powers head.

Back downstairs, he placed the Smith & Wesson on the coffee table and poured himself a small single malt, he needed to keep his wits about him. For a while he had debated with himself as to whether he should consult with Ray Cole, after all, Cole was the "man", but he was his *own* man, wasn't he? Tough, respected in the criminal fraternity, the decision was he could handle Powers on his own, without the help of outsiders.

The wind ripped across the wooden deck of Victoria Pier, waves from the murky River Humber crashed against the wooden timbers. The adjoining streets were almost deserted. Powers sat in the driving seat of the BMW, fingers tapping on the steering wheel to the music on the radio. He was good at waiting, always had been.

For once Powers had been outwitted, Conway was already there, watching. For a fat bloke, he was more agile than his build suggested as he approach the BMW on Powers blindside and banged on the passenger side front, briefly throwing Powers off kilter.

He pressed the switch and the window opened. 'Nice approach, Patrick, almost took me unawares.' Powers opened the door, climbed out and locked the vehicle. He pulled the collar of his jacket up around his neck. Ignoring the wind blowing off the river, the two men walked onto the timber deck. The murky water of the River Humber could be seen between the gaps in the planking.

'Shall we?' Powers asked, stopping near a wooden bench. They sat side by side with a comfortable gap between them. 'Not much of a view today.' The clouds appeared to hang low in the sky and the drizzle of fine rain made it difficult to see the opposite river bank.

'Before you start demanding my life savings, I want assurances Rachell is safe,' Conway told him as he increased the gap between them.

'I wouldn't have expected anything less. May I?' Powers replied, his hand reaching toward his pocket.

As he did Conway stood up, with his back to the river directly in front of Powers. His hand disappeared into his own pocket and produced the Smith & Wesson.

Powers raised an eyebrow and tut, tutted. 'No need for firearms, Patrick.' He took his Smart Phone from his pocket, selected the image folder and with an outstretched arm passed the mobile over. The image showed Rachell sunning herself on a sunbed. He flicked the screen, others showed her in pool, drinking a cocktail, sat on the beach with the musician.

'What the hell are these?'

'Exactly what they look like,' Powers paused for effect, 'a young girl on holiday having a whale of a time.'

'I may be thick, but it doesn't make any sense, explain.'

'If I had suggested a meeting and the possibility of working together, what would your answer have been?'

'I would have told you to fuck right off, I wouldn't go into business with you if my life depended on it.'

'Precisely, leading you to believe you daughter had been abducted was the only way I could guarantee that a meeting would take place. Look, Patrick, can we not carry out this conversation somewhere more amenable,' he said as salty spray blew off the river.

'Rachell?'

'I've told you she's fine, don't worry she'll be home soon.'

Conway nodded towards his vehicle. 'I need some answers.' He opened the door and sat behind the steering wheel, placing the Smith & Wesson on the dashboard.

'And answers you will get,' Powers said, as he opened the passenger door on Conway's Range Rover and climbed in.

'Rachell?' Conway asked once more.

'I have contacts in many places, high and low, she wasn't too hard to seek out. As far as the girl knows, she won an AirCanada, inflight competition, a fourteen-day break for two to Tenerife, all inclusive of course with five hundred pounds spending money. My man told her the only stipulation was that she had to leave the same day. She jumped at the chance.'

Conway took out one of his miniature cigars and lit up, the blue smoke whipping away over the river.

'So, what are you after,' he said as he put the cigar to his lips again, ignoring Powers obvious discomfort.

'A partnership in your business.'

'Are you fucking daft, why would I go into partnership with you?'

'As I said, I have the contacts available to ensure things always run smoothly, and I mean always. And you, Patrick have the business acumen to make it worthwhile for both of us. What's more, I have information that as you said yourself, your life may depend on.'

'Piss off, there is nothing you can say that can be detrimental to my life expectancy.'

Powers turned to face the man behind the wheel and spoke in soft voice. 'Is that so?'

There was something in the voice that un-nerved Conway.

'Let me ask you a question, what do you know about your associate Raymond Cole?'

'Cole, I've worked with him on more than one occasion, he's as sound as a pound.'

'So, if I told you Cole isn't all what he seems?'

'I'd say you're off your head. I know everything there is about Ray, you can't tell me anything I don't know already.'

'I thought you'd say that.' Powers reached into the inside pocket of his jacket and took out a folded A4 sheet. 'Take a look at this.' It was a copy of Greg Warrens police personnel file.

Conway was quiet as he read, the face he was looking at belonged to Ray Cole, or did it? he couldn't be sure. He folded the sheet and handed it back to Powers.

'How do you know all this?'

'As I told you, Patrick, I have friends in very high places. Contacts you wouldn't believe possible. So, what we have here, is proof, Gregory Warren, Detective Sergeant is Raymond Cole. Don't you get it Conway? He's been playing you all along.'

'You're serious, aren't you?'

'Oh yes, deadly serious.'

'I find it hard to believe, he's done right by me so far.'

'On the surface, maybe, but are you willing to continue taking the risk' Conway didn't answer. 'Remember, Jimbo? Of course, how could you not? You practically raised the lad after his old-man topped himself.'

'What about Jimbo?'

'Now I'm sure this *will* surprise you, he's working with the police as a Civilian Advisor.'

Conway was speechless, he didn't know how to respond. There was silence, then he gathered himself together. 'They're dead.'

The seed had been sown, if things went how he hoped they would, Warren would be dead and if Conway did survive he would be locked up for a very long time leaving behind him a void that Powers himself would fill.

Powers stood up. 'So, Patrick, do you think we might be able to do business? I do. Think it over and call me - sooner rather than later. Talk soon, Patrick.'

He climbed out of Conway's Range Rover and walked away. Since becoming embroiled in the seedier side of things, Lieutenant Neil Powers had become accustomed to the finer things of life, the things that were not affordable on Regular Army pay, definitely not on what a Lieutenant earned, he wasn't prepared to give up the money, the car and above all the status. What difference would it make, it was all power for the cause - wasn't it? He saw taking over Conway's already established business as a way of securing his future, once Conway and DS Warren were out of the picture.

Standing facing the Humber he took out his mobile and dialled. There was one last loose end he had to tie up.

'Listen,' he said into the receiver, 'I'm sending you a photograph and an address, it's time he was removed.'

One hour and thirty minutes later, as Philips stepped out of his front door, joyriders in a stolen Vauxhall Vectra mounted the pavement and ended the career and life of Bernie Philips.

Chapter 34

Warren stood up and walked across to Jimbo.

'I've just had a strange conversation with Pat.'

'How do you mean, strange?'

'He wants a meet.'

'What's unusual in that?'

'Where does he have all his meetings?'

'The flat.'

'Precisely, he wants a meet in the old town, some place down Scale Lane, tonight.'

'I wouldn't read too much into it, knowing Pat he'll have a good reason.'

'Hmm, we'll have to wait and see.'

'You want me to tag along?'

'No, it'll be fine, you go and have a pint and I'll fill you in when it's over.'

Warren parked the Ford Escort close to Silver Street in the old town. Rain had been falling steadily for the past hour, making the cobble road surface of Scale Lane slick underfoot. Scale Lane still retained the character of days gone by when the area had been a hive of activity for the ship's merchants and chandlers.

As usual Warren arrived early and did a recce of the nearby streets and buildings, everything looked to be okay. The address Conway had given him turned out to be a disused shop, the previous owners a high-class milliner was long gone. The place looked as if it hadn't been occupied in decades. Warren put his hand on the front door knob and turned, the door was unlocked and opened, he cautiously stepped inside. The street light directly outside the shop cast a gloomy pale glow through the dirty glass window, enough to illuminate the interior. Conway was already there waiting.

'Evening, Pat,' Warren said, as he walked across the empty room and stood in front of the old wooden counter, his hands behind on the warm timber as he gave out the appearance of being relaxed. Conway didn't speak as they stood facing each other in the half light, almost as if in a kind of pissing contest, waiting for the other to falter.

'So, Pat, what's this all about, secret meetings at the dead of night, all seems a bit sinister?'

'All in good time, Ray.'

'Why here?' He had an uneasy feeling.

'Just bought the place as an investment.'

'Very nice, I like what you've done with the place,' he said looking around.

Conway smiled. 'The jobs off, me and you we're finished.'

'What's brought this about?' He said watching for any sudden movements.

'Well, if you don't know Detective Sergeant Greg Warren why should I enlighten you?' It had been totally unexpected, Warren was caught off guard. That was when Conway stooped slightly and picked up a two-foot length of scaffolding pole from the debris.

Warren had heard the words but didn't believe what he was hearing.

'Like fuck I am, who's been filling your head with this shit?'

'I've got it on good authority, no point trying to deny it. Ever since your so-called prison break you've been playing me, oh, yeah, I know everything about you, Detective, everything and not forgetting the little shit Jimbo.' Holding the cold metal in his right hand he playfully tapped it in the palm of his left hand. 'Tell me, did you top the real Cole yourself?'

Warren didn't answer. He had questions of his own.

'So, let's cut to the chase, Pat, when did you decide to get into the arms trade?'

'Sort of fell into it, it was never planned. There was a market and I saw the opportunity.'

'You know, I always thought of you as a decent villain, not someone who'd sell third rate converted guns to kids and pyschos.'

'Don't go pointing the finger, I always had you down as a crook, murderer and nasty piece of shit, and I was right, the only difference between you and me is that you do it legally.'

'That's it then, a parting of the ways, you go back to which ever rock you've crawled out from under and me, I disappear from your life forever, is that how you see it? Well it isn't gonna happen, Pat, I can't let it.'

'You're right there, that's not what's going to happen.' Conway lunged forward, the metal pole held in both hands high above his head like a club. The counter to his back restricting his escape, Warren lifted his arm to fend off the blow, he not only felt the bone shatter, he heard it. He tried to shift position when the pole struck again, missing the side of his head and landed heavily on his shoulder shattering more bones.

Conway stepped back dropping the pole to the floor, this was not how it was going to end. He was enjoying seeing his onetime friend squirm in agony, he took pleasure in Warren's pain.

Warren watched through tear filled eyes as Conway put his hand in his pocket and produced a handgun. Although the pain was excruciating Warren managed to get to his knees, his right arm hung by his side totally knackered, it probably would have hurt less if Conway had shot him, instead of pulverising him with a length of scaffolding pole. He shuffled backward, and struggled to his feet, leaning back against the shop counter. The Smith & Wesson was pointing directly at him.

'You do realise if you blow my brains out with that fucking thing,' he managed to say, nodding towards the Smith &Wesson, 'there's no coming back, not when you've topped a copper.'

'That's a chance I'll have to take.' The gun was still pointing towards Warren. 'You know, I much preferred it when you were Ray Cole. So, it ends here.'

He took a step nearer and raised the weapon.

'You haven't got the balls to pull the trigger,' Warren said, although he knew Conway *did* have the balls. He knew he was only a matter of seconds from death.

The fat man levelled the weapon in a direct line with Warren's head and released the safety catch.

BANG.

A single shot. The closeness of the blast obliterated the back of his head, grey brain matter sprayed through the expanded wound where his forehead used to be. His arms flew out, his feet lifted of the ground as the force pushed him forward. Warren slid down to the floor.

Tears rolled down Jimbo's cheeks, he'd never killed before, now he had ended the life of the man who, had at one time been a surrogate father to him. Pat Conway was dead.

'You are such a bastard,' Jimbo said as he lets his Glock fall to the floor, then close to sobbing he dropped to his knees.

'How did you find me?'

'The GPS tracker I took off Neil's car, I put it on the Escort. I wasn't going to let you come alone, you mad fucker.' He looked towards Conway's body. 'How did he find out?'

'Don't know, Jimbo, don't know but I intend to find out. Look I don't want you mixed up in this shit, get out of here, take the Glock and get rid of it. Before you do go, use Pat's mobile and call it in, I could do with an ambulance myself.' Warren reached out with his good arm and pulled Jimbo close in a man-hug. 'Thanks,' was all he said before he passed out.

Neil Powers was expecting a call. The clock ticked around as he sat, patiently staring through the picture window as the rain ran in rivulets down the glass. He was on his second glass of malt whiskey when his mobile rang. The caller ID showed an unlisted number, he knew who it belonged to. He listened to the short message and hung up. It was not what he wanted to hear. Greg Warren was still alive. Powers swapped his mobile for the glass of malt. 'Until the next time Greg, until the next time.'

The End

Also by Alfie Robins

DCI Marlowe novels
Reprisal
Snakes and Losers
A Winning Hand Loses
Harry Blackburn novels
Just Whistle
Funeral Rites

Short Stories
Why Won't You Stay Dead.

Coming soon,
Heads She Loses – Tails She Loses. A DCI Marlowe novel.

www.alfierobins.co.uk
www.facebook.com/alfierobinsbooks